TERMINAL IMPULSES

a twisted suspense thriller

MICHAEL MCDONALD-LOW

with Dr. Jeremy Senske, PsyD

TERMINAL IMPULSES

LCCN 2018905758

Publishing Date: May 2018

DELTA SIX PRODUCTIONS, LLC

Terminal Impulses is a Delta Six Production, LLC

www.unaccounted.net

Cover Design: Sheridan K. Low

Warning: This book contains explicit language and sexual situations.

Dedicated to the Empty Girl.

Table of Contents

"All things truly wicked start with innocence."

Ernest Hemingway

Chapter 1 • Snapshots

Stephanie Courtland was antsy and fidgeting in her seat as the Southwest Air 727 banked left around the hills of San Francisco and swooped in for its landing just feet above the Bay. She gasped slightly as the big jet bumped and bounced upon impact with the tarmac and then violently braked; she closed her eyes and waited for it to slow before heaving a small sigh of relief as it gradually made its way to the arrival gates.

She heard *Beth say, You'll be fine, we're on the ground. Relax, we have this.*

Tiffany just giggled, nervous as a cat, but ready to see what adventures lie ahead. Happy as a monster just released from her chains, she reveled in what could happen next.

Her boss had booked her into first class and she reveled in how well she was treated but she was so excited it was difficult for her to enjoy the comfort and amenities of the flight. She was thrilled to be attending the West Coast Advertising and Design Expo and couldn't wait to see all of the latest computers and design software that would be on display. She was also impatient to see what the most creative minds in her field were developing, hopeful that they would provide her the tools and ideas to become a more skillful designer.

She took a taxi from the airport to the Marriot Marquis, which was within walking distance of the Moscone Center where the Expo was being held. The Marquis was spectacular and her suite on the twenty-fifth floor was the nicest she'd ever stayed in. The view from her windows overlooked the heart of San Francisco and it was wondrous, almost fairytale-like. After unpacking, Stephanie took a short nap and when she woke, she enjoyed a luxurious bath. She then dressed carefully for dinner: she was shimmering in green. She was thrilled to be dining at the View Lounge on the thirty-ninth floor. She'd read all about it and the pictures they displayed in the hotel directory made her even more captivated.

The View Lounge was elegant. She selected one of the plush red leather chairs at the end of the semi-circular marble bar. It was early evening but there was a nice buzz to the restaurant with waiters bustling between the tables situated around the bar and in the several Cove dining areas. She could see that each had views of the downtown, though not as spectacular as the private tables centered in front of the giant, semi-circular, spider web-like window situated directly across from the bar. She estimated the window to be at least fifty feet wide and twenty feet tall, and it provided an unprecedented panoramic view of downtown San Francisco and the Bay. It's where she first spotted him. He was sitting with two other men having dinner. She was immediately attracted to him and she had to be careful not to stare. He was tall and handsome in a rugged sort of way, broad shouldered and extremely well built. He had curly dark hair, a thick blackish-brown mustache and a smile that could light a building. He was dressed expensively though casually and seemed very self-assured.

She spied upon him throughout dinner and inadvertently caught him glancing at her. He smiled, but she turned her attention away and ignored him throughout the rest of her dinner. She had been *told by the girls* to mind her P's and Q's.

When she saw him the next day at the advertising conference, walking booth-to-booth at the trade tables, her fears of him being a dangerous stranger were eased. Unable to stop herself, she trailed behind him for a few minutes when he suddenly turned around and grinned at her.

"Are you following me?" he asked with a smirk.

Her knees buckled slightly and she blushed nervously through her smile at him.

"Hey, relax. I'm only kidding, but I've seen you here and at the hotel. It's really nice to finally meet you. I'm Ben."

They hit it off right away and over the course of the next two days they spent much of their time together at the conference. They both enjoyed the intimacy they shared in a strange city, until it suddenly ended on the second night when he invited her back to his room for a nightcap. It was the night that *Tiffany* had come *forward* with *Beth*. She vaguely recalled something about an argument but the details eluded her other than how it made her feel: not sad, not angry, not anything. She really hadn't been very involved with him anyway.

The next morning, on her flight back to Portland, she reflected upon her time in San Francisco and the things she'd learned and experienced at the convention: it had been exciting and empowering and she believed it was time well spent. She was confident the various computer design classes and demonstrations she'd attended would make her a better designer. With the comfort of that thought Stephanie settled into the plush cushions of her seat in first class and relaxed. She closed her eyes and slept until she felt a nudge on her arm. It startled her and made her jump. She opened her eyes to find an older gentleman seated across the aisle from her looking quite concerned.

"I'm sorry, Miss. You sounded terribly distressed and when you called out I felt obliged to wake you. You appeared to be quite frightened."

She was flustered and deeply agitated, but managed a sheepish smile at the man. "I'm sorry I disturbed you. I watched a horror movie on television last night and I guess I shouldn't have."

"It's quite all right. I've done that myself. Those types of movies are not my favorite way to end the evening."

She laughed politely, now fully awake. "They shouldn't be mine either."

The man nodded to her with a small smile and returned his attention back to his book.

She glanced around the cabin and was relieved to see no one else seemed to have noticed her. She folded her hands on her lap and noticed a small drop of blood on the back of her wrist. She nervously wiped it away only to have it smear and spread a red, shiny wetness across the back of her hand and fingers. She closed her eyes tightly, counted to three, and then opened them to see that the blood was gone. "It's happening again," she said softly to herself as she hurriedly undid the seat belt, picked up her purse and walked to the restroom. She closed the door behind her and turned towards the small sink and mirror. She stared at herself in the mirror and was terrified. She hadn't watched a horror movie at all, but it had seemed that way. She couldn't remember the details, but the blood on her hand worried her. Imaginary or not, she'd seen it before and knew what was coming.

"Click...click...click...click," she said to the mirror, each word softer and more hesitant than the one before.

She suddenly felt sick to her stomach and retched violently into the sink. She dropped her purse and gripped the cool edges of the aluminum. She bent and spit bile into the sink and experienced a sickening paleness wash over her. She shook and quivered, barely able to stand, her eyes closed.

The imagery began without her being able to stop it.

Click...Ray glaring at her as he kneels over her mother lying lifeless against the stove - her eyes wide open, the blue's faded, empty, staring at the end.

Click...The deep, dark wood paneling, quiet yellow portholes, and the soft rocking of the boat - her laughter turning from fear to outrage at the betrayal.

Click...The warm blues and blacks of a sandy beach at night and the craziness of the booze and pills - the sand between her toes as she walks into the ocean to wash away the chaos.

Click...The incredible, multi-hued, sparkling display of the city and the biggest lie she'd ever been told - a smear of blackness ending the night.

Click...click...click...click.

Her knees buckled and she collapsed to the floor, a cold sweat breaking out on her upper lip and forehead. Her legs were splayed in front of her next to the small toilet. Her chin drooped against her chest. In a heartbeat, she gasped and suddenly straightened, hearing the voice within her.

"Get a grip, girlfriend. This is no time for you being all girlish and fucked up. We're on an airplane for Christ sakes," Beth said harshly.

"Come on, Stephy. We've got this," Tiffany soothed.

She listened, but it took her several minutes to compose herself. Once she did, she stood and turned on the water to wash away the mess she'd created and wondered if removing the disturbing images would ever be that easy.

"Those were just bad thoughts, Stephy. Part of a dream. You know we love you and we'll always be here for you, now and forever. Now relax and enjoy the rest of the flight, it's just your style." Tiffany cooed to her.

She took comfort from the words and was suddenly relieved, though truthfully, she didn't know why.

"Fix yourself. You'll feel better." It was Beth, determined to right the ship.

She picked up her purse and removed her make-up bag. She carefully freshened her foundation, mascara, and then her lips. She leaned forward and carefully examined herself in the mirror. Satisfied that she was presentable, she returned to her seat. The remainder of the flight passed slowly and at times she wanted to scream and cry out but knew better than to cause a scene, *Beth* repeatedly warned her not to and the consequences that would take place if she did.

When the flight landed, she rushed to her car and drove home as quickly as she could. Her mind struggled to concentrate and she could barely contain her physical movements to drive. She was distraught, but one searing thought kept burning in her - check the Internet.

She pushed through her front door and literally threw her suitcase on the floor. She frantically ran to her desk and turned on her new iMac.

She thrummed her fingers impatiently until the white-framed monitor opened and when it did, she went to the Google search site and entered 'SF News.'

Before the page could freshen, *Beth came forward and told her, "Let me check. I'm a faster reader than you are and I don't need glasses. Gimme a sec." Beth paused a few moments before saying, "Nope, nothing about a Ben or anyone else we know."*

"No news is good news," trilled Tiffany. "I told you, Stephy, there's nothing to read and if there was don't be afraid. We never become so involved that we don't pay attention to the details. Chill out, this is not the end of the world."

Stephanie didn't quite understand what *Tiffany* meant, but she was suddenly terrified by the implication. Her body began to tremble and her hands began to shake uncontrollably. She felt the rush of paleness wash over her, draining her. She wanted to faint, disappear, or fade into nothingness, but she couldn't. Instead, she stood up, closed her eyes and started to whirl in a circle; her arms stretched wide and open. Faster, and faster, and faster she spun, until she wobbled, lost her balance and fell to the floor. She sat and held her head tightly with her hands, letting the spin come down. When she began to think of what was next, she stood up and remembered.

Click...click...click...click.

She stumbled as she ran to the bathroom desperate to find the Ativan anxiety meds she'd borrowed from Evan. The bathroom mirror hiding the medicine cabinet shattered when she threw the door open. She didn't care. She clutched the yellow-gold plastic prescription bottle and pushed down on the white cap. Opened, she shook two of the tiny white pills from the bottle and cupped them into her mouth.

It took twenty frantic minutes for the medication to take effect, while she lay on the bed talking with Diana and blubbering things she could hardly comprehend. When the pills finally did kick in, her sister assured her that everything was fine and to not take her flings with men so seriously.

Click...click...click...click.

Chapter 2 • Counting the Days

Collapsing onto the lumpy mattress that covered his metal bunk in the gray, dimly lit, eight-by-ten-foot concrete cell, Ray Franklin was weary from another day of trying to teach computer skills to a bunch of illiterates from the Aryan Brotherhood. It was the price he paid for their protection and also their drugs. The AB was his source for steroids inside Washington State Penitentiary and they insured he had an unending supply of his personal favorites: Anadrol and Equipoise. The steroids helped define his body and they made him bigger and angrier, but not dumb. He'd had enough of dumb.

He relaxed against the coolness of the cement wall, closed his eyes, and thought of the rain earlier in the day that he'd seen through the skylights of the library. It was one of a thousand things he'd missed and how simple of a pleasure it was to lie in bed and listen to the rain beat against the window at night, the trees rustling, their branches swaying to the rhythm of the winds. "Soon," he hoped. And he knew it would be. He'd already been moved to an out-processing cell on the first floor, out of the commons and Gen Pop. It wasn't any better but he was finally alone.

A sudden, but all too familiar impulse struck him and he flinched from the mind-numbing, claustrophobic closeness of his imprisonment. Nineteen years and ten months behind bars seemed an eternity and he hated it more than ever. He scratched and rubbed his closely shaven head, the frustration building within him. He flexed and pumped his arms feeling the veins in his neck expand like thick, red cords as his body began to throb and pulse. He threw his head back and screamed in silent rage at the steady cacophony of men talking, shouting, farting, grunting, arguing, belching, and snoring; the mind-dulling buzz of his intimate surroundings only quieting to semi-stillness in the dead of night.

Franklin stopped, lowered his head and took a deep breath. "Chill motherfuckers," he ordered his demons. "Not now."

He concentrated on his breathing, slowed his heart rate, and let his mind wander to the drift and his favorite fantasy, Alice Courtland. He remembered everything important about how they began: he'd first spotted her waiting tables at the Flitter Inn and he was immediately attracted to her. She was blonde, blue-eyed, gorgeous, and built like a brick shithouse, albeit a softer-edged one. Her low-cut blouses and tight-fitting pants accented her figure and added to his carnal interest. She had an easy, inviting demeanor, and he liked the way she talked to him - her lips pouting and suggestive. He soon discovered that she was his kind of woman: a happy drunk, emotionally damaged from a recent divorce, and anxious to find a man to take care of her and her three kids. She was also sexy as hell. He wanted her, but knew better than to rush into a bad decision that would saddle him with too many responsibilities, and worst of all, cost him real money.

It didn't take him more than a couple of weeks of drop-ins at the Flitter to set a date with her. She was anxious to go out with him and he'd gone out of his way to make sure she was impressed with his wallet. He'd made it a point to order the best bourbon and he always bought her a matching cocktail that included a twenty-dollar tip. It worked.

He'd selected Mariposa, a small, intimate Italian restaurant and its extensive and expensive menu delighted her. He ordered appetizers and drinks and they settled into conversation about their lives and backgrounds. He learned she'd been dating on and off since she began working at the Flitter and if anything, she was tired of it. Alice candidly admitted to him she was barely making ends meet, and that it was becoming harder for her to find the time to work, meet and date someone, and be a good mother.

When he asked her what her hopes were for the future, he wasn't shocked or surprised by her answer.

"I want, no, I need a man who isn't boring and predictable like my ex-husband. Most of all I need a man who has the drive, the money, and the passion I desire."

She wasn't kidding.

He remembered how he smiled at her when she talked of her need for passion. They spent the next twenty or thirty minutes talking about sex. Certainly, the drinks had loosened their tongues, but she felt quite comfortable and even enthusiastic when he intimated his need and hunger for her.

They hurried through dinner and finished with a shared Spanish Coffee. When they stepped out of the restaurant it was freezing cold and their breath rose in the frigid air like smoky puffs from small dragons.

"Brrr. It's nasty out here. Come here and warm me up," she said, stopping in front of his car smashing her lips into his and pushing her wet tongue into his mouth.

He kissed her back roughly. The aroma of her heavy perfume encircled them, and he tasted the lingering sweetness of the coffee and rum on her breath and mouth. To him it was nectar, and it made him helpless to his needs and desires.

She pulled back from his embrace, her red lipstick smeared across her lips from the kisses. She then said softly, "I really like you a lot, Ray. I'd invite you to my place, but it's small and the kids are there."

"I understand, darlin'. I have a room nearby. I didn't want to drive this late after drinking. We can go there if you like."

"Ummmm. Let's do it. I'm pretty buzzed."

He had to take it slow when he escorted her to his car because she was weaving and stumbling. He knew she was ready for anything when he poured her into the front seat as she giggled and squirmed and went out of her way to tease him with her exposed thighs and quick peeks of her red, sheer panties.

He smiled at her antics. She was funny and she made him laugh.

After finally getting her buckled in, he drove slowly away from the Mariposa. There was no real need to rush. He'd picked the Motel 6 because of its nearby location, along with its convenient car-to-door access to the room. When they arrived in front of the door numbered 135, he parked. He helped her out of the car and guided her to the room. She tittered and laughed, wobbling and clutching his arm for balance as they made their way to the door.

As soon as he keyed and opened the door she ran to the bed, ripped the comforter back, kicked her shoes off, and flopped down on the white sheets, raising her hands and calling to him. "Come on, I want to kiss you. Don't make me wait," she pouted.

He sauntered over to her, bent down, and she wrapped her arms around his neck and pulled him close, kissing him hungrily.

He gently extracted himself from her embrace, grinned at her, and confidently suggested, "Alice, hold on a minute. We're not in a hurry. Why don't you relax and take off your coat? You can make yourself comfortable and I'll be right back. I'm going to use the bathroom for a sec, and then we can have us some fun."

She pouted again and with reluctance said, "Okay."

She didn't mean it.

She laughed, took off her coat and threw it across the padded chair next to the bed. She coyly pulled her sweater over her head, stripped it from her arms, and tossed it on top of the coat. Still sniggering with delight, she reached behind herself to unclasp her bra. She fumbled for a moment before dropping the black lace garment and exposing her large breasts, her nipples taut, shaking them at him. With a wicked smile she then lay on her back, lifted her butt, and removed her skirt and panties.

She was pink and wiggling like a baby, squeezing her hands at him the way hungry babies did. "I'm ready, Ray. Come and get me," she taunted as she lifted the sheets up to cover herself, while beckoning to him with her index finger.

"I'll be right back. Hold that thought," he said, smiling and leering at her remark and playfulness. He then turned and went into the bathroom.

He hurriedly stripped off his clothes and removed the heavy leather belt from his pants. He rolled it and stuffed it into the pocket of the black robe he'd left hanging on the door hook. He shrugged into the robe, tied its belt, and checked the pocket for the condom. Satisfied he had everything, he opened the bathroom door and saw that she was still stretched out on the bed, partially covered by the sheet. Her blonde hair lay sprawled on the pillow behind her head and her eyes were closed. Her arms lay languidly across her body, her long fingers interlaced, the tips of her painted nails sharply red against her pale skin. Her legs were stretched out in front of her, her feet relaxed and sticking out of the bottom of the white sheet. Her painted toenails sparkled like red Christmas lights.

He wanted her more than he expected, but he wasn't in a hurry. He slowly walked to the side of the bed and pulled the belt from the pocket of his robe. He carefully laid the coiled black leather next to the pillow beside her before removing his robe and climbing onto the bed, next to her. He kissed her as he straddled her waist with his knees, his arms straight, next to her shoulders. He bent down, nuzzled her ear and kissed her neck.

She opened her eyes, yawned, and stretched her arms above her head, her legs flexed, her toes pointed.

"Bout time, baby. Now, it's my turn."

She pushed up and out from underneath him and rose from the bed. He could tell by the way she swerved and stumbled to the bathroom that the evening was shaping up nicely.

A minute later he heard the toilet flush and then the door opened. She paused in the doorframe, her hands on her hips. "Do you like what you see, Ray?"

Before he could answer, she was quick to the opposite side of the bed from where he lay, his head propped up by his hand, arm bent. She sat and slipped her legs onto the bed. With a movement he could only think of as sliding on a sheet of glass, she was quickly next to him, face-to-face.

"Let me have you," she said hungrily as she slid downward, her mouth open and reaching for him.

He let her do what she wanted. And she was very good at it, he thought, as he reached for the belt. He then bent down and said softly to her, "Hold on there, girl. Slide up a bit, I need to have a better view."

She stopped and scooted forward under him.

He moved his knees inward and roughly pinned her hips, his hands pressing down on her shoulders.

She squeaked, gazed somewhat drunkenly at him and said, "I like it when you're rough with me."

"Well, darlin', I do too. And I've got something for you. It's a belt, like we talked about. Do you mind if I try it on you?"

She shook her head slightly, her tongue licking her lips.

He slipped the belt around her neck, threaded the pointed end through its notched opening and pulled it until it clicked a few times, and then a few more. It was firm, but not tight. "How does that feel? It's not too tight is it?" he asked, attempting to sound concerned. He didn't want her to bolt from the bed screaming that he was trying to kill her. He wasn't. He just had his own ways of doing things. Things he liked.

She reached up and felt the roughness of the leather and said with a lazy smile, "It's real nice. Now, make love to me."

He didn't need to hear anymore. He hurried to put on the condom and penetrate her. She was enthusiastic and didn't hesitate to vigorously demonstrate she wanted it as much as he did. He pounded her and felt his lust and passion building and he let it spin up right until he pulled the belt tight enough to make her gasp.

The effect was what he expected and wanted; she shuddered and started to struggle against him, but she moved her hips in a frenzy grinding against his thrusts. He pinned her arms down forcefully and watched her carefully as he continued to ravage her convulsions.

She came when he climaxed and to him it was exquisite. He then quickly released the belt and watched her cough and gulp for breath. She soon smiled. "That was yummy," she said, her voice hoarse from the belt, her blue eyes dreamy and unfocused.

Right at that moment, the fantasy ended and Franklin sat bolt upright on the bunk. He was in a sweat, his pulse jammed. "Fuck me," he hissed to the prison walls, his voice nothing more than a whisper against the cement.

He recalled how it all ended for him at a time when he had everything. Blurred images of Alice's death against the stove, his arrest, the trial, the fucking girl's lies, and the newness of prison all flashed through his mind. He hadn't wanted to kill Alice. She had everything he wanted: the body, the looks, the kink, the hunger. Hell, she made him nothing but money from the photos he took of her and sold to the underground porn mags. She loved posing for him in naked, salacious positions. The video they produced took it to another level and she was totally into it. Her death was an accident, but that's not what the girl said. Oh, no. Her testimony had been damning, and it almost doomed him for life, but that was ending. He'd outsmarted all of the wheat-growing fools on the parole board. Idiots.

He'd never been stupid, but he had been reckless. For almost twenty years he'd thought about the mistakes he'd made and the redheaded bitch that betrayed him. He fumed at the memory of her, but suddenly checked himself. He'd have plenty of time for her soon.

He stood up, flexed his shoulders, and imagined life without the dismal, black steel bars of his cell and him wearing a fucking orange jumpsuit and a bad attitude. "Not much longer," he assured himself. "Not much longer."

Chapter 3 • Dream Reels

Stephanie walked into the bathroom and turned on the cold water. She popped the *crazy pills* into her mouth, bent over and washed them down. She turned off the faucet and placed her hands flat on the counter. Leaning forward, she peered into the mirror and thought of her many therapy sessions with Dr. Stoltz and the reasons why she needed the pink, yellow and blue tablets: they allowed her to cope with day-to-day life and endure the recurring nightmares she'd had for twenty years. Not to say that some didn't occur when she was awake, they had. The haunting memories of the twelve-year-old girl she'd been were always the same though, and they'd changed her in ways no one suspected.

She pushed back from the mirror, removed her glasses, and reminded herself that her dreams were merely remembrances of who she had been, not who she was now. *Beth* and *Tiffany* were tranquil and for the most part, happy and acquiescent. They'd never really been a problem for her anyway. They were just there to help. She was sure of that, if nothing else. They were her best kept secret.

Stephanie brushed her long, thick, red hair and relaxed into the rhythm of the strokes. Without her make-up, freckles sprouted and smudged across her pale skin everywhere and there was no denying or avoiding their continuing spread; they budded and flowered under the brightness of the sun. She closed her eyes against the imaginary glare and sighed. It was at these times, in the silence that she appraised her life - and it was good. Her career was on the upswing and she loved going to work. New projects kept her mind occupied and focused. They rejuvenated her.

She hesitated with the brush and opened her eyes. Reality check. There was no man in her life, but that was fine with her. Not that she didn't want a serious romance, she did. But men always seem to come with issues and that was a real problem.

She shrugged her shoulders, placed the brush on the counter and ran her hands through her hair. No, she didn't need the kind of baggage that seemed to accompany men; the few flings she'd allowed herself had proven that point, as best as she could remember.

She yawned and turned away from her reflection. She padded barefoot to the bed where Skinnykitty was already sleeping. She slipped underneath the covers, told "Alexa" to turn off the lights, and closed her eyes. As her breathing slowed, the images of her childhood stuttered forward like an old movie; the cue marks flashed, signaling it was time for the reel to begin . . . She was eleven when her mother and father suddenly separated and announced that they were getting a divorce. It changed her life profoundly and made her afraid. She was no longer sure of anything or anyone. They didn't have much money to begin with and now that her father was gone, her mother was forced to take a job working nights as a waitress at a tavern. Her shift was over at eleven, but rather than come home to a quiet, sleeping house, she would stay at the tavern until it closed.

When she asked her mother why she was getting home so late, her mother was defensive. "I'm lonely, honey. I need the company. Without this job and the people I meet there, I'd go crazy. I'm doing the best I can to get us ahead."

It didn't make her feel any better or more hopeful and there was no one she could talk to about her feelings of loss. She hid her parent's divorce and her mother's job from her friends at Parker Middle School and invented stories about their happy family life, but they were only fantasies of how she wished it were. She wanted to be like her friends and fit in, but she really didn't. Not in her mind. She was nothing more than a ragamuffin. That's what the mother of one of her friends called them: "They were the poor little ragamuffins who lived down the block."

In her heart she knew it was true.

They soon moved from their house to an apartment. It wasn't long before the boyfriends began, and her mother's drinking seemed to grow worse with each new, brief relationship. Her sister and she lost all of their school friends because of the move, and her mother put most of their furniture in storage. She hated it and wished one day it would change and things would be back to *almost* normal. But it didn't. It continued to grow worse as they moved again and again, each new apartment shabbier than the previous one.

Then her mother met Ray and he changed everything. She couldn't guess when they'd started dating, but when her mother took her shopping and spent $300 for her new school clothes, she knew something was different. As soon as they reached the car with their packages she asked, "Mom, what's going on? How can you afford to do this? Did you get a raise at work?"

"No, honey. I've met a man who's a promoter and he has a great opportunity for me that will help us get back on our feet. His name is Ray. Ray Franklin." Her mother was giddy when she mentioned his name.

Days later she met Ray when she'd arrived home from the hair salon after having her long hair shortened into a blunt cut. She hated it. It wasn't like the pictures in the magazine she'd seen. She was crying when she left the salon and was still crying when she stumbled into the apartment.

A man was standing with her mother in the kitchen.

Her mother quickly came over and hugged her. "Stephy, what's the matter?"

"Oh, Mom - it's my hair. Look at it. It's awful."

Her mother stepped back and wiped the tears from her face. She then gently placed her hands on Stephanie's shoulders and turned her slightly to the left and then right. "Oh, sweetie, I'm so sorry you're disappointed, but I think it looks great on you. I like it. Give it a few days. It'll be better. You're just not used to it."

Her mother hugged her again. She still wanted to cry, but she was now curious about the man. Before she could ask, her mother introduced him. "I want you to meet my new friend, the man I told you about. Stephanie, this is Ray."

When her mother said his name the man smiled wolfishly, one eyebrow raised, his dark eyes squinting as he scanned her up and down. His critical examination caused her to shrink within herself and she averted her eyes. Her foot began to bounce nervously and she fidgeted, snuffled and wiped her nose with the back of her hand as she stole glances of him.

She didn't know exactly why she felt as she did, but she sensed an intensity and cunningness about him that made her insides squirm. She could only imagine the devil or Dracula standing before her. His coal black hair was combed straight back and it glistened with an oily sheen. His dark eyebrows framed penetrating blackish-brown eyes, and his olive complexion was sharpened by the shadows of his heavy stubble. He was taller than her father, she guessed about six foot two, and more powerfully built; his blue, V-necked sweater hugged his chest and heavily muscled arms. He wore black jeans that were pressed with tight creases and his black shoes gleamed like wet plastic.

He stepped over to her and said, "It's nice to meet ya, Stephanie. Hey, don't worry about your hair. Your mom's right. It looks cute and it's modern. I tell you what. Let me pay for the style job, maybe you won't feel so bad." He reached into his pants' pocket and removed a gold money clip thick with folded bills. Her eyes bulged at the money; she'd never seen so much cash in her life. He pulled two twenty-dollar bills from the clip and passed them to her. "Here ya go, kid. I hope this helps."

She immediately thought he was being a show-off for her mother but there was more to it than that. She couldn't put her finger on exactly what it was, or why she was reacting in that manner, but he made her skin crawl.

She took the money from his hand and then quickly excused herself, polite as she could be. "Thank you, Ray. It was nice meeting you. Mom, I'm going to my room for a while."

Her mother smiled and said gently, "Alright, sweetie. I understand. I'll check on you later."

Stephanie hurried to her bedroom and closed the door behind her. She leaned against the cool wood and shut her eyes. She couldn't believe her mother could be with a man like Ray. She sighed and made a wish, her hands clasped, praying. "I hope you're just another two-week boyfriend like the others, Ray. Please, please, let it be so."

Like so many other times, her wish didn't come true.

A few weeks later they were moving into his house with their family furniture. Her mother assured her it would be just like it was before with her father and they would be a family. Only they weren't a family, because Ray wasn't her father.

Ray's three-bedroom house was similar to the one they lived in with their father, but it didn't have a basement and Ray's did. Diana and she discovered the room when they were first moving in and exploring the house, while Ray and her mother were busy unpacking the U-Haul moving truck.

The stairs to the basement were off the kitchen and they were dark, narrow, and made of rough unfinished wood. As soon as they started down the steps, she smelled the dankness and mustiness of the room and it made her scrunch her nose. The ceiling was low, its wood rafters covered in dusty cobwebs. A single bulb snaked down from the ceiling on a black wire partially illuminating the room while casting shadows into the corners. The gray cement walls were bubbled and cracked in places from where moisture had seeped in and scarred them. In the middle of the concrete floor there was a metal drain where dark stains stretched and writhed towards its opening. A coiled hose, mop and a metal bucket sat in the far corner of the room. Underneath the stairs there was a rusty washer and a dented dryer. Above them hung an old-fashioned school clock; a big round black framed one with black numbers on its white face. A slender, red, pointed sweep hand loudly and relentlessly counted the seconds. "Click...click...click...click," it echoed.

"This place scares me, Steph. I don't like it. Let's go," her sister pleaded at the bottom of the steps.

She tried to sound brave and big sister-like so Diana wouldn't run to her mother and spoil their search. "It's okay, Di. It's just an empty room with a washer and dryer. It's no big deal, but we'll go. Okay?"

Her sister didn't wait to answer and ran up the steps to the open doorway where she stopped, turned around, and said with a quiver in her voice, "I bet monsters live down there at night and I don't like it. Don't make me go again."

When she joined her sister in the kitchen, she assured her with what she hoped was the truth. "There are no monsters down there, Di. It's just a basement."

She didn't realize at the time how wrong she was.

Two days later, on Saturday morning, they'd been roused from their sleep by men's voices. She had Evan and Diana put on their slippers. She took Evan by the hand, and with Diana close behind they tiptoed downstairs. The voices were coming from the kitchen where they found their mother sitting next to Ray with a cup of coffee in her hand. She was barefoot and wore her pink bathrobe wrapped tightly around herself. She frowned when she saw them and then shushed Ray and scolded him.

"Now see what you've done? The kids are up."

Ray and four of his friends were drinking beer and laughing about the deer, 'coon, and bear they'd killed the night before. Their clothes were dirty; they smelled bad and were slurring their words. Ray was especially filthy, his shirt and trousers smeared with dark, brownish-red stains.

He put his arm around their mother and pulled her close. "Don't you worry about it, little lady," he said. "Ol' Ray will give your babies a little lesson in how we provide meat for the table and trophies for the home, man style."

The other men laughed and sniggered.

Ray stepped away from Alice and scooped up Evan, who began to squirm and cry. Ray squeezed Evan closer, glared at him and said gruffly, "Stop your crying boy. It's about time you man up. I'm gonna show you and your sisters something you'll think is cool."

Holding Evan tightly, Ray led Diana and Stephanie to the wooden stairs leading to the basement. Her mom didn't say anything.

A wild, moist, iron-tainted odor hung in the air and it made Stephanie crinkle and scrunch her nose as she walked down the steps. It didn't take but an instant before she discovered its source. It was the most hideous thing she'd ever seen. Blood was dripping and oozing from gutted, dead animals that hung by their feet from the rafters on big steel hooks. Their bodies were shiny and whitish pink having been stripped of their skins, which lay in bloody, furry clumps on the floor. She tried to look away, but her eyes were magnetized to the horror in front of her.

Two of the animals were deer, but one was a fawn that was no bigger than a skinny, long-legged dog: its small pink tongue flopped between yellow teeth from the side of its mouth. A raccoon hung next to the deer and it still had its fur, but its brown and black-striped tail had been garishly chopped off and was nailed to the rafter beside it. The one that sickened her most looked like a big, fat baby, but it didn't have a head, hands or feet, and its chest had been split open, its insides removed. The body glistened pink and wet, hanging by its legs from two hooks running through them.

"That one is a black bear," Ray proudly proclaimed, but she knew by its size it had to be a cub. Ray then pointed to a lumpy, green tarp underneath the carcass. "Check this out," he bragged. He bent down and flipped the tarp back revealing the little head, paws and pelt of what she first thought was a teddy bear, except all of its stuffing had been cruelly torn from its body.

Diana screamed and ran upstairs. Evan just stood there next to Stephanie, transfixed by the gore.

"Why would you show us this, Ray? It's awful," she said to him in disbelief.

Ray stepped over to her and touched her arm. He was so close to her she could smell his liquored breath on her cheek. "Well, little girl, this is what men do for their family. And guess what? If you're real nice to me, I'll make this bear skin into a rug for your bedroom. Would you like that?"

All she could do was shake her head at his lurid suggestion. That strange wrongness she suspected about him she now knew was true: Ray was a weird, creepy, long-fingered, leering, soul-devouring monster. He terrified her in a way that made her cringe in naked fear . . . A dog suddenly began barking somewhere outside of her dream. She moaned in her sleep at the sound as the dream ended, the transparencies flapping rhythmically as they slowed. She turned in the bed, her feet kicking free of the covers, and she slowly opened her eyes.

"It's just the dream," she said lazily. She sighed before drifting back to a dreamless sleep.

Chapter 4 • 2017

Stephanie appraised the woman in the mirror. She tugged at her gray silk blouse and straightened her black Armani skirt. They fit perfectly. She thought about her presentation as she considered her make-up for the second time. She was somewhat nervous, but when she checked her watch she relaxed. She had plenty of time. She also knew she was ready. She'd worked hard on the concept and design and it had come easy to her. She would be proposing the Graham Developments Columbia Gorge Resort and Waterpark be named "Islands in the Stream," reflecting the diverse water features and habitats, which she described as "moods" of the park. There was KidSide, Interlude, and Gale Force. She didn't know what the competition would be presenting, but she wasn't worried. She'd tailored her designs based upon what little she learned from Susan about Marcus Graham. Susan described him as a *mover and shaker*. Graham took over the firm four years previously in 2013, when his father died. The company, under his leadership, had been fast tracking ever since. She also knew he was a West Point grad, a war veteran, and he was single; his biography had been documented with great flattery in Portland Magazine. His written request for creative input had been their only contact with him, other than when Susan confirmed their meeting.

She returned her attention to the mirror and took a deep breath. She fluffed her hair a bit and strolled out of the lady's executive washroom, her high heels clicking towards the conference room. As creative director of Synergy Advertising and Design, this was her moment and she wasn't about to let Susan and the agency down.

Susan was waiting at the conference room door. She was wearing a dark blue blazer, skirt, matching pumps and a cream-colored blouse that accented her buxom figure. Her dark hair was a long, curly sprawl.

"All set?" Susan asked, smiling, her brown eyes gleaming. At forty-six, Susan Arcadia was a powerful, driven woman with a direct, no-nonsense reputation.

"Yes, I believe we are. I feel very good about the direction we're presenting. I hope Mr. Graham agrees."

"I do as well. Just remember to smile and be cordial, Steph. I want this one." Susan then turned and opened the door to the conference room where Marcus Graham was waiting.

•

He watched the two women come through the door. He could easily guess the all-blue number with the curly hair was Susan Arcadia. His eyes moved quickly to the stylishly dressed, long-legged, willowy redhead following her. She was strikingly beautiful in a pale, freckled way. Slender, large breasted, with long red hair that contained streaks of blonde, he was instantly interested. He surveyed her closely as she walked purposely towards him. She had blue-green eyes, graceful arms and hands, and perfectly manicured nails. Her glasses matched her demeanor. "She's all business," he mused to himself.

He rose from his chair and greeted the two, his mouth curved into a smile. "Ladies, it's a pleasure to meet you both. I'm Marcus Graham," he said, extending his hand.

The older woman shook his hand and said, "Mr. Graham, thank you. I'm Susan Arcadia and this is our creative director, Stephanie Courtland."

•

Stephanie studied him carefully. He was dressed in a tan suit that appeared hand-tailored, and his white shirt, brown tie and reddish loafers were impeccably matched; he obviously took great care about his appearance. He was over six foot tall, lean and athletic. He had a lightly tanned complexion, brown eyes and dark, longer hair combed straight back. A small thin scar ran from the corner of his left eye to his hairline. His smile was engaging, and it radiated when she made eye contact with him. She thought he was very handsome and vaguely familiar. The familiarity startled her, but she quickly brushed away the thought.

He shook Susan's hand first and then hers. "Please, call me Marcus. I very much look forward to seeing what you have for me today."

"Thank you, Marcus," Stephanie said coolly, appraising him.

Susan gestured Marcus towards the chair he'd risen from and said, "We're delighted to share with you our ideas for your Columbia Gorge Project, Marcus. We call it 'Islands in the Stream.' Please, let's sit. Stephanie will be presenting."

•

Graham knew what he wanted and wouldn't be easy to impress, but Stephanie Courtland captivated him. When she imparted her ideas for the park her voice was soft, almost breathless. When he questioned her motivation for the various habitat themes, she confidently spoke of the "moods" that could be created in each. She wasn't afraid to defend her ideas and he admired that. She was also cool and unflustered in her responses and he wondered if he was having any effect upon her at all, other than business.

At the conclusion of the presentation, Graham paused and reflected quietly for a moment before responding. "Ladies, I have a lot to think about, but I'm encouraged by what I've heard and seen today. I'll be making my decision within the next few weeks. Susan, please send me your numbers on media projections and final costs. Thank you so much for your time."

He stood and turned his attention to Stephanie. "I want to personally commend you on your presentation today. I very much enjoyed our time together."

He then nodded to her and left the room, escorted by Susan.

•

Stephanie watched them leave as she began to cover and re-assemble her poster boards. She took her time, lost in thought over her presentation and his reactions.

Her reverie was broken by Susan re-entering the room, who she caught mid-sentence. "And Stephanie, you were wonderful and he had nothing but eyes for you. He's quite a package. So well-spoken and handsome - let alone rich. I'm thinking we have ourselves a new client." Susan was gleeful, almost giddy.

"I'm glad you feel that way, because I believe his questions were very challenging. He's very specific about what he wants and appears to be quite controlling. Don't get me wrong, he's very charming and smart, but I think he comes across a little strong."

"Oh, come on, Steph. He was just being focused and his questions during the presentation were appropriate. It's a lot of money he'll be shelling out. Remember what my mother used to say: don't look a gift horse in the mouth."

She followed Susan out of the conference room thinking of him. Her curiosity was aroused, as were the yellow caution flags she imagined waving in warning before her. She was surprised *Beth* and *Tiffany* were so quiet. She didn't think it would last.

That evening she brushed her teeth and took her *crazy pills*. In the bedroom she found Skinnykitty curled up asleep next to her pillow. She crawled into bed, pulled the covers up to her neck, relaxed and quieted her thinking. She closed her eyes as the dream reel spun and the frames began without her being able to stop them . . . She'd slipped out of bed to remind her mother that she had to be at school early the next day to register at Parker Middle School. When she arrived at their bedroom door, she saw it was partially open. She peeked in and saw Ray on top of her mother. They were both naked. Her mother's hands were tied above her head and her feet were tied tightly across each side of the bed. Her mother was groaning, and saying words to Ray she didn't want to know or hear. There was something over her mother's eyes so she didn't see her standing there, but Ray did. He glanced back over his shoulder at her and smiled lasciviously. He didn't seem to be surprised. He then pursed his lips together and blew her a kiss.

She turned and ran as fast as she could from the door and back to her room. Her heart was beating so hard it seemed as if it was going to explode. She didn't know what to do, so she climbed into bed and pulled the covers over her head. She tried not to think of what she had seen, but she couldn't get his face or how her mother looked out of her head. All she could do was lie there, shake, and hope the door wouldn't open. She couldn't understand why her mother would let Ray do that, but she would never ask. It would be too embarrassing and her mother worshipped Ray, which she also didn't understand.

It only became worse.

He enjoyed catching her alone, coming up from behind her and pushing his body close against hers, while he touched her hips and shoulders and whispered in her ear that she was pretty and so grown up. It was in those moments she felt totally helpless. She couldn't move or say anything. All she could do was wait until it was over, trying not to be there in her mind. As bad as those brief encounters were with him, her most horrifying experience occurred in the basement.

Her mother had left for the market with Evan and Diana, leaving her behind to do the laundry. The laundry was her main chore and it was the only reason she ever went to the basement. She didn't want to be down there if she didn't have to, but the washer and dryer were there and she had no choice.

She'd waited impatiently for the washer to end its cycle and come to a stop. When it did, she opened the lid and was shocked at what she saw. The clothes she'd been doing were all whites, but now they were a light pink. She discovered why when she reached into the mound of wet clothes and found a pair of Evan's red socks hidden inside.

She slammed the washer door shut and then reopened it, afraid of what she had found.

"What the fuck is going on down there?" she heard yelled at her from upstairs in the kitchen. It was Ray.

"Nothing. Everything is okay. I'm doing the laundry for Mom," she said, trying to sound upbeat.

She soon heard his footsteps coming down the stairs and wished that she could disappear.

Ray stomped from the stairs around to where she was standing in front of the washer. He glanced at her and then examined the clothes. "What the fuck have you done?" he said angrily. "Why are my t-shirts and BVD's pink?" He held a wadded, very pink t-shirt and shook it at her. "How am I supposed to wear this shit?"

"I-I made a mistake. There was a pair of Evan's socks hidden in the middle. I didn't see them. I'm so sorry, I can fix it," she said, trying to keep the fear from her voice.

"You're sorry? You're always fucking sorry. It's all I ever hear from you. By the way, I saw you watching us the other night. Did you enjoy the little party your mom and I were having? I knew you would."

He paused and moved his eyes slowly over her body. "Now, take off your dress," he ordered abruptly.

She was afraid to understand what she had heard.

"I said, take off your fucking dress or I'll take it off for you!"

She glanced at the steps thinking she could run, but she knew she'd never make it. She could scream, but there was no one at home to hear her cries. She was trapped. "Why? Why do I have to take off my dress? Don't make me, Ray," she pleaded.

"You take it off now or I will goddammit! I think it's time you learn a lesson about following instructions."

She started to cry. "Please, Ray. Don't make me do this, please."

He paused, smiled, and dropped his voice. "Relax, baby girl. I'm not going to hurt you, but I'm not going to tell you again. Now do it!"

She sobbed as she clutched the hem of her dress and lifted it over her head. She slowly dropped the dress to the floor in front of her. She was left standing in just her panties and bra. She hugged her arms across her chest trying to hide herself.

He went over and stood intimately close behind her. He waited a moment before saying softly, "You look real good, you know that? I was hoping we'd have the chance to spend some time together. I think you know what I mean."

She stopped crying. She focused on the clock and its relentless click...click...click...click.

"You're so silky and smooth. You smell nice too," he said as he placed his hands on her shoulders and gently rubbed them. He then traced his fingers down her arms and he pushed his body against her hips. He pulled her closer to him and brushed his fingers against her ribs, just under her breasts. He was breathing heavily and when his whiskered cheek brushed against hers she could smell his stale breath. She shuddered. Goosebumps raised along her arms, the panic immobilizing her.

"You like that, don't you, girl? I can tell," he whispered.

She felt his right hand slip inside her bra and cup her breast, while his other hand slid inside the back of her panties and caressed her bottom. Her heart jumped to her throat and she wanted to scream, but she was frozen with fear. His fingers softly glided across her as she shuddered under his touch and her legs began to shake.

It was then they both heard the car arrive. Her mother was home!

Ray reacted immediately and pulled away from her. He was suddenly infuriated and frustrated. "Say one word to anyone about our time together today and you, your mom, and your brother and sister will be back to living in some shitty apartment. You don't want that kind of trouble for them, do you?" he asked meanly.

Stephanie shook her head as footsteps sounded above them in the kitchen.

Ray reached down and grabbed her dress. He held it up, crumpled it into a ball, and threw it into the washer, staring at her as he did it. He then dropped his voice and quietly said, "Maybe next time we'll have more time together." He smiled and winked at her before turning and heading for the stairs.

As he walked up the steps, he said in a voice loud enough for her mother to hear, "Maybe if it's your clothes in there you'll be more careful. The next time, pay attention. Now wash everything again and make it right. Don't come up until you've also dried and folded them."

Seconds later, she listened to Ray greeting her mother in the kitchen as if nothing had happened. "Stephanie had a screw-up with the laundry, but she's taking care of it. How was the shopping, baby? Did you get something for lunch?"

The door shut and she collapsed to the floor, crying. She didn't want anyone to hear her, so she buried her face in the heap of laundry piled there. No one had ever seen her almost naked or touched her. It was so wrong, but she knew she couldn't tell anyone. They'd be without a home and her mother would be devastated. She didn't know what to do, but if she did nothing who would stop him?

She pulled away from the clothes pile and took a deep breath. She wiped her eyes and then her nose with the back of her hand. She stared at the clock and listened to the second hand make its relentless hollow echo: click...click...click...click.

She suddenly shuddered and heard, *"I'll stop him from ever doing that again to you, Steph. No doubt about it."*

The voice and response startled her. Stephanie looked around the room and didn't see anything or anyone, but when she closed her eyes she imagined a girl sitting on the dryer. The girl appeared to be about thirteen or fourteen and she was big: she was no girly-girl. She had a sharply chiseled face, thin lips, and freckles. Her short dark hair was neatly brushed and her deep-blue eyes were framed by dark eyebrows. She was dressed in a red-striped t-shirt, blue jeans, and black Converse hi-tops with white laces. Her arms and legs were muscled and her overall appearance was one of toughness.

"Don't forget me. I'm more like you than she is," said a sugary sweet, lilting voice. It was another girl about the same age. This one had long red hair and she was thin and pretty. She wore a blue and white dress and had on shiny white shoes. She was standing under the light bulb and was rocking back and forth as she twirled her hair with her right hand.

When Stephanie opened her eyes she saw no one, but she felt surprisingly at ease. "Who are you and what are you doing down here?" she whispered.

"I'm Beth and she's Tiffany," the dark-haired girl replied. *"We're here because you need us - to protect you. And trust me, that Ray bastard will never touch us again."*

"She's right as rain, Stephy. You're too nice and quiet, just like me," Tiffany added, giggling as she wrung her hands by her side.

Beth hopped off the dryer, shook her finger at Tiffany and scolded, "No, she's not! Tiffany sounds all gooey and nice, but she can be very, very bad. I know the way she thinks and I'm here to make sure she doesn't make a mess we'll all be sorry about. Trust me on that one."

Tiffany looked at the floor and quietly said, "Uh-uh. I'll be good. Promise."

Stephanie stood up and wiped her nose. She thought about what the *girls* had said and smiled with relief. The funny thing was she felt as if she'd known *Beth* and *Tiffany* her whole life, but she'd forgotten about *them.*

The dream reel ended suddenly when the cat snuggled up against the back of her knees, partially waking her. She rolled over onto her back and slowly opened her eyes. She glanced at the red numbers of the clock beside her bed: 4:38 a.m. She turned away from the display and stared into the darkness. She wondered if the dreams would ever stop.

Chapter 5 • The Devil in the Details

Graham considered Stephanie Courtland as he drove back to his offices in the Tower. He'd always had an affinity for redheads and he wanted to find out more about her. He'd have Hank do it. Powell and his team specialized in discreet background work and he'd depended upon them more than once. Powell never let him down. "Can't be too careful," he mused, looking up and smiling to himself in the rear-view mirror of the Mercedes. At the same time, he was also thinking of his last tour in the Middle East and when he'd been less than careful there more than once. "Ain't no big thang," he reminded himself.

Turning into the underground entrance of the Tower, he cautiously made his way to his reserved parking stall. He jumped out, locked the 650, and strode to the elevator. He punched 22, his lucky number.

He hummed to himself as the elevator glided up, dinged, and then opened with a quiet shush. He advanced to the double maple doors and admired the simple bronze plaque sitting next to them engraved with two initials, GD. "Home sweet home," he said to himself, a subtle sigh of relief escaping his lips.

Before he could insert his key card into the lock, the door clicked and opened: Gretchen was watching from the video monitor, ever diligent.

"Good afternoon, Marcus," she said, rising from behind her desk and gliding towards him. She was beautiful as ever, but definitely not on his hit list. Even though Gretchen was absolutely drop-dead gorgeous with a personality to match, "Don't screw the help" had been drummed into him at the Point, and he knew better than to mix business with pleasure. "Hmm, that's a contradiction," he thought, thinking of Stephanie and her agency.

"Hello, Gretchen. I'm happy to be back. Any messages? And please get Hank on the phone for me," he replied, looking over the waiting room, which he'd designed to resemble a fine library with leather couches, brass floor lamps, and tall palms.

"No, Marcus, there are no messages. Clay and Robert are both in their offices. All is good. I'll get Hank on the phone momentarily. How was the meeting?"

"I'm pleased and somewhat impressed. I think we may do some business with the ladies of Synergy."

"Shall I add them to our VIP list?"

The list had been his idea. If you weren't on the list, you'd get the courtesy of one message to leave behind with Gretchen. One only. If you were on the VIP list, then your call would be placed through with screening. If you were on the "M" list, the call was forwarded directly to him.

"For now, let's go with VIP. I'll be in my office. Ring Hank as soon as you can."

"You got it, LT," she said sternly. The LT reference was her way of telling him to lighten up, because she wasn't in his "platoon."

Graham gave her a wink and a thumbs-up as he pushed past her desk and through the door that led to his office and home. There were three offices and a conference room sitting astride the green-carpeted hallway. At the very end of the hallway were two large maple doors that had another card slot opening to the right against the wall. On each of those doors was a simple brass M - his home.

The largest of the three offices was his, and it was on the same side of the hall as the conference room. On the other side of the hallway resided the workspaces of his broker, Clay Turner, and his architectural designer, Robert Cothren. Both were busy at their desks: Rob was bent over his computer and Clay was on the phone.

All of the offices sat behind glass walls, and each had a glass door with brass hinges. The walls partitioning the offices were opaque. Graham's office and the conference room also shared ceiling-to-floor windows that could make even the hardiest viewers have an attack of vertigo.

The intercom buzzed and he heard Gretchen say ever so politely, "I have Hank on the line, LT."

Apparently, she was still miffed. He leaned over his desk and pushed the respond button. "Got it. Thank you, Gretchen."

He settled into the high-backed, black leather chair behind his desk and tapped the blinking light. "Hank, my man. Thanks for calling. How are you and the troops?"

"LT, I'm good and so are they. I haven't heard from you in a while. I take it all is well in the land of the Tower?" Powell's deep bass voice boomed over the speakerphone.

Everything about Henry Salomon Powell was large including his personality, demeanor and service record. Powell was a recipient of the Congressional Medal of Honor and was a legend in the Special Forces. Broad-shouldered and heavily muscled at six foot five and 260 pounds, he was a "presence with a menace," as he liked to say. Blue-eyed, square-faced and strong-jawed, Powell's graying blond hair was cropped military-style. His choice of clothing was carefully selected by him to complete what he called "the look."

"Everything is copasetic here. I've been busy reviewing agencies for the Gorge project and I need you to check out someone for me. You have the time?"

"LT, are you kidding me? Time is never an issue."

He could hear the genuine delight in Powell's voice and it made him smile. They both enjoyed the relationship. It was something only a grunt shared with another grunt that nobody else could understand. Both wore their Combat Infantry Badge close to their Purple Hearts and it was a bond between them. They'd spilled blood together and they possessed a brotherhood forged by fire.

Powell was older by six years at forty-two, and he'd spent twenty of those in the Army, most of them in Special Forces. He was on his third tour in the Middle East as a senior First Sergeant when he met Lieutenant Marcus Graham. The LT and his merry band of infantrymen helped extradite him and his badly shot-up A-team from a mountainous position in the middle of nowhere in Afghanistan. It was where Powell won his MOH. He recalled what he said to Marcus on their way out: "We were lucky. The only reason they didn't kill more of us was because there weren't more of us there."

They'd been tight ever since.

Powell remembered when he retired from the military and was discovering there weren't many jobs that held an interest for an ex-Special Forces NCO with his skill set. That's when the LT had called and asked him to come up and check out Portland for a few days. But it wasn't for a visit. Graham had a reason for the invite and it was an idea right up Powell's alley. Graham financed him into his own private investigation business: Avalanche Investigations. But their partnership was not just a monetary one.

"Hank, grab a pen and write this down." Graham paused briefly and then continued, "Stephanie Courtland. Works for Synergy Advertising and Design. She lives in Portland, and she's in her early thirties. I did my typical prelim search on the agency before I met with them, but I didn't see much info about her. Now that I've met her, I want details. I think we'll be working together and you know how I am when it comes to beautiful women. Oh, and she's a redhead and gorgeous with a big G."

Powell cut to the chase. "Sounds serious. And yes, I do know. Your caution doesn't surprise me, LT. We both remember Nancy and her gold-digging ways. You don't need any more of those in your life."

"You've got that right. Anyway, find out what you can about her and get back to me ASAP."

"You've got it, LT. I'll get on it. Give me a few hours."

It didn't take him long after passing the info to Andy Hines, the computer guru of Avalanche. It was 5:30 p.m. when Powell punched the call button next to the key card slot at the doors of Graham Developments. He suspected Gretchen was watching on her video monitor as he stared up the camera and mocked the words, "Really?" He'd forgotten his entry card, again.

She buzzed him in.

Pushing the door open, he marched towards her desk. "Gretchen, my love. What's up?"

Powell was dressed in a black safari jacket, the long sleeves rolled up, the pale blue MOH ribbon with the five white stars pinned to his lapel. He wore the jacket open over a light blue shirt that hugged his powerful physique. His khaki pants and black loafers completed "the look." He carried a thick manila folder in one hand.

"Everything is very good, Hank. How are you, big man?" Gretchen replied.

"Big man is it, Gretchen? So, it's more about my body than my brains?" he said with a mock look of concern. "Is the LT available? I think he may be expecting me, love."

"Yes, he is. And Hank, I think you have very nice brains." She smiled and gave a small wink.

He grinned back at her. "Thanks, Gretchen. It's good to know what I'm respected for."

As Powell headed toward Graham's office he considered Gretchen Hilde: she was the only woman who possessed everything he wanted, including smarts. Blonde with long legs and a devastating figure, the only thing keeping him from her was their work. He didn't want to upset the apple cart at Graham Developments and it certainly could if they became an item. Marcus wouldn't be happy if he had to find a new Gretchen; he knew how the LT wanted everything in his life "just so."

Graham was standing and leaning against his desk when he saw Powell push through the glass door of his office. He was quick with his greeting. "Hank, good to see you. I take it your search was successful?"

"It's always good to see you too, Marcus. Yes, there's quite a bit of info on Miss Courtland. As you'll read, she had a particularly tough childhood," he said, passing the folder to Graham, who flipped it open and began scanning through the pages.

Powell stood quietly and admired their pictures from Afghanistan hanging on the office wall along with Marcus' West Point diploma, commissioning certificates, and a boxed display of his medals and awards from his military service.

"There's a lot here. Anything I should be worried about?" Graham asked, peering up from the pages of the folder.

"It's a little more complicated than that. She's thirty-two. She has a sister, Diana, who's twenty-nine and a brother, Evan, who's twenty-six. She's a college grad. Above-average grades. No criminal history. Good credit. Never married. I've given you all the Facebook and social profile info - printed those, though I'm sure you've already seen them. She's been on the dating site, Match, still is. Nothing unusual, but it's easy to see why you're attracted. She's very, very beautiful. But, and here it is, there's a big, dramatic family history and you're not going to like it."

Powell paused and then continued. "In '96 her mother was living with a man named Ray Franklin, who one night beat her up and killed her. Miss Courtland was also beaten when she tried to defend her mother. She was only twelve-years old at the time, but she had it together enough to protect her brother and sister and call the cops for help. Franklin swore it was an accident, but he'd been in trouble his whole life. Petty theft, drugs when he was younger, and there was an accusation of rape, but nothing came of it."

Powell paused again, letting Graham absorb the story.

"Miss Courtland crucified him at the trial. It was reported she recounted things about Franklin that were so terrible they had to be taken in closed court. They didn't say exactly what she testified to because of the censure, but during the trial, when she was asked if she was afraid of him, she answered without any emotion at all. She said she wouldn't be afraid of anyone, anymore. I've put the press clippings in the folder for you."

"Miss Courtland and her sister and brother ended up living with their dad and stepmom. Franklin received fifteen to forty at Washington State Penitentiary for second-degree manslaughter, with circumstances. There may have been allegations of sexual abuse, but it was unsubstantiated. In the transcripts, the judge only insinuated to it when he passed down the verdict and sentence. It's all in there."

Powell paused, shrugged his shoulders and slightly shook his head. "But there's something more and it's a big one."

Graham shuffled the pages within the folder for a few moments and then said, "Ok. You've got my attention. What is it?"

"When Hines was digging up the info on Miss Courtland, he took a hard look at Franklin, too. The accused-rape thing proved to be the lynchpin to unlocking a secret that's hard to believe. Hines researched the girl who was involved with Franklin and discovered she wasn't a rape victim at all. The yearbooks of her high school revealed she and Franklin were not strangers, but were quite an item together in their junior and senior years. Franklin had been an athlete and lettered in several sports, and Kathleen Reardon was a cheerleader. Photos of them together at dances and other school events didn't portray the picture of a rapist and his future victim. Quite the opposite."

"It was the State of Oregon that provided most of the details for Hines. He discovered the Multnomah County Health Department maintained all records of official births and deaths in Oregon. All records of marriage and divorce were also recorded there. They were online and Hines considered them quite helpful when he carefully examined the relationship of Franklin, Reardon and the baby they conceived. His research disclosed that adoption records were secret and information on them was difficult to obtain until a few years ago. It was then a new Oregon statute was put into law that allowed people involved in an adoption to receive copies of pertinent documents from the Oregon court where the adoption finalized. A further link on the site guided him the Oregon Adoption Search and Registry Program. Its database recorded adoptions going back to the early 1920s. It was easy for him from there. Within fifteen minutes he'd found everything and it wasn't good. Hines made a list of his conclusions."

Powell passed a single sheet of paper to him. "Marcus, this is going to be tough on you, so hang on."

Graham read Hines' report:

1) Kathleen and Ray were high school sweethearts who were having sex and had been for a while. It was the 70s.

2) Kathleen became pregnant.

3) Her parents were furious and called the police to have Ray arrested for rape.

4) When interviewed, Kathleen disputed her parents and said she loved Ray and wanted the baby. Ray was released.

5) The parents sent Kathleen away to have the baby and insisted that she put it up for adoption, which she did. Ray didn't object, or didn't care.

6) Kathleen fell into a deep depression over the loss of her baby and six months later she killed herself with a drug overdose.

7) The baby was adopted by Walter and Rose Graham, who named him Marcus.

Powell watched his friend and could only guess how he felt. He couldn't imagine what it would be like to learn that your father abused your potential new girlfriend and then killed her mother. "What were the odds on that?" Powell wondered.

Graham slowly shook his head as he finished reading the list.

"Are you okay?" Powell asked.

"I am. Thanks, Hank. I'm not sure how I feel about all of this," Graham said, worry settling on his face. He then slipped the paper Powell had given him into the report folder. "I need to do some reading."

"I get it, LT. Take your time. It's a lot to digest. If you need to talk, call me."

Graham only nodded at him.

Powell knew when it was time to leave. "I'll be in touch," he said as he left Graham to his reading.

Graham sat down in his chair and opened the folder.

Chapter 6 • Avalanche

Powell drove the big, black Ford Raptor to his office in north Portland. The vehicle was more of a statement than it was practical, but Powell preferred the image - just like their HQ. The old brick building of Avalanche originally housed a boxing gym and laid unoccupied until Graham purchased and then renovated it for the company. It sat on the street alone with large vacant lots on either side of it and across the street; the burgeoning growth that gentrified much of northwest Portland had yet to reach the industrial north side.

The twin glass doors at the front of the building were signed in black letters with a blue shadow: AVALANCHE. The line underneath read: *Licensed Private Investigations / Security / Personal Protection.*

The company had grown rapidly because they'd solved a crime that stumped law enforcement for years. "The Invisible Man" is what the press called Frank Morton, and he'd been responsible for a three-state killing spree that began with prostitutes and ended with teenage runaways. Powell's involvement in the investigation began shortly after opening Avalanche. He had one employee at the time, Andy Hines. They both took immense pride in what they'd accomplished and it earned them an early reputation for being smart, capable and tough. They'd also received great press. When the media discovered Powell's MOH and service background, he and Avalanche became the focus of intense, albeit brief, praise and recognition. It proved to be enough to bring them the clients they needed and within three years there were a team of six.

Powell pulled into the Avalanche parking lot at 6:30 p.m. and counted vehicles to see who was still at work: Hines, McGee, the Kirkpatrick brothers, and Mac Kierney were all still at base camp. The full crew. He jumped from the Raptor and marched to the entrance doors. When he entered the small lobby he saw Mac look up at him from the receptionist desk.

"So, we have the second meanest dude on the compound playing receptionist?" Powell asked gruffly.

Kierney frowned and responded, "You said second meanest, Top Sergeant? Why, I believed I was a good third or fourth behind you and those mean ass badger boys. But then again, I could be ready to be champ."

Powell laughed at the giant African American as Kierney stood and began taking mock swings at an invisible opponent. Kierney, at six foot five and 245 pounds, was wedge-shaped and powerful. His sand colored polo shirt and black slacks hugged his muscular frame. He had the biggest hands Powell had ever seen. Kierney was a former Army combat engineer who had qualified as a sapper. He was trained to build bridges and defenses, lay and clear minefields, and use demolitions. He was the Avalanche handyman. He also served as a personal bodyguard and surveillance specialist. His grizzled appearance was accented by a five o'clock shadow he always seemed to have. He was forty-five and had two combat tours under his belt.

"Easy there, big fellah. You might pull something," Powell warned.

Mac grinned at him all toothy and in an easygoing Carolina drawl said, "That's good stuff, big man. For the record, there are no messages or events to deal with. Hines and McGee are in the computer room and those crazy fuckin' badgers are working out in the gym like usual - probably trying to kill each other again. Those boys are nuts, but I love'em."

"We all do, buddy. Thanks for the update. Plans for the weekend?"

"The wife and I are taking the kids to the beach Saturday. We enjoy the coast and our girls like flirting with the boys they see in Seaside. Very exciting stuff, don't you know?"

"I'm sure you're watching out for them," Powell said, laughing again.

"Those two will be the death penalty for me. They're too smart and way too good lookin' for their own good. God help me."

"Yes, He should, Mac. I hope He does. You have your hands full. Now, get outta here and go see your family. Just lock up on your way out."

"You got it, Top. See you Monday."

Kierney rose from the desk and strode to the front door, nodding at Powell, eye-to-eye.

Powell watched the big man leave. He then pushed through the door leading to the interior sanctuaries of Avalanche. It first opened to the old gym, the elevated boxing ring still standing under its screened chrome lamps and rotating fan. The ring had been refurbished, as had the gym, which now sported all the latest fitness machines, recumbent bikes, treadmills, weight systems, and climbing ropes of any top-flight training facility. On the big wrestling mat he could see the Kirkpatrick brothers facing each other in the prone push-up position. They were wearing shorts and were shirtless, their bodies glistening with sweat, straining, red-faced with grim, determined expressions.

Both were Irish-handsome and obviously brothers: dark-haired, buzz-cut, and short bearded. Aiden Kirkpatrick was five foot ten, heavily muscled and appeared twenty-two, although he was ten years older. Liam was six foot two, 200 pounds and three years older. Powell considered them his toughest, most capable, and certainly the most dangerous of his men.

The brothers were born and raised in Oregon and had served in the special operations community. Aiden had applied to Avalanche when Powell first advertised for 'specialists' from the ex-SpecOps community. It was just after Powell's success with the Morton investigation. Liam followed once he'd heard from his brother that Avalanche offered their kind of work. Both were hired without hesitation.

Liam Kirkpatrick spent ten years in the U.S. Marine Corps, his last four as a captain in the Marine's elite Force Recon. He'd been to the Middle East on three tours. His many awards and decorations included the Distinguished Service Cross, America's second highest award for heroism in combat.

Aiden Kirkpatrick served twelve years with the U.S. Air Force. His last six years he spent as a master sergeant and combat controller. Powell knew most people didn't know what a combat controller did or that they were ranked among America's most highly trained special operations forces; their mission was to deploy undetected into combat environments to establish assault zones or airfields, while simultaneously conducting air traffic control and fire support. His combat assignments included Iraq and Afghanistan. His numerous decorations were highlighted by a Silver Star for gallantry in action.

Powell walked over to the edge of the mat and shook his head as he eyeballed the two brothers. "Let me guess. First, you ran five miles to warm up. Then you pumped weights for forty-five minutes and polished those off with 200 matching push-ups. Now you're seeing who can hold their up-position the longest. Am I right?"

Liam glanced up at Powell and nodded with a frown.

Aiden, sweating profusely said in a strained voice, "I'm gonna kill him this time, Top."

Powell shook his head and said, "Well, I wish you both good luck in this endeavor. Please don't damage yourselves. I know it's after hours and your time, but don't you two have women to chase or beers to drink? Something besides this?"

They both shook their heads.

Powell laughed and headed for his office at the rear of the gym and boxing area. At the back half of the building stood six doors. One led to the shower, lockers and restroom area. Another went to the Ready Room where the weapons and gear were stored. The third opened to the bunkroom, which was set-up for rest and relaxation given the odd hours the team members worked. The fourth room contained an elaborately outfitted kitchen with attached dining area.

Powell peered through the wire-meshed glass window of the fifth door, the Operations / Legal center of Avalanche, and saw Hines and McGee focused on the computer monitors, furiously typing away.

Andy Hines had been a counter-intelligence computer analyst during his three years in the Army and afterwards, for another three, at the Department of Defense. Hines was the youngest member of the Avalanche team at twenty-eight, and at five foot eight and 165 pounds, he was also the smallest. Blonde-haired and blue-eyed, he had a narrow, boyish face and wispy beard. His round, wire-rimmed glasses accented his intellectual demeanor. Hines was hired after responding to an ad Powell placed in the Army Times: "Computer specialist wanted for complex private investigation work - military experience required." Hines fit the bill perfectly, though Powell found his taste in rap and hip-hop music disturbing.

John McGee was the newest member of Avalanche and the only one with no former service background. Powell was initially suspicious of adding an attorney to the Avalanche team, but when Graham explained McGee's background, skills, low-income requirement, and employment aspirations, Powell couldn't resist. McGee was a Harvard Law grad and was gifted with a photographic memory. Six foot three and lanky, McGee had a long face, was brown-haired and balding, and where on other men it was distracting, on McGee it imparted a look of wisdom and maturity. His nose was crooked: Powell was reminded of a fighter he'd once seen. The glasses he wore were similar to Hines' wire frames, except McGee's were rectangular and Maybach's. Powell guessed they were probably worth $2,500 or more. The glasses went well with his steel and gold Rolex Sky-Dweller, which made even Powell envious.

Graham had met McGee by chance when he was paired with him for a round of golf at Columbia Edgewater Country Club. They were both members but had never played together. During the course of the day Graham learned that McGee was fifty, recently divorced and bored with his practice. He was also wealthy, having explained to Graham he was looking for a new career and money wasn't the object. When Graham inquired what interested him, McGee said he always wanted to be a private investigator - digging into backgrounds and facts is what he enjoyed most when he was practicing law.

Graham didn't hesitate to introduce him to Powell the next day.

McGee's contacts within the legal community immediately produced a wealth of new business for Avalanche. It began when Powell asked McGee why attorneys typically hire an investigative firm, because most of their work came from private individuals. When McGee gave his photographic recital of the multiple ways in which attorneys utilize private investigators, Powell was somewhat surprised. He'd always believed they could do a better job with attorneys, and McGee's suggestions only helped to drive home the point. McGee wrapped up his advice by saying, "Hope this helped. If you want, I can prepare a letter for Avalanche that can be sent to several firms and attorneys I know who may be able to utilize our services. We can include our profile and personnel assets."

The effect of the letter was almost instantaneous. Avalanche was now working on six new cases from four different attorneys. Initially, Powell was forced to spend the time and money to officially license everyone, and it had slowed them down, but it was required when working for their new clients. It also justified their higher fees, which he enjoyed, as did the team. Hines was particularly busy, but seemed oblivious to the increased workloads. In fact, he hadn't seen the man happier.

The last door opened to his office. It was very similar to Graham's: it was both his office and private apartment. It'd been Graham's idea. Powell considered it smart and convenient. His life at the moment was his company and he found combining his residence with his business worked perfectly. He'd never been married, mainly due to his military service, but he'd been close a few times. In each relationship the Army eventually won out, usually by transferring him to a new post.

He made his way through the office to the door of his apartment. When he entered, lights automatically came on illuminating the living room, the kitchen and the hallway that led to his bedroom. The lights were Hines' handiwork and were adjustable by voice as was the audio and television. Powell could also communicate to the operations room through the same system by saying the key words, "On my six."

Powell wandered into the kitchen, opened the fridge, and snatched a bottle of Budweiser beer. He slugged half the bottle back and considered the report he'd passed to Marcus. He worried for his friend and wondered again what he would do. He had a hunch that if Courtland became important to Marcus, trouble wouldn't be far behind. The LT loved reclamation projects and he sensed this could be a big one.

Chapter 7 • Playing the Doctor

The next morning, Stephanie was still upset from her dream of Ray and his creepy, long fingers pawing and dwelling upon her body. She shivered at the thought as she slipped into the steaming shower. She turned her back to the spray and let it massage her with its warmth, washing the nightmare away. Lost in the sensuous touch of the water against her skin she was reminded of her first session with Dr. Stoltz.

Dr. Jean Stoltz had not been her first choice. She'd originally selected Dr. Jim Galloway, but he was booked out for months. Dr. Stoltz did come highly rated; she was just unsure about an older female psychiatrist prying open her head when all she wanted was to sleep better and stop the dreams of Ray. *Beth* was concerned the doctor would intuitively know that *they* were watching and listening. *Tiffany* wasn't the least bit concerned.

She turned and faced the warm spray and remembered that Dr. Stoltz was dressed somewhat casually that day in black slacks and a green sweater. She was a trim brunette with sparkling eyes and an expression Stephanie could only recall as caring. When she was shown into Dr. Stoltz's office she was greeted warmly with a handshake. "Stephanie, how nice to meet you. Please let's sit."

Dr. Stoltz sat opposite her and quietly asked, "Stephanie, how can I help you today? I understand you've been having difficulties sleeping. Nightmares?"

"Stick to the basics, Steph. No clicking." Beth warned her silently.

"Yes, I've had trouble my whole life it seems. I have dreams, nightmares. They're about Ray Franklin and what he did to me, my sister and brother, and my Mom. And they're always the same."

Stephanie paused for a moment and then slowly recounted her history with Ray and all that it entailed.

Dr. Stoltz made frequent entries on her notepad as Stephanie talked for the next ten minutes.

She remembered how Dr. Stoltz reacted when she had finished describing her mothers' death. "I'm so sorry you had to endure that, Stephanie. I can see why it still upsets you. I do have one more question though. Would that be all right?"

"Yes, that would be fine."

"If Ray Franklin weren't in jail, how would you feel?"

Beth was immediately suspicious. She quickly whispered to Stephanie, "Answer calmly. No mistakes. She's prying."

"I would be bothered if he was out and about, and if I saw him, or if he tried to pull something, I would be on the defensive. I'm not a kid anymore. I'm sure you would feel the same way, or at least you should, Dr. Stoltz. He's a child molester and a murderer. I'm equally sure he'll never get out of prison for what he did," Stephanie said coldly, but there was no mistaking the anger in her voice.

Dr. Stoltz nodded silently and wrote on her pad.

Beth silently approved.

At the conclusion of their time together, Dr. Stoltz explained to her that it was a good start and that all things begin with small steps. She passed her a prescription that she said would help her sleeping and hopefully limit the nightmares. The doctor reminded Stephanie that she would see her the following week to see how the medications were helping.

Stephanie doubted that the doctor had been aware of *them*: *they* had been very careful, knowing fully well that if the doctor discovered *their* existence it would complicate matters and she would be more closely examined. If that were to happen and *their* secrets were to emerge it wouldn't be a good thing. No, that wouldn't do. *Beth had been very clear about that.*

Stephanie stopped at the Walgreens for the meds on her way home. There were no objections from *Beth* or *Tiffany*, quite the contrary.

Tiffany, unable to hide her enthusiasm, exclaimed excitedly, "Party at our house tonight!"

Arriving home, Stephanie went immediately to the bathroom and stood before the mirror. "Dr. Stoltz seems very confident that the difficulties I experience sleeping are the indirect result of my interactions with Ray Franklin when I was twelve. She believes the meds will help with the dreams."

It didn't take but a second for *them* to emerge.

"Stop the Ferrari! She's so right Stephy. It took her a while, but she nailed it. Brilliant. Ray Franklin is the devil! Just look at how smart she was to figure that out. Good work on the meds," Tiffany thrilled to Stephanie.

There was a shudder and Beth said calmly. "Tiffany is right for a change. Dr. Stoltz seemed very cooperative and helpful."

Beth paused, rolled her shoulders and slowly popped her knuckles, one at a time. She then said determinedly, "Stephanie, please remember I'm the voice of reason when there is none. You can trust me to always tell you the truth."

The physical transformation between *Beth* and *Tiffany* happened as quickly as *Tiffany's* response. This time there was no shudder. It was as if *Beth melted into Tiffany.*

"Big surprise," Tiffany said scornfully. "Voice of reason, huh? Well, listen to you. What does that make me? Unreasonable? I'm the fun one, Beth. Or did you forget? If it weren't for me, Stephy would be boring and alone, like you. Poor baby."

"Easy. Lighten up," Beth warned Tiffany. "Watch what you say. Don't be so . . . you," Beth scolded.

"Shut up. I know what I'm doing," Tiffany snapped. "I'm trying to tell Stephy that everything is fine and you deflate it. You just suck the wind out of it. Let me be."

Stephanie smiled unconsciously at the memory, amused by the back and forth drama that always seemed to take place between *them*. "It is what it is," she said aloud, continuing with her shower.

Chapter 8 • Victory Lunch

Stephanie was joining Susan for lunch with Marcus Graham at the Heathman Hotel in downtown Portland and she was hopeful for good news, but reserved at the same time. She squeezed the steering wheel, worrying about the what-ifs, and then relaxed. She stole a glance at the rearview mirror and reminded herself of the time and effort she'd invested in other projects only to have nothing come from it. She recalled the advice her father had given her. "Don't ride a high horse. Stay on the low pony. It's not so far to fall."

Susan hadn't been so reserved in her expectations.

It had been two weeks since their "Islands in the Stream" presentation and Susan was anxious to meet with Marcus to discuss their proposal. "I think we're going to seal the deal," Susan told her confidently. But it wasn't all business for her friend and boss. Susan was always trying to match her up in a situation where she would meet "Mr. Right" and she'd insisted the day before Marcus Graham should not be overlooked. She also told her for the umpteenth time it was just as easy to marry a rich man as a poor man.

Susan was right, of course. She was looking for the right man, the perfect man, but she wasn't in a hurry. She believed she knew what she was doing. Her experiences had taught her what to watch out for: the control, the arrogance, and the lies. She had her own issues after all and she didn't need a new one.

When Stephanie arrived at the Heathman it was lightly sprinkling as it sometimes did in June, and her dash from valet parking to the hotel entrance was made with her frowning, her purse clutched in the air above her head. She'd taken special care with her appearance this morning and had worn her new, gray spiked heels, a matching gray cashmere sweater and black pencil skirt. "Thank God it's not pouring," she whispered as she pushed through the revolving, brass-framed, glass doors of the hotel.

She worried again about her hair and make-up after her brief run through the summer rain, but she shrugged away the thought. She shook the raindrops from her purse and searched the lobby for Susan, who'd decided to come in her own car from the office. Susan told her earlier that she was going shopping after their "victory lunch" with Graham Developments. She hoped her boss was right.

•

Graham watched Stephanie run from her car to the hotel entrance, shielding herself from the rain with her purse, and it made him smile. "Smart girl," he said aloud to himself. Now that he knew her history and his, thanks to Powell's detailed report, he was even more interested in her than before. He didn't know if it had to do with guilt given their connection, but he didn't think so. He suspected how fragile she might be, and yet, she was so composed, strong and sure of herself, let alone beautiful.

He saw Susan Arcadia enter the same lobby doors and the two women greet each other. Susan was wearing an all-blue jumpsuit and was removing her black raincoat when he walked up to them and said, "Ladies, it's nice to see you. Thanks for joining me today."

"Thank you for inviting us, Marcus," Susan said. She beamed at him as he helped her off with her coat.

"Yes, it's very nice," Stephanie replied, smiling shyly at him.

"Let's go in and get settled," he said, guiding them to the left of the lobby and up a small ramp to where a placard stood in front of an open, wooden door. The sign stated, "Lunch at the Headwaters."

When they entered the entrance alcove, the maître d' glanced up from his station, smiled and came over to them. He was dressed casually in dark blue slacks and a blue and white pinstripe shirt. His carefully combed brown hair was graying at the temples and he had a neatly trimmed gray mustache. "Mr. Graham, it's always a pleasure. I have your table prepared for you and your guests. First, let me take care of the ladies coats."

"Thank you, Carlton. It's good to see you."

The man slightly nodded his head and said, "Ladies, Mr. Graham. Please, follow me."

Headwaters at the Heathman had recently been renovated and now had large windows running the length of the dining area. Artworks by Michael Schlicting were tastefully positioned on the walls. Recessed lighting accented the interior's graceful vaulted ceilings and tiered dining room. The long, open kitchen was immaculate, manned by bustling chefs. Each four-person dining table was very private; a glass backdrop separated each dining space. On one side of the table resided a moss green banquet seat and positioned on the other side were two, leather-padded chairs. The tables were set simply with silverware, a tall water glass and a white linen napkin covering a white plate. Graham already knew the menu featured risqué dish names that were inspired by *50 Shades of Grey*, the novel with scenes set inside the Heathman.

Each table they passed in the main dining area was set similar to the others until they reached one with a large black vase containing a dozen long-stemmed white roses. "Mr. Graham, ladies, I hope you enjoy your lunch," Carlton said, guiding Susan and Stephanie to the banquet seat, while Graham sat in the chair facing them.

"Thank you, Carlton, everything looks wonderful. Would you please set the flowers aside for the ladies? They can retrieve them after lunch. I can barely see across the table," Graham said, moving the vase to the side.

"Of course, Mr. Graham. I'll have them removed and prepared for travel. In the meanwhile, please consider our menu at your leisure," Carlton replied, passing out black, leather-bound menus as another waiter appeared, silently filling their water glasses and deftly removing the vase and roses.

Graham didn't know how Carlton did that. Telepathic powers, he guessed. He then focused on his guests. "Ladies, I'm not someone who enjoys holding back good news," he said. "I'm very much impressed by your 'Islands in the Stream' concept, and I've decided to go with your agency. Congratulations."

They both broke in large smiles and grinned at each other before returning their attention to him.

"Thanks so much, Marcus. I'm delighted to hear you've selected us. We'll do our very best for you," Susan responded enthusiastically, her smile gleaming.

"Yes, that's wonderful news," Stephanie added in a slow, breathless manner, each word sounding twice as long.

"You're both welcome. I also have something else for you. I want you to take a look at our entire media budget for all of our various properties. I'd appreciate your analysis. I believe we've not been getting the numbers we should for the money we've been spending, and I know we can do better."

He reached into his sport jacket, pulled out a thick envelope and passed it to Susan. "Here's our media, creative expenditures and budgets. I'd appreciate your review and input as soon as possible."

Susan broke into a broad grin and reached across the table for the envelope saying, "Thank you again, Marcus. What a wonderful surprise. We'll get right on it and find out what's been going on. I assure you."

"I appreciate it, Susan. I'm delighted to be working with you both. Now, why don't we order lunch?"

•

The lunch was delicious and the news couldn't have been better. Susan was exuberant and very animated during their meal, smiling and laughing, buoyed by their success. Stephanie just smiled and tried to fit in a positive word here and there, happy at the prospect of working on the "Islands" campaign.

Marcus was charming and upbeat, exchanging small stories of business and people. Stephanie enjoyed looking at him, and it was easy for her though she still felt there was an odd familiarity to him. He'd worn a blue sport jacket with a silky white shirt open at the neck, black jeans and black loafers. A black handkerchief peeked out of the breast pocket of his jacket. She thought he was very alluring, so GQ and out of her league; they were as different as their lifestyles and bank accounts - he was a multi-millionaire and she was a working girl at an ad agency.

When they were finishing their coffees, Susan excused herself to the restroom. Stephanie was alone with him and she remembered to be cordial, as Susan suggested.

Graham turned to her and with a sincere expression said, "Stephanie, I have to admit I'm very impressed by you and your work. Your presentation was wonderful and I thought your images of the various park themes were as beautiful and captivating as the artist who designed them."

She looked away and tried to compose herself. She didn't know how to react. It was the last thing she expected. It wasn't the way it was supposed to be with her. She liked distance and now there wasn't any. Her heart seemed to be beating loud enough for Marcus to hear, so she took a small sip from her water glass and mustered her smile and strength. "Thank you, Marcus. That's very kind."

He broke into a broad grin, amused by her shy response. "Well, you're welcome, Stephanie. That's very kind of you to say as well."

"What's so funny you two?" It was Susan, returning to the table.

"We were sharing a small joke and I was telling Stephanie how much I enjoyed her work," he said, exchanging a small wink with her as he stood and helped Susan with her chair.

Stephanie could tell Susan didn't buy what he said by the way she peeked at her out of the corner of her eye, but she didn't say anything.

Marcus then announced to them both, "Ladies, I have enjoyed our lunch, but I'm afraid I have other appointments. Thanks so much for joining me today, and congratulations again on your proposal. Susan, please contact me when you're ready to talk about our media. Stephanie, it was a pleasure as always."

She watched him turn and walk away, surprised and a little shaken by his interest in her, but intrigued. She wasn't afraid. She wasn't sure how she felt, but for the first time in a long while she wanted to find out.

"I do too. He's scrumptious. He makes me all slippery inside." Tiffany secretly said to her.

"Wait a minute." It was Beth. "He obviously has everything he could possibly want, so why isn't he married? He's either a player, or trouble."

Beth was right. She would have to very careful. There were just too many connections - most importantly the brand new one with Synergy.

The rest of the day passed quickly as she worked on refining the designs on the "Islands" project. Susan and the media girls were a flurry of activity pouring over the media budgets Graham had supplied them. They didn't even respond when she told them all goodnight.

When she arrived home, Skinnykitty greeted her at the door, his tail flicking back and forth in pleasure. She stooped and stroked his fat, furry body.

"How's my boy tonight? You hungry? You miss me?"

The cat arched its back and meowed.

"I'll take that as a yes. Good boy."

She dropped her coat and computer bag on the couch and went to the kitchen. The cat followed at her heels, its tail waving lazily. She took the small bowl from the floor and refilled it from a bag of dry cat food that sat on the counter. She placed the bowl back on the floor and listened to the cat crunching the kibble as he ate hungrily.

An hour later, she had changed and eaten a fried egg sandwich. She was working on her second glass of wine when the text chimed on her phone.

She read the message.

Stephanie, Good evening to you. I asked Susan for your number because I wanted to brief you on another project I have in mind. I also wanted to reiterate how much I enjoyed your company at lunch today. Marcus.

"Oh, shit," she said out loud. He was actually texting her. She paused and took another sip of wine before typing.

Thank you, Marcus. I'm looking forward to working with you, too. I think 'Islands in the Stream' is going to be a terrific project.

I think so, too. Tomorrow morning I'll be sending you our former ad campaign FMG used for our Mt. Hood Villa project. I want your input on how to make it more effective. Let's review at my office on Friday at 11.

Okay, but let me clear it with Susan first.

I don't think that will be a problem. I called her earlier and told her I wanted your review of the Villa project. I'm sure you two will discuss it in the morning. I'm meeting with her Thursday about media. Anyway, have a good evening!

Thanks, you too.

Stephanie sat there and reread his texts. She was excited to be invited to work on a new project, but wondered why Susan hadn't warned her about his plans. It wasn't her style. The new work would be great, but the idea of a private meeting made her pulse quicken in apprehension. She hadn't been to his office and the whole thing sounded a little too intimate and very much preplanned on his part. No, it was controlling. There it was: control. She remembered *Beth's* first impressions of him and her internal alarms began sounding again.

She'd experienced being controlled by Ray, and others had attempted it, and she vaguely remembered that it didn't end well. She'd kept men at arm's length for years and the few relationships she allowed herself, she knew were going to be short lived. She'd never invested in a romantic relationship she couldn't recover from. She believed she was only being sensible and careful. It wasn't any different now, except for her crucial, impossible-to-escape business responsibilities forcing her to be pleasant and charming.

Stephanie turned off the living room lights and made her way to the bathroom. She brushed her teeth and took her *crazy pills*. In the bedroom she found Skinnykitty curled up asleep next to her pillow. She crawled into bed, pulled the covers up to her neck, and wondered why Susan hadn't told her about the arranged meeting with Marcus.

She relaxed and quieted her thinking. She closed her eyes as the dream reel stuttered to a start and the frames began without her being able to stop them . . . Stephanie heard the front door open and the drunken laughter of her mother and Ray. "Please, not again," she said to the girl in the hallway mirror as she heard Evan and Diana running downstairs to greet them. She followed close behind.

They found her mother in the kitchen with Ray.

"Hello, you little bastards," Ray chuckled, his arm wrapped around her mother, who was grinning the way women do when they know they should. Ray then kissed her mother on the cheek and attempted to turn her towards him for an embrace.

"Stop that," her mother said, pushing away from him, swaying and giggling.

"Don't tell me to stop it, Alice!" he ordered, grabbing her arms and pulling her back to him.

"Ray, the children."

"Fuck the kids, they'll be fine. Won't you?" he said, daring them not to be.

Stephanie saw what was happening and clutched Evan by his shoulders. Diana cowered behind them both.

"Stephanie, take the kids and you all get in bed. I'll be up to tuck you in," her mother said to her.

Giggling again, her mother pushed away from Ray saying, "And you mister, off to bed with you while I do my motherly duties."

Suddenly Evan broke away from her grasp and raced forward, grabbing and hugging his mothers' legs. "Mommy, I love you. I want to be with you. Please," he begged.

Ray reached down and seized Evan by the arm, turned him, and smacked him hard on his bottom. "I said get the fuck outta here and I'm not kidding."

"Stop it, Ray," her mother pleaded, frantically grabbing his arm.

Ray turned and violently shoved her mother backwards into the kitchen door, the glass pane cracking from the impact of her elbow. "Goddammit, Alice. Don't tell me how to handle these kids!"

Beth came forward. "I've got this, Steph. A promise made is a promise kept from now on."

When she heard *Beth's* voice, she sensed a comforting familiarity and though new and strange, she relaxed; she instinctively knew *Beth* was there to help. Stephanie felt her body expand, her muscles growing with each heartbeat. She flexed her arms, pumped her fists and without thinking further about it rushed forward and slugged Ray in the nose as hard as she could. It was the first time she had ever hit anyone or was brave enough to do something, but it felt incredible. *"Stop it. Just stop it. It's not fair. Don't do this to my mom and us!" she* screamed at him in a voice she didn't recognize. It was *Tiffany.*

She didn't even feel the brutal cuff of his backhand; all of a sudden she was sitting and blinking, wondering what had happened. Her glasses lay broken at her feet. Her face was numb. She blinked again, reached up and touched her nose and lip. When she pulled back her hand there was blood smeared on her fingers. She tasted it on her lips.

At first there wasn't a sound, then Evan started crying and Diana was holding him, crying too. All Stephanie could do was sit on the floor, touch her face and blink her eyes, which were now filling with tears.

Her mother suddenly launched herself at Ray and began hitting his chest, screaming, "You fucking son of a bitch! Hit my kids? I will kill you!"

Ray stood there, red-faced and angry, his fists clenched by his sides. "Take your best shot, woman. This is my house, my rules," he taunted, a cruel scowl on his face, a bubble of saliva in the corner of his mouth.

Her mother took another wild swing at Franklin only to have him catch her arm and brutally twist it. Her mother screamed and grabbed her wrist, pulling away. Franklin stepped forward and slapped her mother on the face, spinning her around and knocking her into the edge of the kitchen cabinets.

When her mother turned back towards Ray, there was a large red gouge above her eye beginning to drip blood. Her mother reached up and touched her face where it was bleeding. Looking at Ray she showed him her bloody fingers. "You satisfied, Ray? You hit my kids and now me. What a big man you are. So tough," she said bitterly.

"Fuck you, Alice. I told you to stop. You're so fucking dumb sometimes. And your kids aren't much better."

"My kids - you talk about my children? You bastard!" she shrieked at him.

Stephanie couldn't take it anymore and crawled over to Evan and Diana. Diana helped her to her feet. She then took them by their hands and ran for the living room and the phone, Ray's threats and her mother's shouting echoing behind them. She dialed the number she'd learned.

An older female voice answered, "911, what's your emergency?"

"My mom's boyfriend is hitting us and now he's beating up my mom. Help us, please. Send someone!"

"What's your address, honey?"

"5627 North Carlisle Road."

"I'll send an officer right now. Is there a place where you and your brother and sister can go that's safe?"

"I don't know. Please hurry"

She heard her mother scream, "Ray, stop. Please don't hit me anymore. It hurts."

Seconds later there was a crashing and thudding sound. It was silent and then she heard Ray say, "I told you to quit, Alice. You wouldn't. Now look at yourself, what have you done?"

She dropped the phone and ran to the kitchen.

Her mother lay slumped against the oven door, her arms slack by her side. It seemed as if she was sitting, but her neck was at an odd angle and her head hung down, her chin resting on her chest. There was no expression on her mother's face and her breathing had stopped. Her eyes were open, staring blankly, and there was an open, red gouge above her right eye. There was blood seeping from her ear.

Ray was kneeled next to her and pleading, "Don't do this to me, dammit. All you had to do was stop, but you didn't."

She stood there staring at her mother, unable to move and grasp what she was seeing. She didn't know how much time had passed when she heard the door open in the living room and a man's voice shouting, "Police!

Vancouver Police!"

Diana yelled, "They're in the kitchen. He's hurting Mommy!"

Footsteps ran towards Stephanie. A policeman dressed in blue, his gun drawn, came into the kitchen. The officer glanced her and then at Ray who still kneeling by her mother. He then pointed his gun at Ray. "Stand up and step away from the woman. Keep your hands where I can see them."

The policeman peeked over his shoulder at her and asked, "Are you all right, Miss?"

"Yes, but help my mom, he's been hitting her," she said in her calmest grown-up voice, pointing at Ray.

Ray glared at her before saying to the officer, "I didn't mean to hurt her. We were arguing, I pushed her and she slipped and fell against the stove. It was an accident."

"It doesn't look much like an accident to me, shithead. Now I want you to stand up, face me and lock your hands behind your head. Do not attempt to reach for anything." He then yelled over his shoulder, "McHale, need you in here!"

Another officer quickly entered the kitchen. She intently watched as he approached Ray, handcuffed him, and then sat him back down on the floor facing the wall. "Don't move from there," he ordered.

The policeman who had first arrived turned towards Stephanie, holstered his weapon and said, "Now, let me see if I can help your mom."

But she knew her mother wasn't going to need help. Not ever again.

The last reel of her dream sputtered to a stop: the film crumbling and yellowing with age. The cue marks flashed, indicating that it was time for reel one to begin once more.

Chapter 9 • Working Together

Stephanie was rarely early to work, but today was different. She couldn't wait to see Susan. When she arrived at 8:45 a.m., Susan was standing in the reception area, tapping her foot and sipping from a steaming hot cup of coffee. Susan pulled the cup from her lips and held up her hand. "Before you say it, let me tell you that I wanted to call and give you a heads-up, but Roger had friends over for dinner and I was trapped."

"I was a little surprised I didn't hear from you," Stephanie replied, the disappointment evident in her voice.

"Hey, it's good for us and what's to lose? He's not Jack the Ripper," Susan scolded, obviously happy at the prospect of more new business. "And he could be your Mr. Right." Susan then pointed at her and said, "Better get busy. Friday is only three days away."

She considered Susan's remarks her as she made her way back to her office. There was no doubt there was a challenge in what her boss had stated and it concerned her. Marcus was going to be in her life for a while, and she couldn't blow him off even if she wanted. She couldn't let Susan down either. She was caught, but why did she want to smile?

She was still smiling when she strolled through the doors of Graham Developments on Friday, and while other people were impressed with Marcus' wealth and good looks, she wasn't at all concerned, even though she'd taken extra care with her appearance and scent. "Nothing ventured, nothing gained," she said confidently to herself, while worrying at the same time about the consequences: *Beth* and *Tiffany* would be watching.

She expected his offices to be fabulous, but she didn't expect Gretchen. Gretchen was blonde, blue-eyed, tall, and incredibly beautiful. She was the type of woman who sparkled, but there was no mistaking the mark of extreme fitness upon her physique; she was more a sentry than a smiley-faced greeter.

"I'm Stephanie Courtland. I have an appointment with Mr. Graham."

"It's nice to meet you Stephanie. I'm Gretchen Hilde, Marcus' personal assistant. You're expected. Let me show you to his office," the woman said coolly.

She followed the blonde past her desk and reception area through a door that opened to a green-carpeted, glass-walled hallway. She had to hurry; the pace she could only think of as power walking. Gretchen was muscled, but sleek. Her legs were highly toned and defined, as were her arms. She moved like a big cat down the hallway, only big cats didn't wear a green Yves St. Laurent' blouse, black Gucci pencil skirt and Manolo Blahnik alligator pumps. She was just guessing, of course.

"Here you go," Gretchen said, effortlessly opening the glass door with her fingertips and looking at her with an expression of *we shall see.*

Marcus rose from his desk, the buildings and bridges of downtown Portland at his back. He was wearing a long sleeve black shirt, the sleeves rolled up to his forearms exposing a tattoo that wrapped his wrist. He wore gray slacks that matched his tie. A gray sport jacket hung over the back of his chair.

Graham's office was breathtaking in its simplicity and maleness. Photos and military memorabilia were framed on the walls. A leather couch, coffee table and lamp were positioned off to the left of his desk. Behind his desk and to the right, near the windows, stood an oversized, chrome and glass drafting table with two matching high-backed chrome-framed chairs with black leather seats.

"Thanks, Gretchen. Good to see you, Stephanie. Please, come in," he said, walking towards her and extending his hand.

She shook his hand, surprised at its warmth. "Thank you, Marcus. I appreciate your invitation to review Mt. Hood Villa. I have some ideas I hope may interest you." She sounded confident, but only about her work. He was another matter.

She'd found FMG's creativity on the project to be lackluster and their message somewhat off-target. She knew the FMG ad agency and their work. For over two decades Foster, McWillis, and Grant had been the heavy-hitters in the Portland market, representing the biggest and wealthiest clients. Now, brighter, fresher, younger minds were challenging the conservative, old school agency and it was taking a toll on their client list.

"Stephanie, let's work over here," he said, pointing to the tall, glass table. "You can set up your computer and also anything you wish to show me from your portfolio."

Graham's attention was glued to her as she took her computer from its case, opened it and set it on the table. He watched her unzip her portfolio and remove several poster boards, each covered by heavy, white paper. He couldn't take his eyes off her. She was stunning. She'd parted her red hair on the side, and it cascaded down her shoulders, partially concealing her right eye. She wore a cream-colored blouse and green skirt. Her patterned green and cream heels completed the package, showing off her long legs.

When she finished with her arrangement of the poster boards, she asked him in her best all-business voice, "Shall we begin, Marcus?"

Stephanie's presentation for Mt. Hood Villa focused on the audience more than the property. She explained to Marcus that their marketing targets' lifestyle was the result of their hard work, and the Villa was an appropriate reward for their effort. Her ad layouts and brochure examples focused on people between the ages of fifty and sixty-five enjoying life in their luxury homes and lavish estate grounds. Ad copy was more strategic with an emphasis on guarded and gated entrances that insured privacy and security.

He really didn't expect it to be as good as it was. And it was better than good. He had to ask, "Stephanie, what was your inspiration for using questions as the way to reshape a potential buyers mind? It's very good. So empathetic."

"Thank you. I believe personal questions can evoke ingratiating responses, and I believe it would be particularly effective with your target audience of upper-income, older adults. Our theme is very powerful and focused. 'Don't you deserve the best for all you've accomplished?' That sounds so much better than FMG's 'Luxury residences for discerning adults.' It's night and day. The two are very dissimilar."

"Well, you've got the job. I'm impressed with your work. I couldn't be more pleased."

He then gazed out of the windows and said, "It's quite a view, isn't it?"

"It is, but it's also a little scary. I'm a little uncomfortable to be so close."

"I was too, at first, but you get used to it after a few days. Now, I see it as a beautiful painting that has the ability to transform itself from one moment to the next. I've grown very fond of the movement from morning till night."

She nodded and smiled. "I'm surprised by you every time, Mr. Graham. And yes, the view is wonderful."

"I'm glad you enjoy it." He stood and turned to her. "I have to tell you how impressed I am with you, Stephanie. I feel very confident about where we're heading on everything. I also wanted to thank you again for coming by today. I hope we can see more of each other in the future. I'd like that."

"I would enjoy that too, Marcus," she said, trying not to sound as impulsive and excited as she was.

"Excellent. Let me walk you out."

She stood and gathered her poster boards and computer. She was relieved the meeting was ending, but she was also excited about what could be next.

Chapter 10 • Outside

"Fuck all of you," Franklin spat hatefully towards the closing steel doors of the Washington State Penitentiary. He was pissed, but stoked to be out after almost twenty years. He'd suckered in all the true believers at the parole hearing claiming Jesus had come into his life and he was a reformed man. His earning a bachelor's degree through the prison education rehab system and then helping teach other inmates computer skills also helped convince them.

He'd survived prison the same way - he'd outsmarted them all. It hadn't always been easy, especially in the beginning. He was nothing more than a scared white man when he came to "The Walls," which was what the inmates called the brick and concrete structure since it first opened in 1886. It was also the home of the death penalty in Washington State, where they either hung you by the neck or lethally injected you.

When he first entered the gates in 1996, it had an inmate population of 1,753. Now, it was almost five hundred over its maximum capacity of 2,200. Most inmates were violent offenders or drug felons, and many of them were gangbangers. The Crips, White Supremacists, Sureños and Norteños were the main players. He was a nothing, but not because he wasn't recruited. Not at all. The Aryan Brotherhood wanted him because he was built like a bull from his tireless iron sessions in the yard, and he carried himself with a *don't fuck with me* attitude and demeanor.

It was his smarts and his earned time that eventually saved him from becoming a full brother of the AB. He'd already been in for ten years and had earned his BA when they first recognized the importance of his position within the learning department of the prison. He soon became their passport to computer skills and he guided them through prison-approved study programs with a focus on accounting, management, marketing and communication. The end-result was that it helped them to refine their organization, thereby expanding their drug empire. They were also smart enough to know that if he became an AB member his time with the computers would end. They couldn't own him, but they ensured no one else was able to get close enough to leverage him or gang stamp him. Nobody messed with their geek.

"Fuck them all," he said aloud, stuffing the bag containing his shaving kit and old clothes into the trash barrel that sat outside the steel doors. His only possessions were the clothes on his back and his prison money, and he was good with that. The clothes he'd checked in with back in '96 were two sizes too small and he laughed when he saw them. He had to buy boots, denims, a blue shirt, a blue denim jacket and a belt at prison supply just so he had civilian clothes on his back. The bastards who worked in the supply room joked about him, but they were only jealous. He was going free and they were going nowhere.

He marched with a swagger, his new black boots slapping the pavement of the road leading from the prison to the highway. It was sunny and hot. His shaved head was beginning to glisten with sweat when a green four-door Ford pickup pulled up in front of him and stopped.

His older brother Randy was smiling at him from behind the wheel. He then opened the pickup door and jumped out. "What's up, brother? It's good to see you."

He'd only seen Randy three times since he'd been in and he appeared to have gained some weight, which was good because he'd always been on the thin side. His brother's face had also grown rounder and his dark hair was now gray.

"What's up? Is that a real question, brother?" Franklin said, approaching the man and embracing him.

"Dude, you're like hugging a fucking piece of steel. Prison food must have been real good."

"Are you're shitting me, Randy?" he retorted, stepping back and giving his brother his best hard-ass look before breaking into a broad grin. His brother still had the same easy, upbeat attitude he remembered; his eyes squinted when he smiled and it was an expression he found contagious. "It feels so good to be out, man. Everything feels so big out here. I can't fucking believe it! I made it!"

"Yes, you did, bro. Let's get the fuck outta here. And yes, before you ask, I brought all your shit."

"Good deal. I knew you would." Franklin said as glared one last time at the now-closed steel door before walking to the pickup and climbing in.

Once seated, his brother fired up the truck and asked, "What time do you have to check in at the halfway house?"

"Not for a while. Let's go to a restaurant so I can get some real food and I can take care of some business with you. Then you can hit the road. I'm sure you need to get back soon."

"You got that right. Don't get me wrong I don't mind picking you up, but I can only trust those fucking knuckleheads at the shop for so long. The weekend is always big for us and we're a lot larger than when you last saw us. I've got twelve guys now and we're washing about three hundred cars on a sunny Saturday."

"Not bad. It's cool you did it all on your own."

"Thanks. But we both know I didn't do it on my own. Without you I would've never had enough dough to make it happen. You got me started and I'll never forget it, man. I'm happy. Doris and the kids are too. Amazing stuff. Anyway, let's get some food. I'm starved."

As his brother wheeled the truck away from the prison and towards town, Franklin settled back into his seat and stared intently out of the windshield marveling at cars he'd never seen and people dressed in fashions and colors totally unfamiliar to him. He rolled the window down and took a deep breath.

"Randy, I have to tell you it smells so fucking good on the outside. I didn't realize it until just this moment. It smells so green and fresh. I think I know what they mean about the sweet smell of freedom. Or is that success? Fuck, both the same to me, man. The other thing is, everything is so colorful. I'm so used to seeing the guards in black uniforms and the cons in orange it blows my mind to see reds, greens, yellows and blues, let alone women."

His brother only smiled as he drove down the highway and then turned into the parking lot of Big Bear Diner. "How about this place, Ray? I've eaten at their other locations and they're always good. Plus, we can get anything we want from breakfast to steaks."

"Sounds good to me. Hell, anything I don't have to stand in line for with a fucking metal tray in my hand is good to me. And don't even get me started about seeing a woman serve me. My dick might jump out of my pants! But yeah, let's eat here. I can get some work done while we talk. Then you can go."

"Don't worry, bro. I'm good on time. Let's eat and I'll catch you up on what I know."

They exited the truck with Franklin carrying the Wilson sport bag his brother had brought for him. For the next hour they ate and reacquainted themselves, catching up on life and what was ahead. Ray assured his brother that he knew what he was doing and that he had a solid plan. Randy wasn't as sure, but said he could count on him.

When they saw the taxi pull into the parking lot, they paid their bill and walked from the diner to where a taxi was parked next to the pickup. Ray looked at the driver and held up his hand mouthing the words, "I'll be right there."

Franklin embraced his brother. "Thanks again, Randy. You're the only person I trust and that's a big deal for me right now. I appreciate it. Thanks for finding about her for me. I can't wait to see the Internet for myself."

His brother pushed slightly back, and holding his arms said, "No worries, Ray. I just hope you know what you're doing. The last thing you need is trouble in your life again. I'll do what you've asked and mail those photos to her, but shit, I'm worried for you."

"I get what you're saying, but man I'm owed what I'm fucking owed. It's just to get her attention and freak her out. Thanks for doing that for me."

Randy dropped his hands to his side and shrugged. "Okay. Keep safe. I'll see you when I see you."

Franklin passed the sport bag to his brother, turned and stepped over to the cab. He opened the door to the taxi and bent his heavily muscled frame to get into the cramped rear seat. He grunted when he sat down, satisfied the first part of his plan would soon be in motion, thanks to his brother.

"Where to mister?" the cabbie asked him.

"Take me to the closest stripper bar," he ordered. He hadn't seen real tits for almost twenty big ones, and he needed to get laid. He had twelve hundred dollars in his pocket from his work in prison and he couldn't wait to spend it.

"Yes, sir. I know a place you'll like," the cabbie replied as he slipped the cab into gear and drove out.

When Franklin pushed through the pink doors of the strip club, he was stopped by a man the size of a small mountain who was dressed in a black turtleneck sweater and black slacks. His arms and legs bulged and distorted the fabric. His head was the size of a basketball and he scowled when he said, "Welcome to the Pink Pearl, buddy. Good drinks and fine ladies. Just follow the house rules. There is absolutely no touching of the merchandise allowed. Enjoy yourself."

Franklin nodded and made his way to the bar. He sat down on the barstool and watched a scantily attired, unattractive brunette approach him from behind the bar. She had dark circles under her eyes as if she'd been up all night. Her pasty white make-up and bright red lipstick added to her garish appearance. She set her elbows on the bar and leaned forward, exposing her ample cleavage. "What's your pleasure, handsome?" she asked in a gravelly, cigarette-stained voice.

"Whiskey Seven," he ordered, putting a twenty on the counter.

He didn't sense her until her hand gently squeezed his elbow. The scent of her perfume quickly followed. He turned to see an absolutely gorgeous twenty-something blonde with a big smile. She was dressed in filmy lingerie that did little to conceal her naked charms.

The blonde leaned into him, licked her lips, and put her hands underneath her breasts, lifting them up provocatively. "Do you want me to dance for you, baby? I can do almost anything, especially when I'm horny."

He'd waited twenty years to hear a woman talk to him that way. He turned on the bar stool to fully face her. "You better believe it, baby. I'm gonna dick you down," he said as he slid his hands around her waist and pulled her into him. Without waiting, he kissed her on the lips and began to feel her ass.

She squirmed and attempted to pull away from his grasp. "Wait, stop," she said, obviously frightened.

Suddenly his arms were clamped by vices and they pulled him powerfully away from the woman. Franklin stared at what stopped him. There were two of them. Another equally large, bald headed hulk dressed in the same black attire had joined the big-headed heavyweight from the club entrance. They towered over him menacingly. Big head growled at him. "I warned you about touching the merchandise, bud. Now you're gone!"

The two didn't wait for him respond. They each grabbed one of his arms and dragged him on his tiptoes to the front door and out. When he reached the pavement they released him. "You're not welcome here! Don't come back," he heard sneered at him as the two monsters walked back through the pink doors.

Franklin shook his arms, stared at the doors and spat, "Fuck you. Fuck your club."

He turned away, looked around, and spotted the cab he'd arrived in sitting just up the street. He had nowhere else to go and he knew he'd better chill out. He was also on a time limit for check-in at the halfway house and he sure as hell didn't want a parole violation on day one.

He stomped towards the taxi. "It'll get better," he promised himself.

Chapter 11 • News

She was exhilarated. Her meeting at GD had gone even better than expected. But there was more to it than that. Marcus had been gracious and engaging. He was also fastidious and driven by perfection. Controlling would be another word she might use. Everything was so precise in the beautiful world of M. His office certainly reflected his personality, she mused, as she entered the doors of Synergy.

Melody peered up from her desk, pushed down the microphone of her headset, and said, "You have a message, Stephanie. I've placed it on your desk."

"Thanks, Mel. Susan in?"

"No, she isn't. She's at lunch and afterwards she has a three o'clock meeting with American Business Machines. I'm not sure if she'll be back. It's just me and the media girls slaving away."

"Ok. Thanks."

When Stephanie entered her office, she thought it small after being at Marcus' expansive quarters. Reaching her desk, she pushed the start icon on the Mac and sat down. While it booted up, she glanced at the pink message slip and picked it up.

Her blood froze at the name listed above the phone number: Janice Snowman. Her body involuntarily shuddered at the memory connected to the woman's name; she was the prosecuting attorney at Ray's trial.

She wondered what the woman wanted as she slowly dialed the number and heard a voice she hadn't heard for almost twenty years say, "Hello, this is Janice Snowman."

"Ms. Snowman, this is Stephanie Courtland," she said, the words almost catching in her throat.

"Stephanie thanks so much for calling me back. It's been many years. I hope you and your brother and sister are well."

"Yes, yes we are. Are you still working for the Vancouver district attorney?"

"No, not any longer. I'm now the district attorney for Yamhill Country. I've been here almost twelve years, since I worked in Portland. Stephanie, I'm calling for a reason. Ray Franklin is being paroled and I wanted to notify you. He's being released today."

She could hardly believe what she was hearing. "Ray's getting out of prison? He's going to be free? That can't be possible."

"I'm truly sorry. I attended the parole hearing and he was very convincing about his reformation. He even obtained a degree in prison. In any event, I thought you should know. Of course, by the terms of the release he isn't permitted to contact any of you, for any reason. The restraining order is very clear. He'll also spend six months to a year at a halfway house in Walla Walla where he'll be closely supervised."

"Oh, my God. I didn't think he'd ever get out for what he did," she said, her eyes closed as she shook her head in disbelief.

"I'm sorry to bring you the news, Stephanie."

"Thanks," was all she could manage before ending the call.

Her hands were trembling and the word "No!" was repeating over and over in her head. She'd always been afraid Ray would be released and now it was happening.

It was then the all too familiar echo of the clock began. "Click...click..."

It didn't take a heartbeat for Beth to say, "Stop with the clicking, Stephy. I'm not afraid of Ray. I've been waiting for that bastard for years and now he'll soon be ours."

"It would be good to see Ray - good to see what's inside him," Tiffany sneered diabolically.

"Shut up, Tiffany. This is my deal. You can come, but just shut up for now," Beth ordered.

"Don't be so sensitive, I just want to help and help I will."

"You will if I say it's okay. I know what you want to do, I've seen it."

Tiffany giggled. "Oh, come on, Beth. You know it was the right thing to do. We're not going to let anyone mess with our Stephy."

Their talk ended as quickly as it began.

She sat there in a daze for several minutes. She then packed up her computer, grasped her purse and walked out of her office. She gave Melody the excuse that she didn't feel well. She drove straight home and by the time she arrived, she was more in control, more herself.

Skinnykitty was there to greet her at the doorway, rubbing his fat, white, gray-and-black body up against her legs as she hung up her coat. She bent and caressed his big head, listening to his purrs. "Come with me, big boy, and I'll get you some fresh food and water," she said softly. The cat meowed back and happily followed her to the kitchen.

She prepared his food, mixing dry and canned food together and then sat it on the floor, next to the wall. She poured herself a glass of wine and headed for her bedroom. Her iPhone toned and she saw a text from Marcus. She took another sip of her wine, took a big breath, and read it.

Stephanie, I very much enjoyed our meeting today. Your ideas are great for the Villa. It must be because you're so empathetic.

She sat on the bed and waited to respond, thinking about what he had said. She shook her head and took another drink of the Chardonnay. "Focus," she said aloud to herself.

Thank you, Marcus. I always try to place myself in the viewpoint of the buyer in my work. I believe being sensitive to the needs and wants of the target buyer will produce positive responses. I consider empathy to be very important in communication.

I think you've also said that about yourself on Match. I thought your profile was truthful, revealing and amusing.

My Match profile? Are you on Match? Are you stalking me?!?

She took another large sip of her wine. "What is he up to?" she wondered as she waited for his response. Her phone chimed and she read his answer.

No, I'm not on Match, but I have my resources. (I'm laughing). Match is not exactly the way we used to do it, is it? You could tell if you bumped into someone interesting, on a chemical level, back in the day. Now, we have to contend with photos, profiles and our ability to determine the best choices on a computer monitor. And in terms of stalking, absolutely.

⋯ You're very funny. Do you use your resources to check out everyone you work with?

⋯ I actually do. Probably, my military background, and it's worked for me. But truthfully, I reserve my "resources" exclusively for special projects. Like yourself.

⋯ So, I'm a project? No. *We* are working on a project.

She paused and typed, "I'm a little uncomfortable with this and." She stopped and erased the text. "Careful," she warned herself, thinking of the business complications. The cat jumped on the bed and she smiled. "I better lighten this up," she said to the cat. She then entered her text.

⋯ To be honest, Marcus, there are a couple of things you've said that make me go "hmm."

⋯ Well, I hope they're good "hmm's." Let me prove to you I'm worth it. I was hoping we could celebrate our progress on "Villa" and "Islands" tomorrow night. If you don't have plans, I would enjoy your company for dinner at Ringside. We can meet at eight in the bar. What do you think?

⋯ Hmm. (Knew you'd enjoy that). Okay, see you there. It'll be fun to get to know you better.

⋯ Great! I look forward to it. See you tomorrow night.

She was somewhat surprised by her own texts when she re-read them. She guessed immediately that *Tiffany* had subtly injected *her* own ideas into the responses, or maybe it was just her. It was always difficult for her to tell. She'd gone from warning herself about a relationship with Marcus because of its potential for disaster with Synergy to being downright fascinated about a possible romance with him. "Must have been the wine talking," she rationalized. But she knew that wasn't entirely true. She then tapped in Diana's number and listened to it ring. She had other things on her mind than Marcus Graham.

Fifteen minutes later, her confidence was restored. Another glass of wine hadn't hurt either. Diana was always so sure of herself and though concerned, she believed Ray didn't pose much of a threat.

"It doesn't really matter," Diana reminded her. "We have no control over what he does, but I think the police will keep their eye on him. We also have the restraining order, so if he ever does show up, all we do is call 911 and he's back in jail."

Diana didn't even want her to call Evan, saying she would, because it was really no big deal. Diana did, however, think her encounters with Marcus and their forthcoming dinner date was a big deal and she was excited to hear all about him. She even told her a man in her life was long overdue and Marcus seemed perfect.

It all sounded so easy and simplistic to Diana, and it always had. She'd been the popular one and never seemed to struggle with anything, least of all boyfriends. But she wasn't the one who'd testified or endured what she went through with Ray. She thought of the basement, but quickly shook the remembrance from her mind. "Don't do this to yourself," she scolded.

The cat meowed at her.

"I know. I won't go there again. Let's get some sleep, shall we? I better take my meds first. Almost forgot."

The cat watched her when she came back to the bed, crawled underneath the covers, and ordered "Alexa" to turn off the bedside light. The cat waited for her to settle and then sauntered across the bed, following her legs and body until he curled up next to her head on the pillow, purring.

She let her thoughts of Marcus Graham lull her to sleep.

Chapter 12 • Ringside

It was Saturday night and Marcus was feeling invincible. Business was good, the new agency was money in the bank, and Stephanie - lovely, soft-talking, reserved Stephanie - was joining him for dinner at Ringside. He was looking forward to their first real date, especially after their business meeting together. He wasn't sure if it was guilt, lust, or a chemical reaction that was inspiring him, but he was intrigued and it drew him to her. "Improvise, adapt and overcome," he said aloud to himself. The phrase had been drilled into him at the Point; it had been his method of operations in the Middle East and he believed it would still work for him now.

Graham glanced at his Apple Watch and saw that it was time to leave. He wanted to be early, settle into the atmosphere of Ringside and relax with a cocktail before she arrived. He checked his appearance in the hallway mirror. He was wearing a hand-tailored white shirt under a blue Hallsworth jacket. He'd chosen black gabardine slacks with the black, Bass Weejun loafers. He checked his jacket for the Mercedes' keys and headed for the door. All was quiet when he passed the conference room, offices, and through the now Gretchen-less reception area.

Riding down the elevator he hummed to himself. It wasn't uncommon for him. He did it when he was waiting. He'd spent much of his life waiting. Waiting to get through high school. Waiting to graduate from the Point. Waiting for his second combat tour to end. Waiting to get out of the Army. Now, he was waiting to find a true companion: a woman who was beautiful, strong, sexy, smart, and funny. A woman he could share his triumphs, dreams, joys and deepest desires with. A woman strong enough to stand by his side and find strength in his actions. *Companion* - the word was very special to him and he knew most people would not be appreciative of its depth of meaning. It was everything to him, and he'd searched for it in every romantic encounter he'd experienced. He had yet to find his.

The elevator stopped and slightly recoiled when it reached the parking garage. He strode to the Mercedes, fired it up, and drove away from the Tower.

It only took him six minutes to reach valet parking at Ringside. It was packed as usual with nicely dressed people coming and going. The valet took his keys, passed him a claim ticket and slowly drove the 650 to a parking slot directly across from the entrance.

Pushing through the doors of the restaurant, Graham could hear the busy activities of the bow-tied, black-suited waiters and the guests they were serving. Frank Sinatra crooned quietly behind the mixed sounds of conversation. He loved the place. Ringside was one of Portland's oldest and finest dining and drinking establishments. It had opened in 1944, its name originating from boxing matches that took place at a nearby stadium in the '30s and '40s. A ringside seat, or front row, was the best in the house, and the name was appropriate.

He stepped towards the small bar, which was located off to the right of the entrance. It was small, intimately lit, and had eight small tables that ran opposite the curving, dark wood bar.

"Mr. Graham," he heard from behind him.

He turned at the sound of his name. It was Casey, the manager of Ringside. "Good evening, sir. It's good to see you again. I have your table ready. When your guest arrives, may I direct her to join you?"

"I appreciate it, Casey. It's good to see you, as well. I'll be in the bar."

He excused his way around two couples and found a leather stool at the bar. He admired the two sets of boxing gloves hanging from the heavy wood beams of the ceiling above the bar. The brown leather gloves were weathered, cracked, their laces yellowed from age. They had belonged to local boxers Carl 'Bobo' Olson and Denny Moyer, two top contenders in the '50s and '60s. He found the gloves to be the perfect and appropriate mementos to the restaurants' rich history. The only thing missing, he reflected, was the smoky haze of fine cigars. It reminded him of the many times he'd come here with his parents.

"Mr. Graham, it's very good to see you again," he heard from across his shoulder. It was Jim, the senior bartender for Ringside, a veteran of twenty-five years. White-haired and in his sixties, he was dressed in black pants, black vest and a white long-sleeved shirt with a black, hand-tied bowtie. He was an icon at Ringside and possessed the memory of an elephant; he never forgot a face or a drink.

"Russian Standard on the rocks, olives on the side?" he asked with a knowing look on his aging, round face.

"Yes, thanks, Jim. It's good to be here."

He felt a small tap on his shoulder. He turned to find Stephanie standing before him, smiling. She leaned in to him and whispered, "Did I surprise you?"

"You did, but in a very pleasant way. I'm happy to see you," he said, leaning in and kissing her lightly on the cheek. The fragrance of her perfume was sweet and light. "You're lovely," he said, holding her arm and appraising her up and down. He was really thinking she was scrumptious. He then added, "You're definitely quite a package, Steph."

He meant it. She was wearing a body-hugging emerald green dress that had a demure, v-shaped front, a swooped, low-cut back, three-quarter length sleeves and small, angled cutouts near the shoulders. Her necklace, hoop earrings, shoes and clutch were all in black. Her red hair was gently curled running in thick, red and auburn ribbons down her bare, beautifully freckled back. She carried a black coat over her arm.

When he kissed her cheek, her pulse jumped and an electric tingle ran from her neck to her feet. The hairs on her arm stood up. She shivered with delight at his touch, surprised by her own physical reaction. "I'm pleased that you're pleased, Marcus. I'm happy to see you, too. You look very GQ."

"Thanks. Let's get you a cocktail. What's your pleasure?" he asked, guiding her to the empty stool next to his.

"I think I'll try a Cosmopolitan," she said softly.

"May I make that with the Russian Standard vodka, Miss?"

Stephanie turned her head; surprised the bartender had heard her.

"Jim's very good at listening, Stephanie. Be careful what you say here at the bar."

She smiled and said, "I believe you're right, Marcus. He seems to be very attentive and I'm sure he's a man of many secrets. And yes, that would be fine, Jim. Thank you."

Graham looked at the bartender, who was grinning fiercely as he vigorously shook the chrome cocktail shaker.

He enjoyed that about her. She was quick and funny without being boisterous or loud. And her voice - it was breathless, soft and so rich. Every word sounded as if it had been stretched by too many vowels and consonants.

"Cosmopolitan, Miss," Jim said with a broad smile on his face as he placed the drink on the bar in front of her. "I hope you enjoy it and your evening."

The man turned to Marcus and said, "Mr. Graham, it's always a pleasure."

Marcus nodded and then said to her, "Your drink is beautiful."

"I know, right?' she said, sipping the Cosmo, her tongue lingering on the sugary rim of the glass.

"Are you hungry? The steaks are absolutely the best here. All of their beef is hand-selected and the best cuts are aged for sixty days. It tastes unlike anything you've had before. You're a meat eater, aren't you?"

"Yes, that sounds fine," she said, but she was actually thinking, not very often.

"Well, we have a number of tasty treats ahead of us this evening. We can always share one of their steaks."

"That sounds perfect, Marcus."

Turning his attention back to the bar he said, "Jim, can you tell Casey we're ready for our table."

"Absolutely, Mr. Graham. I'll have him come right over."

The restaurant was packed and their table, which sat against a dark wood wall opposite the entrance, was perfect for people watching. There was a vase of white, long-stemmed roses sitting on the round table. Their drinks were already waiting for them.

"The white roses are beautiful, Marcus. You're very sweet," she said softly, tucking her hand inside his elbow and leaning in toward him. "Thank you."

"You're most welcome, Stephanie. I prefer this spot because I can keep everything in front of me," he said, holding her chair while she sat.

She smiled, raised her eyebrow and asked, "Is that a control thing? You know, where you need to know everything that's going on? Is that one of those hmmm's we texted about?"

"If you only knew," he said to himself as he smiled back at her. And he did. He knew everything and he'd have to be very careful where their conversations led them. The last thing he wanted to do was frighten her.

He took a sip of his drink, held it for a moment, and then said seriously, "Well, I'm hoping I can set aside some of those hmm's for you tonight."

Without expression she quietly replied, "I guess we'll see, won't we?"

Inside she was in turmoil. She was more worried about how much he really knew about her than anything. She'd been careful to avoid talking about her family or her past and she'd been successful thus far, but Marcus and his resources were a big concern. He seemed to be catering to her in every way and it both pleased and frightened her. If he knew the truth about her, would he still be interested?

The manila envelope she'd received only heightened her concerns and worry. It'd arrived in her mail at home that morning and when she opened it, she'd been totally unprepared for the photos of her mother. Her eyes had burned when she examined the pages from the old porn magazines. Her mother was in full-page color photos doing things to other women and men she could only think of as lascivious and wrong. And yet, her mother seemed genuinely titillated and involved. She couldn't imagine what Marcus' reaction would be if he saw them.

He gave her a smile and wondered what she was thinking. She'd been cordial but cautious with him, and he wasn't used to women reacting that way. She was so dissimilar and it fascinated him. First things first, he reminded himself. This evening was his opportunity to make an impression upon her, exclusive of business. He needed to set her at ease and more importantly, learn what made her tick. What was she really thinking? At this moment he wasn't really sure so he stuck to the basics. "Ringside has the tastiest onion rings and salads besides their great steaks. I can order for us, if you don't mind."

"See, there's that control hmm I talked about."

"No, not at all, Stephanie. I know the menu and thought you may enjoy some of my favorites." He turned on the charm. "I want our evening to be perfect and you to learn a bit about me. You can trust me with this, can't you?"

She folded her menu and said seriously, "All right. But I'll tell you something Marcus." She paused and then said seriously, "I get to order dessert."

He laughed and smiled at her. "You were going to say something else there for a second, weren't you?"

"Of course not. I'll trust you, but just this once." Her smile was barely beginning, but her eyes were laughing.

"Ok. It's a great start," he said, gesturing to their waiter, who was passing nearby.

The waiter quickly came over and stood before them. "Yes, sir. Ready to order? Perhaps some appetizers?" he inquired.

"Yes. We'll begin with your fabulous onion rings followed by the spinach salad with raspberry vinaigrette. I believe for our main entrée we'll go with the aged Porterhouse, baked potato and baby asparagus. We'll share that."

"Thank you, sir. I'll have it up momentarily," the waiter replied, turning and heading for the kitchen.

"What you ordered does sound delicious," she said softly, looking at him.

"I know, right?" he said, somewhat mimicking her. "Now that we have a moment, let's get to know each other a bit. I'll give you three questions you can ask about me, and then I get three. What do you think?"

"Oh my God, you're not really serious, are you?"

"Sure, why not? You must have at least three things you want to know about me, don't you?"

"Okay, okay. Give me a second to think," she said, taking a sip from her cocktail.

She was much more concerned about his questions than hers, but experience had taught her that she could always brush off any question with a smile and a polite "not that." The last thing she needed was him poking around inside her head; she was afraid of what he might find.

She'd decided to keep it light and fun. "Okay, question number one, Marcus. Do you always attempt to romance the people you hire?" A good start, she thought. Maybe it'll put him off balance.

"Only the beautiful ones," he said confidently.

"That's not fair."

"I'm being truthful!"

"Fine. I see how you want to play this game. Question two. When was your last serious romantic relationship?" she asked in her best prosecutorial style, one eyebrow raised.

He smiled slightly and momentarily shifted his gaze to the ceiling before looking back to her. He then reached for his glass and after taking a large drink he said, "I've had many relationships over the years, Stephanie, but none have initially affected me like you."

She blinked and blinked again. She wasn't ready for his response, but she considered it to be very clever and sweet.

He leaned towards her, touched her arm, and asked with mock concern, "Are you okay? Was my answer that good?"

"Yes. I was thinking about how clever you are. I'm afraid I could never do as well, so I'm at a disadvantage." She wasn't kidding, at least not to herself.

"I doubt that. You still get one more question. Make it a good one."

"All right, okay. Why are you interested in me, and what have your resources told you about me?" She was afraid of what she was about to hear, but was unable to stop herself from asking.

"That's two questions," he bantered. "I'll answer them both, though. To the first one, I'm interested in you because you're beautiful, smart, and well spoken. I also love your voice. I could listen to it all day. Secondly, my resources are the same as yours: Facebook, Google, Match. The basics. It's all good. That's why I'm here."

He then reached across the table and squeezed her hand.

Her head was spinning with his answers, and she was relieved until she heard him say, "Now, it's my turn."

"That was too easy," he thought. She was so fragile and afraid; he knew he had to be gentle with her. "Okay, here we go. Number one. Do you have cats?" he said with great seriousness.

She sighed with relief and smiled.

He could tell she expected something totally different.

"So you think I'm a crazy cat lady, huh?" she said with a frown. "As in, all I have are my cats and me? Very funny, but to answer you, yes, I have a cat. Only one. His name is Skinnykitty, and no, he isn't skinny."

He was laughing, surprised by her answer to his cat question. "All right, I'll try to get tougher with this one," he managed to say.

He paused, wanting her undivided attention. "Number two. What are the three things you hold closest to your heart?"

She glanced down and up, and then at him. "My sister, my brother, and my cat," she said with a small laugh.

"That's a very catty response, Stephanie. Good answer. Okay, here's my last one. If I invited you back to my home for a drink after dinner, would you be interested?"

"As much as the idea intrigues me, I believe it's too early in our friendship for 'late night drinks at your place.' However, I'm flattered you would ask, Marcus. Thank you," she said sweetly, her eyes open and truthful.

"Well, it's early," he said confidently, but he'd expected her answer. He was testing the waters of what he suspected about her.

The waiter arrived and placed a heaping plate of golden-brown onion rings in front of them. He set two small dipping bowls containing a mixture of ketchup and horseradish next to the onion rings. He then positioned a small plate in front of each of them with an accompanying fork and knife.

"Please enjoy," he said with a small bow as he left their table.

The time flew for her during dinner and before she was knew it she had white roses in her arms and they were walking from the restaurant to where her Lexus was parked on the street. She hadn't used the valet; it wasn't practical.

"Marcus, the dinner was so good; I don't think I've ever enjoyed a better steak. I had a wonderful time. Thank you for the roses."

"I'm really delighted you enjoyed yourself, Stephanie. I certainly did."

She stopped in front of her car and pushed a button on her key fob. The Lexus' lights flashed and the door locks clicked open. He reached down and opened the door for her. He then touched her arm and turned her gently towards him. "Thank you for tonight," he said.

He kissed her and she kissed him back. What started as a polite first kiss turned into something much more. She emptied herself into his lips and his kiss, her tongue touching his, exploring. He responded and pulled her closer to him, but the intense chemical reaction between them made her suddenly stop and pull back. Her knees were shaking and she was flushed. "That was very nice, Marcus, but I have to go," she said breathlessly. "I'm afraid if I continue I won't be able to drive."

She turned and with a rustle of her skirt, dipped to get into the Lexus. She placed the roses on the seat next to her, fastened her seat belt and started the car.

He leaned down and said to her, "Good night, sweet girl." He then closed her door, turned and walked back to valet parking.

Her hands were shaking when she drove away. She tingled.

Chapter 13 • The Three

Diana slipped off her headband as she pushed out of the doors at SuperFit in downtown Lake Oswego. "That was crap," she said to herself.

She usually did the spin class, but tonight she'd missed it, so she ran on the treadmill and lifted some free weights. "Boring with a capital B," she said aloud. But it was better than nothing and that would never do. She'd been a gym rat since her college days and now at twenty-nine she still wanted and needed the burn. If she had to miss more than one day at the gym she could get real bitchy. Withdrawals, she guessed.

Her colleagues at Uptown Real Estate believed she went to the gym to meet men, but they were wrong. She was all business at the gym, and that's why she preferred the spin classes - there was no time for chitchat. She did her workout and then hit the road. When it came to men, she had as many dates as she wanted. In fact, if anything were true, she had too many.

She smiled, thinking about how hard it was to even keep them separated. She couldn't remember how many times she'd called James - Robert, or Robert - James, or some other mix-up of things they'd done or places they'd been. She wasn't trying to be mean or forgetful; she was just too busy and none of them had caught her interest enough for her to care. At this point in her life most of her time and energy was centered on her career, not men. Her client list was bursting at the seams with buyers and the luxury properties of West Linn and Lake Oswego didn't last long. She felt like she was printing money lately - enough to buy her new BMW 5 Series sedan for cash. It went perfectly with her new wardrobe and townhouse.

Her phone chirped as she climbed into her car. She closed the door and read the caller ID. It was Stephanie.

"Hey Steph, what's up? I'm on my way home from the gym."

"Di, how are you? God, I wish I had a cigarette."

Stephanie sounded more scrambled than usual. "I'm good. You sound a little wound up. And FYI, you don't smoke anymore. How was your date? Where are you?"

"Di, my date was so good. I'm on my way home. Ringside was perfect and wonderful. Marcus was very attentive and so handsome. He makes me swirly."

"It sounds like you might be head-over-heels for the guy, Steph. I don't think I've heard this from you before. Did you kiss him?"

"Oh, yes. Di, there was this electricity thing. I think he experienced it, too. We were both surprised. I'm not sure if he is trying to charm me or conquer me. You know he has a military background, in combat? He may have that take-the-hill mentality, with me being the hill. I'm worried about what happens when he gets to the top."

"Steph, don't start that shit. You said you liked him. You said there was chemistry with him and now you're starting to look for things to question. Give him a chance. He certainly has gone out of his way to romance you. Don't mess this up. Just enjoy it." She wanted to sound encouraging. The last thing Stephanie needed was any seed of doubt or worry.

"You're always so upbeat and positive, Di. I love that about you. I'll do my best. I do really like him, you know. But I'm nervous. I think we may be too dissimilar. It scares me. I'm also worried about Ray. When I was home today, I went through my mail and there was a large, unmarked envelope. There was no return address, but it was mailed from Portland. In it were old pages from a porn magazine. The photos were of Mom. They were terrible."

"What? Photos of Mom in a porn magazine? How's that possible? Maybe they were Photoshopped."

"They don't look like it to me, Di. I know Ray sent them. I know in my heart he did."

"He's in the halfway house and can't leave Walla Walla. You know that. How could he send them from Portland?"

"Well, who else would? I'm worried about what it means. What does he want from me?"

"I don't know, sweetie. What can we do?" Di asked, quiet and calm.

"I know what to do," Beth said silently to her.

"Just leave that bastard to us, Stephy," Tiffany added.

Stephanie paused, letting *the talk* within her subside. "Nothing, that's what. I can't even prove who sent them or why. I can't really tell anybody, especially Marcus. What would he think of Mom and us? I can't even imagine."

"Steph, I don't like the idea either, but you can't panic about this. Ray's still in lock-up. Focus on Marcus. Just be brave and let your heart guide you. You know, that hard, little, goofy thing beating inside your chest?"

Stephanie laughed at her comment. "Yes, thanks little sister. I'll do that. I'm almost home now. Any other words of advice?"

"No, I believe I've said everything I could on the matter. You go girl. I'm on my way home as well. Talk soon. Love you."

"Love you, too. Bye."

Diana considered what her sister had said and worried for her. Stephanie was so breakable and skittish; she desperately needed someone she could trust and love. She hoped Marcus Graham was the right man.

As she drove, she called Evan.

He answered on the second ring. "Diana, I was wondering when you were going to check in. Coming home from the gym a little late, aren't you?"

She could tell he was high on weed from the way he slowly enunciated his words. It was one of the ways he got through each day and she believed it helped calm him.

"You know me so well. How was your day, Ev?"

"It was okay. I'm so bored. It makes me crazy to be inside and sit. I haven't given a lesson or played a round in a week. The weather sucks."

Crazy wasn't good for him. He couldn't concentrate if he had to be indoors and sit for any length of time. Evan had struggled in grade school, but he had the hardest time in high school. He was constantly in fights or breaking up with some girl. His grades were awful, largely because he couldn't focus long enough to do the work. It really wasn't his fault; he had never been the same since their mother had died.

However, he did have a skill. He was a natural when it came to golf and his report card D's didn't prevent him from leading the Grant High School golf team in his junior and senior years. He'd even received a scholarship offer from a college, but he hated school. The first job he applied for was where he worked still: Lakemount Golf and Country Club. He'd been there eight years and had worked his way up from taking care of the clubhouse to now managing the pro shop as the club's assistant pro.

Evan once explained to her the only time he ever relaxed was when he was playing golf. He said the order of the manicured fairways and greens eliminated any distractions for him. It was when he felt most at peace and genuinely happy. He didn't know why, but it had been that way since he first stepped onto a course with a club in his hand to see what it was all about. He'd been in love with the tranquility ever since.

Diana knew he still felt this way and she was happy for him. "Yes, the weather does suck, but look at it this way, you're inside where it's warm and your life is pretty damn good. You'll get your rounds in, you know you always do," she said, trying to sound encouraging.

"I know, but I hate sitting and waiting. You know that. So, what else? What's Stephanie up to?"

"I'm glad you asked. She's been seeing this guy with megabucks she met at work. He has some big development company and he hired her agency to do some work for him. He sounds very nice and Steph, for the first time in her life, sounds like she's almost ready for a real relationship."

"Really? Almost? I didn't think she'd ever find someone. She's so aloof and picky. I've never even seen her with a man. Never even heard talk about one."

"That's definitely true, but our big sister has always been in her own little world. You know that as well as I do and why."

"I don't need reminding. Thanks. Anything new on Ray?"

She knew Evan didn't need the drama of their past. It haunted them all in their own ways. The damage and memories would remain forever. She decided to skip telling him of the porn photos Stephanie had received. She hadn't seen them and she really didn't want to talk with him about them. For some weird reason it embarrassed her.

"Nope, all's quiet. But back to Steph - I'm happy for her and I have my fingers crossed she's finally found someone she could fall in love with. What about you? Any new love interests?"

"I'm happy for her, too. And no, I have no new love on the horizon. Anyway, it's good to hear from you, Di. I'll chat with you later. I'm hitting the sack."

"Okay. Keep your chin up about the weather. Remember, you play golf for a living for Christ's sakes," she said with a laugh, trying to cheer him.

"That's very good, like it's not a job. Good deal. Later, Di."

Diana turned into the drive and pulled into her parking spot. She turned off the car and sat there for a moment. Life was really good for them right now, she reflected. She hoped it would remain, but dreaded what could be next as she unconsciously crossed her fingers.

Chapter 14 • Judith Fischer

When Powell drove into the parking lot at Avalanche, he wondered who belonged to the sleek, black Audi S8 parked out front. He didn't have long to figure. Mac Kierney was talking with a woman in the lobby when he pushed through the glass doors. They both looked at him. He surmised she was the 2:30 appointment Mac had reminded him of earlier.

Kierney gestured with his hand to the woman and said, "Hank, this is Judith Fischer. She's come to us for some help regarding her brother. Ms. Fischer, this is Hank Powell, the senior investigator and owner of Avalanche."

Powell stepped towards the woman and extended his hand. "It's a pleasure, Ms. Fischer." He guessed her to be in her fifties and by the looks of her car and attire - wealthy. She was raven haired, finely featured and attractive. By the set of her jaw and her determined expression, Powell surmised it was serious matter.

The woman smiled slightly and shook Powell's hand. "Mr. Powell, I'm very pleased to meet you. I've come to you based upon the recommendation of Matt Givens. He said you might remember him."

Powell smiled. "Of course. Matt's a detective with the Seattle Police. I met him on a case I was working a few years ago. He's a good man."

"He said the same about you, Mr. Powell: that you were a good man who didn't mind ruffling a few feathers to get the truth. And that's what I need - the truth about what happened to my brother." The woman's tone was serious and again for Powell it was another tell about her: Judith Fischer was used to being in charge and getting her way.

Powell replied cordially, "Please accompany me to my office, Ms. Fischer. We can discuss the details of your concerns in private. Mac, please have Hines stand-by. I'll buzz him if I need him."

Kierney nodded. The request by Powell was more than just a heads-up for Hines. "Stand-by" was actually an in-house alert for Hines to record the conversation that would soon take place in Powell's office.

Kierney returned to his desk to call Hines as Powell guided Judith Fischer through the door that led to the interior spaces of Avalanche.

"I know it's not what you were probably expecting, Ms. Fischer, but it suits our style. We're a working company, with the emphasis on being ready to do our jobs 24/7. Most of our investigators are also ex-military."

He observed her as she strolled up to the elevated boxing ring, its drama highlighted by the yellow light shining down from the hanging lamp above it. The fan above the ring spun lazily. She touched the mat of the ring and looked over to where the weight machines, recumbent bikes, treadmills, weight systems, and climbing ropes sat ready for use.

Powell pointed to the right of the ring. "Over there on the other side is our self-defense and offensive tactics training area. In addition to detailed investigations, some of our services include personal protection and we take pride in being highly capable at it."

"I'm sure you do, Hank. You don't mind if I call you Hank, do you?" she queried with a small smile.

"Not at all, Judith." Powell smiled at her, responding to her familiarity. "Please follow me," he said as he headed for his office at the rear of the gym. Powell pointed as he walked. "Each of these other rooms is where our investigators can rest, eat, and re-arm."

Powell then gestured to the wire-meshed window in the middle of a heavy, steel door. "That door leads to our computer operations and legal center."

"Here we are," Powell said as he stopped in front of his office and opened the door for her. "Please come in."

Powell watched her quickly chose one of the two plush leather chairs sitting in front of his desk. He joined her as she sat. "I don't take notes, Ms. Fischer. With your permission I'll record our conversation so I have an exact record of your request and all of the details you'd like to share. We'll transcribe these for our reference should we both decide to enter into an agreement."

"That's fine with me. Do you mind if I smoke? I see that there's an ashtray on your desk." she said bluntly, while opening the clasp of her handbag and withdrawing a lighter and a silver cigarette case.

Powell wasn't concerned. "Certainly. Not a problem. I enjoy a cigar every once in a while."

She lit her cigarette and slowly blew the smoke towards the ceiling before beginning. "Hank, my brother was murdered in Maui, Hawaii in 2008. I've stressed about his death for all these years foolishly believing that someday I'd receive a call from the police saying there'd been a breakthrough and they'd caught his murderer. That never happened."

She took another drag and continued. "He was on vacation with some friends after graduating from the University of Washington. His body was discovered near a beach in Kihei. He'd been drugged, robbed and then castrated. He bled to death. The police investigation discovered little, other than he'd been seen having drinks with several different women at bars that night in Lahaina. They interviewed his friends, but they lost track of him around midnight. The detectives also interviewed bartenders and waitresses at places he'd been seen, but no new information was discovered. For months they posted his picture in Lahaina hoping to find someone who saw him. No one ever came forward."

Judith Fischer paused and inhaled deeply from the cigarette. She lifted her chin, exhaled, and looked Powell directly in the eyes. "Hank, you're going to find the person who killed my brother. I don't care what it takes. Whatever resources you have to employ, do it." She reopened her purse and removed a white envelope. She passed it to Powell. "That's a cashier's check for your retaining fee. Ten thousand dollars should be sufficient. You may bill me for all expenses. I just want answers," she said without emotion.

She peered down at her watch. "I've had my attorney's email you all of the information, including police reports that we've been able to obtain over the years. It should be in your firm's inbox by this time."

Powell's iPhone chimed. It was Hines. "Got it," said the text.

Judith Fischer rose from her chair and looked squarely at Powell. "I know about you, Powell. Medal of Honor and all that. That's one of the reasons why I selected you. I wanted someone who would not be deterred from finding the truth. I'll expect reports of your progress as you achieve them. I'm counting on you, Hank."

The woman smashed her cigarette out in his ashtray, turned and left his office.

It wasn't thirty seconds later both McGee and Hines joined him.

McGee didn't wait to give his overview. "She sounds very determined, Hank. And yes, we have the documents from her attorneys, Courtland and Nash. Good firm, FYI. They only represent the folks with money. Few can afford their services."

"We'll get into the research immediately, Top. It's a big file and we're stacked up right now. We'll have a report for you as soon as we can," Hines stated. He knew Powell wanted the hard facts to examine, but it was going to take some time.

"Let's get to it." Powell said flatly.

Chapter 15 • A Night to Remember

Stephanie was happy to be off work and that it was the weekend. She'd been busy on the Villa and Gorge projects and she had talked with Marcus frequently about both. She felt their personal relationship was growing and he'd been very attentive. She now had white roses on the kitchen table, along with ones in the living room. Marcus had sent them to her every Friday for the last three weeks, ever since their dinner at Ringside.

She smiled to herself thinking of him as she leaned forward towards the mirror and applied her mascara. She had come to know and trust him more, but she was still cautious. She felt conflicted, though more about herself than him. She needed her independence and didn't want to be controlled, but at the same time, she wanted the love of a man who protected her and cared enough to help her make good decisions.

I'm so practical, she mused, and then laughed at herself. She had no idea why she was being so reflective, and yet, so giddy. She was reminded of the song "Drunk on Your Love."

"Well, sober up girlfriend," Beth said to the woman in the mirror.

Stephanie scrunched her nose at the *voice*. Her dates with Marcus the previous two Saturdays had each ended in a kiss that excited and strengthened her interest in him. To make matters worse, Marcus inquired during the course of each dinner if she would afterwards consider coming to his home for a late-night drink and conversation. She had stuck to her guns thus far and had kept him at bay with a polite "not tonight," though in her heart she knew her defenses were weakening.

"Can I be that strong tonight?" she asked the mirror.

Dinner that evening was at their new favorite restaurant, Salty's on the Columbia River. He had answered most of her "hmm's," though not so much by his words, but by his actions. She wasn't completely relieved; Marcus did have his eccentricities. He loved making, as he said, "small suggestions" about her make-up, hair and what she wore. They weren't awful or offensive, but they were unexpected. He was always very polite when he would recommend something to her, usually by saying her beauty was being hidden or improperly accented. In some ways, his attentiveness to her every detail pleased her, but it also concerned her and she had told him.

She recalled his exact reply and his broad smile as he said it. "It's all in how you look at it. I don't consider my suggestions a control thing at all. In fact, I would hope the same from you. It's just us looking out for each other and wanting the best."

"I believe him," Tiffany said aloud.

The woman in the mirror looked back at her and said, "I hope you're right."

She started to apply her lipstick and stopped. Marcus was totally entwined in her life. She saw him at work when he was in for media discussions with Susan. He had meetings and calls with her about ideas and refinements for the new campaigns, and he talked to her in the evenings over the phone and through texts, romancing her. The sheer volume of her contact with him made her feel more at ease. She was learning about his ways and her confidence and trust had grown.

She smiled at her reflection.

She remembered the other brief relationships in her past and how there had been no real chemistry. That was the big difference with Marcus. She'd never experienced real passion and love for a man - that required chemistry and trust. Did she trust Marcus enough to begin letting him see and love her? She had to be cautious: *Beth* and *Tiffany* would be close and watching.

Stephanie leaned closer, peering at the woman in the mirror and asked, "Are you ready for tonight?"

Tiffany suddenly appeared and exclaimed, "That man turns my handles. I'm definitely ready."

Beth wasn't far behind. "Tonight will be fine. I'll be there with you, Stephy."

Stephanie pulled at her sweater, fluffed her hair and carefully applied her lipstick. She checked the mirror one final time before leaving the bathroom headed for her coat, car and Salty's. Skinnykitty meowed at her as she walked out of the front door.

Graham guessed she'd be late. She always was. He believed she couldn't help herself. She also didn't respond to him as other women had. She always seemed to be somewhat reserved and holding back. He'd worked diligently at romancing her to overcome it, and he believed he was closer, but she still insisted driving herself to meet him for their dinner dates. She'd told him it was just easier for her and he hadn't pressed the issue knowing her potential for skittishness. He wanted her more than ever, especially when they embraced and kissed, but she'd remained passionately reserved. "The best things in life are sometimes very much worth waiting for," he reminded himself.

He glanced up from the bar and watched her walk towards him. She hadn't worn her glasses, which she had been doing more frequently.

He rose to his feet smiling and waited for her.

"You look fabulous as usual, Stephanie," he said, kissing her lightly on the lips, inhaling her presence, thinking how wonderful she smelled. "Hmm, is that Candy you're wearing? I think it's delicious," he said, his smile gleaming.

"Settle down there, mister, and isn't "hmm" my line?" she said, pushing gently away from him and smiling.

"In my defense, I'm just happy to see you." And he was. She was intoxicating in her black sweater, skinny black jeans and black stilettos. Her thick red hair was parted to one side, falling provocatively over her eye.

"I see that. Salty's looks busy," she replied, surveying the dining area adjacent to the bar. The large windows of the dining room faced the Columbia River and featured an expansive view of the river and the many boats and barges traveling its currents. She watched as an Alaska Airlines passenger jet made its final approach inbound to the nearby Portland International Airport. The jet was lined up on the middle of the Columbia and it was only about 500 feet above the water when it flew by. The viewing pleasures for the patrons of the restaurant was one of the reasons Salty's was becoming *their* place. She decided that the first time they had gone there.

"It is a little busy, but our table is waiting. I'll have our drinks sent over. You know where we're sitting, right over there next to the windows," he said, pointing across the dining area.

"Of course I do, Marcus. I wouldn't expect to be anywhere else," Stephanie replied coolly, turning and walking towards the dining room.

He told the bartender where they were sitting and then followed her gorgeous backside into the dining area. "She is on it tonight," he whispered to himself. He wasn't worried. He had his own plans and ideas of how the evening would progress.

Cocktails, oyster shooters and bleu cheese iceberg wedges went by with their chatting about West World, books they both had read, and movies they'd heard about. She relaxed, but knew his question would be coming soon. She didn't have long to wait.

"Steph, I know I've asked you before, but maybe this evening you'd enjoy coming back to my home for some drinks and conversation. I know that sounds awfully similar to my favorite line, but I really would enjoy your company. Plus, you've never seen my home and it's kind of fun."

"I enjoy your company as well, Marcus. I think that's a lovely idea this evening, and I would love to see the house of M," she said, watching his face turn from his most sincere expression to one of astonishment. He was grinning.

"That surprises and pleases me. I'll get the check," he said, beginning to stand as he laughed.

She smiled at his sense of humor and laughed with him. "That's funny, Marcus. Don't you think we should have dinner first? I'm just guessing."

In mock disappointment, he shrugged his shoulders and with a matching frown he said, "All right, you've got me. I'm surprised by your answer. I damn near couldn't believe my ears. But yes, we should wait."

"Thanks for your patience. I couldn't agree more," she stated in her calmest voice.

She was anything but calm. She tried to sound confident and composed, but she was deeply apprehensive. To take this next step with Marcus meant a real commitment on her part - a commitment that involved her being truthful with him. She had never wanted anyone to know her family history, but she had to tell him. She didn't want to appear she was hiding something from him and she was worried he already knew everything. She was ashamed, not because of what she did, but because of the circumstances.

Beth came forward in a rush. "Whoa there, girlfriend. This is not true confessions and you really can't tell him about us. Crazy doesn't really make a great girlfriend. Also, Ray and the porn are off limits. He doesn't need to know any more than the basics."

She couldn't argue with *Beth. She* was right. Marcus would have enough to consider, including her poor background and sordid family history. She was nothing more than a ragamuffin and he was brought up by millionaire parents who gave him everything. They weren't in the same league. The socio-economic gap between them was huge and inescapable. She was terrified her masquerade would soon be ending, but she knew it had to if they were to take this next step together. She shivered at the thought. She could only hope for the best and trust in what she had seen in Marcus and that it was real.

Dinner rushed passed them and they were soon in their cars heading for downtown and the Tower. He tried to keep his speed under the limit on the way, even though he wished he was blasting through traffic. He doubted she would appreciate his full-throttle driving style. She was already nervous enough, but she always seemed somewhat skittish around him. He was hoping he could change that this evening.

When they reached the underground parking of the Tower he had her park next to him in Gretchen's space. They took the elevator to the twenty-second floor and entered his offices. He walked her hand-in-hand down the hallway to the large doors marked with brass M's. He pulled his entry card from his wallet, slipped it into the slot, and opened the doors to his home. "Welcome to my home, Stephanie. Come in. I'll get a fire started. Please make yourself comfortable."

She couldn't speak. It was astonishing. The same wall-to-ceiling windows in his office wrapped the complete east side of the living room. The nighttime cityscape of Portland and its bridges over the Willamette River dominated the view. A round, black and gray mottled marble fireplace base sat in the middle of the room, its black metallic, funnel-shaped hood separated from the base, rising to the ceiling. A black, glass ledge about twelve inches wide surrounded the fireplace base. An Amazon Echo sat upon the fireplace ledge. A large, circular jet-black, over-stuffed leather sofa partially encircled the fireplace. To the right of the sofa, a futuristic flame-shaped floor lamp rose gracefully to a height of six feet; a soft reddish-orange glow emanated from its glass, multi-tiered body. On the wall opposite the entryway, a large black and white painting overlooked the room. The painting was of a tree in the shape of a woman's body, her arms gracefully extending upward, her hair forming branches and boughs of the tree. On each side and below the painting sat tall, pyramid-shaped speakers. She could faintly hear a Jack Johnson song playing from them.

To the left of the living room she could see a large kitchen. A beautiful dining table with eight chairs sat to the left of the kitchen, separated by a wet bar. A chandelier reminiscent of a sea urchin illuminated the table. There were two glasses positioned under the light, a vase of white roses flowered between them.

Marcus went over to the couch, the lights and traffic of downtown Portland twinkling and gleaming through the windows behind. He reached for the remote on the table, selected the code and watched the fire start. He adjusted the flames and went back to where she was standing, removing her coat and laying it across the couch with her purse on top of it. He then stepped forward to her and lightly kissed her, squeezing her hands as he did.

He didn't want to hurry, quite the opposite. "Would you join me, while I mix us a cocktail?"

"Yes, of course. I love your home, Marcus. The view of the city at night is wonderful," she exclaimed, staring at the white, green and neon colors of the downtown lights.

"I know. I never tire of the view," he said, admiring her. "I always enjoy looking at you too, Steph. You're a beautiful woman, whom I'm very excited and happy to get to know."

She had those *please forgive me* eyes when she answered him, breathlessly, "I'm happy too, Marcus, but we need to talk. I need you to know some things about me, about my past." She slowly dropped her eyes from him and turned her face away as she began to cry.

He wrapped his arms around her, while she cried. He didn't know how long it lasted, but when it gradually ended, she snuffled and said, "I'm so sorry, I'm a mess about me and us."

"It's okay. We're only beginning, and we'll get through this," he said confidently, reassuring her as he held her.

"Marcus, sweet man. I'm not sure I'm the woman you think I am or want me to be. I'm so afraid that when you know my past . . . I'm so embarrassed," she said, beginning to cry again.

He stood there, holding her, feeling her weep in his arms. He whispered to her, "It's all right. We'll be fine, Steph. I am not afraid of you or your past."

He listened as she recounted the miseries of her childhood and all of its soul-crushing damage. Even though he knew the story, it was like hearing it for the first time. Some things she wouldn't even talk about; she would stare at him with those eyes and start crying again. His combat tours seem to pale in comparison to her suffering. He wanted to kill Franklin.

He wiped her cheek with his thumb and said, "Stephanie, it's okay, you're fine. Thank you for telling me. You're one of the bravest women I've ever met. I admire you so. You know, we have something in common about our backgrounds. My parents adopted me at birth. My birth mother gave me up at the hospital and six months later she died of a drug overdose. I don't even know the name of my biological father, but he must have been a bastard. I learned all of this from my adopted mom, Rose Graham, just before she died. I only found out a year ago. I never knew."

He briefly closed his eyes and considered what he had said to her and the lie contained within it. "So you see Steph, we both came from situations we had no control over. And look at us today. We're both so lucky. I'll tell you one other thing: I promise you that this Ray bastard will never hurt you again, ever."

She could hardly breathe. His reaction and willingness to protect her touched her deeply. She put her head against his chest and softly said to him, "No one has ever stood up for me before, Marcus. Thank you." She meant it sincerely. It was the first time in her life she had experienced someone willing to protect her other than *them*, and she perceived the barriers protecting her heart beginning to soften.

She wiped her eyes and said to him, "I must be a sight. Please excuse me for a minute, Marcus. I need to freshen up." She picked up her purse from the couch and headed for the bathroom. She needed to collect herself.

"Me, too," Tiffany exclaimed. *"He makes me feel dreamy. I think I'm in love."*

Standing in the bathroom she approached the granite counter, placed her hands flat against it, leaned forward and examined the woman in the mirror. She was a mess, again. Her mascara had run from her crying and her cheeks were tear-stained. She removed her make-up bag from her purse and repaired her foundation, then her eyes and finally her lips. *Tiffany approved, excited for the next step. Beth remained surprisingly silent.*

Satisfied with her fresh look, she left the mirror and returned to the living room where she found Marcus holding her phone in front of him. "You've had a call."

She took the phone from him and saw that Melody had left her a voicemail.

"That's weird. It's Melody, from my office. She never calls me, especially at night."

She pushed the voicemail play arrow and listened. "Stephanie, this is Melody. Susan's been hurt. She went back to the office tonight and surprised someone who apparently had broken in. He beat her up badly. Her husband called me. He tried to reach you, but couldn't get through. She's at Providence Emergency."

At first, she was confused and couldn't process the message. But it didn't take long before she was clutching Marcus' arm and trembling. "Susan has been beaten up by someone who broke into our offices. She's at Providence. I have to go."

"I'll drive you. I'm not letting you go alone," he assured her.

Chapter 16 • Wreckage

Graham bulled his way through traffic to get to Providence Hospital, the power of the Mercedes blazing by car after car. He parked next to the red emergency sign, his Purple Heart plates daring a ticket. They ran towards the entrance, through the big sliding doors and over to the reception desk where a man in blue scrubs was looking at his computer monitor, his head down. The waiting room was empty.

"Excuse me. We're here to check on Susan Arcadia. We were told she was admitted," Stephanie said to the man.

The male attendant scanned his computer and said without looking at her, "Yes, we have her. She was admitted at 10:12. Doctors are seeing her now. If you'll have a seat, I'll check on her progress for you."

"Thank you. That's very kind," Stephanie replied.

They walked over to the rows of the hard-plastic chairs and selected two in the front. She took a deep breath and waited. Marcus continued to hold her hands.

A few minutes later the attendant returned. A tall, dark-haired, middle-aged man followed him. It was Roger Acadia, Susan's husband. A pained expression with worried eyes looked at her.

Stephanie stood up and went over to the man. Graham followed her.

"Roger, how is she? What's going on? What happened?"

"Stephanie, it's awful. She's alive, but she's had the royal hell beat out of her. She lost two front teeth, and she has lacerations on her lip, eyebrow and ear. Probably a concussion, too. She did manage to dial 911 before she passed out, thank God. Oh, and the son of a bitch broke two of her ribs. I can't believe somebody would do this to Susan. And for what? It all seems so senseless."

Graham extended his hand to the man and said, "I'm Marcus Graham. I'm a friend and a client of Susan's. I'm sorry we're meeting under these circumstances. If there's anything I can do, please don't hesitate to ask."

"Thank you, Mr. Graham. Susan has mentioned you and how delighted she is to be working with you. Thank you both for coming, but if you'll excuse me, I have to get back to her now. Please don't wait. It's going to be several hours before she gets out of evaluations and surgery. She's tough and I know she'll get through this. I'll call you, Stephanie."

Roger Arcadia then turned and headed back towards the hallway and the dual doors that led to the treatment rooms.

"Excuse me. Are you friends of the family?" Stephanie heard from behind her.

She turned to face the voice with Marcus. A smaller man with brown hair and a dour expression, dressed in a rumpled brown suit, stood facing them. His right hand was holding a gold badge with blue letters stating the words DETECTIVE, Portland Police, 45322 across its front.

"I'm Detective Bill Lane with Portland Police. I'm investigating what happened to Susan Arcadia."

Marcus reacted first. "Detective, I'm Marcus Graham and this is Stephanie Courtland. Stephanie works with Susan, and I am friend and a client of their agency. We were at dinner this evening at Salty's. When we heard the news about Susan we came here as quickly as we could."

The detective nodded and removed a small notepad from his jacket pocket. He wrote on the pad for a moment and then said, "Mr. Graham, I believe I know your business partner, Hank Powell of Avalanche Investigations. I've bumped into him a few times. Good man."

Marcus smiled. "Yes, Hank is a great guy. Avalanche is really his company. I just offer advice from time to time."

Lane made another note and turned his attention to Stephanie saying, "Miss, I'm sure this is a terrible thing for you, but I would appreciate your help in identifying anything missing from the office. It was quite a mess. We have our forensics people there now, but they won't be finished for hours. Could I ask you to meet me there at nine tomorrow morning?"

"Yes, of course," she managed.

"Thank you. Just one quick question - do you know of anyone who may have wanted to hurt her? Was she having trouble with anyone you're aware of?"

The question immediately made her think of Ray, but she buried the thought and answered calmly, "No, Susan is liked by everyone. I've never seen her upset or worried about anything other than meeting a client's deadline or normal business things. When I saw her yesterday, she was happy and looking forward to the weekend."

Lane made another small notation on his pad, closed it and put it back in his pocket. "Thank you both very much for your time. Miss Courtland, I'll see you tomorrow morning. Mr. Graham, please say hello to Hank for me."

The detective left them and headed to the glass doors that led to the parking lot.

Graham watched her carefully for signs of stress or worry. He saw none. She had a somewhat blank look on her face as she watched Detective Lane walk away from them. He was thinking of how calm she was when she turned to him slowly and said softly, without smiling, "Marcus, let's go. There's nothing we can do here at this moment. I don't want to go home and be alone tonight. Do you mind if I stay with you?"

"Of course you can. I understand."

She tucked her head into his shoulder, snuggled into his arm, and curled her arm around his as they walked to the parking lot. He needed no encouragement to take her home and he wanted her to feel safe, especially tonight.

She woke slowly the next morning and stretched. She detected the aroma of coffee brewing in the kitchen. She rubbed her toes against the smooth black sheets, her legs extended. She'd slept wonderfully, unexpectedly so, without any reels turning at all. When they had first arrived at his home Marcus prepared tea for her and they chatted about Susan and wondered of the circumstances that led to her being beaten so badly. Marcus reasoned that it was a burglary and Susan walked in on it. He also reassured her that he didn't think it was Ray, because the halfway house prohibited travel other than to and from work, or to a specific pre-approved local destination.

She remembered how he then excused himself and when he returned a few minutes later he told her, "Steph, I've placed some things in the master bath. There's a toothbrush, bathrobe, and a 49'ers jersey for your sleepwear. I hope it's okay. I'll be wearing a suit of armor as any good knight would. So, no harm, no foul, no worries, my love." He was smiling broadly, barely concealing his obvious delight.

"That's my guy," she thought, sliding out of bed heading for the kitchen and coffee. She was buoyant until she recalled the terrible things Susan had endured. She was suddenly stricken by the contradictory emotions she was experiencing: her best friend had been brutally beaten, and she felt like she was dancing on clouds.

Her thoughts returned to Susan when an evil image appeared in her mind. She could see his face, leering. Could it have been him? Was it Ray looking for her at the office?

She shook her head, tumbling the questions, his face and her fears of him from her mind. A sudden confidence rose in her and at first she couldn't identify why, until she heard *Tiffany say, "Don't you worry yourself about Ray, Stephy. We're not twelve anymore and we've learned how to take care of men like him who are mean to us."*

Chapter 17 • Crime Scene

Stephanie left Marcus with a kiss goodbye, promising him she would call after her meeting with the detective. She was apprehensive and fidgeted during the drive from the Tower to their two-story, brick office building located in the newly gentrified Hawthorne district of southeast Portland. Synergy occupied the entire second floor, and though not expansive, it suited their five-woman staff perfectly.

Detective Lane was waiting for her at the office entrance. "Thank you for being so prompt, Miss Courtland. I appreciate it," he said, lifting the yellow crime scene ribbon for her.

She coolly surveyed the reception area and it appeared undisturbed; the doors to the offices led to the real damage. She imagined a small tornado had blown through each room, whirling papers and desk contents randomly throughout their interiors. The office where the media girls worked was a catastrophe. Their desks had been emptied, the contents strewn all over the floor. She saw the computer hard drives were gone, their cables dangling under each desk. Both MacBooks were also missing, the monitors standing, disconnected. She described what she observed to the detective, who wrote on his pad.

Her office had also been rifled through. Her hard drive was missing, but nothing else seemed to be. Luckily, she had taken her computer home for the weekend.

She stopped at the doorway of Susan's office and stared at the brownish-red discolorations on the beige carpet, and spatters of the same color on the wall. She suddenly felt sick to her stomach and took a deep breath. Her heart was pounding.

"Are you okay, Miss Courtland?"

She turned her attention from the stains to the detective. "Yes, I'm okay. I guess I didn't expect to see blood. That's blood isn't it?"

"Yes, it is. Please, let's focus on what you see that may be missing."

She nodded and went behind Susan's desk. Again, as in the other rooms, the hard drive was gone, and so was the computer. The open drawers of her desk were empty.

"It's the same. He took our hard drives and our computers. I can't tell if anything else is missing, but those are the big ones. We don't keep money or any real valuables here. It's funny though, he didn't touch the computer in the reception area."

Lane wrote as she talked.

Her cell phone chimed at her. It was Roger Arcadia. She didn't wait for him to begin. "Roger, how is she? I've been so worried."

"Stephanie, thank you. She had a rough night, but our girl is tough. She's had a bunch of stitches and her ribs are really sore. The oral surgeon comes this morning. She also has a concussion. My God, the bastard beat the hell out of her. And for what?" he questioned, the stress obvious in his voice.

"I have no idea. When can I see her?"

"Give us another twenty-four hours. Monday would be better. She said to tell you that you're in charge until she returns. I'll tell her we talked. I have to go now."

"Okay, Roger. Bye. Tell her I love her."

Stephanie thumbed off her phone and looked back to the detective. "That was Roger Arcadia. Susan is in rough shape. I don't understand who would do this to her and this," she said, surveying the chaos of Susan's office.

"We don't either at this point in time. Our forensic people turned up very little and there is no video coverage of the building. Here's my card. Please call me if you discover anything else missing. I appreciate you coming down this morning."

"You're welcome. Is it okay if I lock up the office? Can we come to work Monday?"

"Yes, you can. We're done here. Again, I'm sorry for your friend, and thanks for your time."

As soon as the detective left, she called Marcus and told him what she'd learned. She then told him she was going home and she would call him later.

The moment Stephanie rang off, Graham was on the phone.

"Hank, Marcus. There's been an incident and I think we should take a look at it. I'm not satisfied the police will be able to bring the clarity we need. Let me explain." And he did for the next five minutes, telling Powell everything he had heard from Stephanie.

Powell hesitated before responding. "LT, on the surface it appears to be a burglary gone badly. The woman was at the wrong place at the wrong time, but what makes me suspicious is what was taken. Obviously, the computers are a commodity, but shit, it takes a hacker to open one without a password. The other weird thing is the hard drives. What's the point? The drives aren't worth much and it slowed him down to disconnect them. It doesn't make sense, unless they wanted the information on them."

"You know what, Hank? The key will be finding those MacBooks once they surface. We'll probably find them on Craigslist, or being dumped at a pawnshop or a second-hand computer store. And I think you may be right about the motive. Maybe there's more to this than just some computers being stolen for their street value."

"I think it's a possibility, LT. The Macs may surface, if the thief doesn't have his own guy who can crack them. We'll have to see. Other than that, we've got diddly. No video feeds, no prints, nothing unless Susan Arcadia can identify him. I'll check on it when the Blues get their interview with her. I know Lane and he'll share the info with us."

"Roger that. Stay on top of this. It's too close to home. These are my people."

"You've got it, bud. I'll put on the full-court press. Hines will spread his web and find our guy. I'll get back to you when I have something. Take care."

"You too. Later."

Powell's first thought after Graham hung up was Ray Franklin. He checked his watch; it was 10:27 a.m., Sunday. He searched his contacts on his phone. He took a chance and dialed Jim Lowell at the halfway house.

"Jesus, Powell. It's Sunday," the voice growled at him.

"The strong never sleep, Jim. I need a status report on Franklin."

"Good to know, Hank. He's a model duck. He waddles and quacks. We have him working at a corrugated box plant. He's received no warnings or reps. He's quiet. Spends most of his time in his room, either watching TV or on his computer. Oh, yeah, and if he's not doing that, he's pumping some iron. Got him a set when he first arrived here. What's up?"

"Our bird hasn't left the compound unannounced has he?"

"Nope. You know we're on a strict sign-in and sign-out policy here. We have no free-flyers."

"Okay. Thanks for the info, Jim. Let me know if anything new on Franklin should come up. I'll be in touch."

"Always glad to help, Hank. Will do," the man said, but Powell recognized his sarcasm.

"Dead end," Powell said aloud.

Chapter 18 • Time On His Side

Franklin sat down at the small desk in his room happy to be off work from the box plant. The line had been stop-and-go all day, switching from one small job to another. He didn't mind the work, it kept him busy and the money was good. That was the biggest surprise: the money. When Jim Lowell first told him he was going to be working at Corrugated Box Industries he expected to be hired as a janitor or some other factory slave, but instead he was trained on a machine that folded and glued the seams of corrugated boxes. He'd never worked a real nine-to-five job before, let alone one paying $16.50 an hour. In four months, he'd earned $3,500, which allowed him to pay for his room and meals in advance in addition to buying some clothes, a weight set, and a new Mac computer.

Lowell had strict rules at the halfway house, but compared to prison they were easy for him. He was short-timing. Lowell's approval of his computer purchase was a reward for his good behavior and performance at work. Plus, he'd never been late on check-in. He had no intention of fucking up and ruining his plans this close to total freedom.

He'd changed, too. Without the steroids and the time to work out he'd slimmed down to 205 pounds and he felt better. The steroids were his angry edge in prison and they'd helped him survive, but in the real world he didn't need them. His mind was his edge and his power. He was also thinking more about pussy and getting laid again. The steroids did have their price and he wasn't paying it any longer.

He fired up the new Mac, thinking you'd have to be a fool to buy anything else. He patiently waited for it to boot up. He entered his new password and waited again. Once the desktop was up and running, he selected Safari and then Google. He began his search with her name. It was the first time he'd ever accessed the Internet. In prison he'd taught other inmates how to use a computer and its Microsoft Office programs, but they were strictly forbidden from the Internet. He'd read about it and seen it on TV, but he'd never been online. He'd waited a long time to see what it held.

An hour later, he stepped away from the computer and sat on his bed. He was amazed by how easy it was to find people, places, facts, and porn. Randy had told him how quickly he'd found where Stephanie worked and lived, but he didn't quite believe it until now.

Stephanie Courtland was all grown up and wasn't the awkward, skinny, red-haired girl he remembered. She was now thirty-two and as beautiful as her mother. She worked as some sort of creative director for an ad agency, Synergy Advertising. An Oregonian link showed a picture of her with some dude named Marcus Graham, the big wheel at Graham Developments. They were at the Mayor's Ball; she was in a long princess dress and he was in a tuxedo, both mugging like high rollers.

But there was more to it than that.

When Franklin searched the Synergy website, he discovered Graham Developments was one of Synergy's biggest clients. He then searched Graham Developments and learned that Walter Graham founded the company in 1935 and died in 2013, leaving the company to his only heir and son, Marcus. Graham Developments was now a one-hundred-million-dollar company according to Internet news reports. They were also in the process of working for an approval on a major development in the Columbia Gorge.

Franklin sensed he'd hit the jackpot. All he needed to do was threaten her and she'd jump through hoops to avoid having him implicated in a scandal, but he'd have to be very careful. A man with the kind of money Graham had would have plenty of protection at his disposal.

He didn't want to kill anyone. It'd taken him fifteen years of anger and wanting to slaughter her every night before he realized it was nonsense. He'd just end up back in prison, probably forever, if they didn't execute him. When he finally let the thought of murdering her leave his head, everything became clearer to him. His revenge would come in the form of payback from her for a new start, a new life for him. She would be his bankroll, whether she liked it or not.

Franklin suddenly fumed and pounded the bed, his eyes closed, jaw clenched. He hadn't deserved what she'd done to him. He was good to those kids. He took them in, fed them and gave them a roof over their heads. Nobody cared about that at the trial, least of all, Stephanie, the ungrateful little bitch. All she did was whine about him trying to touch her and how miserable he made her feel. Big deal. Did she think about how they were living before he took them all in? Fuck no. They had nothing. Her mother was a fucking bar maid and a tramp when he met her. He saved her and the fucking kids. He hadn't meant to kill Alice; it was just a terrible accident.

Franklin rose from the bed and calmed himself.

He took a deep breath and stretched his shoulders, feeling the stress subside. He rolled his neck and listened to the vertebrae and tendons snap and pop. He reached his hands high over his head until his fingertips touched the white, textured ceiling. "Be smart. One step at a time," he reminded himself.

He turned and sat back down at the Mac. He was ready to begin his next step if he could find the right information. He started his Google search when there was a loud knock on his door.

"Franklin, you've got visitors in the lounge," he heard Lowell say.

"Okay, thanks Mr. Lowell. I'll be right there," he replied with great courtesy, knowing he needed to stay on the good side of his PO.

He walked to the visitors lounge and found two giant carbon copies of men waiting for him, one white and the other African American. The white guy was dressed in sand-colored khaki pants, and a black safari jacket, with a green T underneath. The black man was in blue jeans and a black sweater. His first thought was that some ex-con survivalists had come to recruit him, but he knew Lowell would never allow it. He vetted everyone who visited his parolees.

"Are you Raymond J. Franklin?" the older, square-headed, white guy asked.

"Yes, I am. Who are you two? Police? Feds?"

The two men smiled at each other and then returned their attention back to him.

"No, we're not either of those. We're specialists," the black behemoth replied.

"Specialists, huh? In what?" Franklin asked.

"I'm Hank Powell and this is my associate, Mac Kierney. We're with Avalanche Investigations, out of Portland. Our firm specializes in private investigations and personal protection, among other things. One of our clients is Stephanie Courtland. I received a call today from a very important friend of hers about you."

Franklin noticeably cringed when he heard her name. "Yeah, so what? Why are you here to see me? I haven't done anything."

The one named Powell stepped towards Franklin until he was right up next to him, looking down. The black man had repositioned himself at the same time, moving behind him, blocking the exit to the door.

"We're here to inform you we won't tolerate any interruptions or distractions from you in Miss Courtland's life." Powell thumped the man's chest with fingers like steel pegs. "Listen, bub. If my friend and I hear you've contacted Miss Courtland in any way, we'll be back. But next time, we won't be as polite. We'll catch you somewhere between here and the box plant and I guarantee you it will be a meeting you won't enjoy."

The big black man added emphasis to what Powell said when he stepped forward and grabbed Franklin roughly by the shoulder turning the man around. Inches from his face Kierney said calmly, "You think you're a tough guy? You think twenty years in the big house made you big and strong? Boy, you ain't shit, but you better get some smarts about you real quick. You see me again and I promise you the closest thing to a near death experience you'll ever have. You hear me loud and clear?"

Franklin could only nod weakly at the man and then watched as both of them turned away and walked quietly out of the room.

Chapter 19 • On the Radar

During Hines' military and government service he'd accumulated a broad list of friends and associates who were on the cutting edge of what they all called "geektech." Some made a legitimate living hacking into computer systems containing information that the police or FBI wanted. Others were storefront pro's serving the personal computing community with repairs, operating system issues and the occasional lost start-up password. In Portland, there were only a few techs with the talent to open the MacBooks stolen from Synergy, but it still took almost two weeks before the computers showed up on Hines' radar. As he suspected he found them through one of his connections. The information relayed to him came from a freelance service tech in Beaverton, who told him a second-hand electronics store requested a cleanup and new operating system on three MacBooks they'd obtained from a man who said his business went broke. The store paid $200 for each Mac - well under market value - because the man said he needed the cash immediately. All files on the three computers had been erased. The electronics store owner identified the seller as a man named Catters, Kitts, Cutters, Kitters - something like that. The tech told him the owner didn't ask for an ID and could only describe him as a dark-haired man about six-foot-tall with a medium build. He also said the guy looked like a hard-hat worker and was in his late forties or early fifties.

Hines ran the names through his DMV search program. He came up with twenty-two hits for Catters, Kitts, Cutters, and Kitters. He discarded the women and concentrated on the men. That cut it to twelve. He next removed anyone under the age of forty and anyone who didn't have dark hair. There was one name left: Carl Kitters.

Hines immediately conducted a deep background review of Kitters to develop a detailed profile on the man. There was plenty of info, but what caught his eye when he dug deeper was the wife. Carl Kitters was the husband of Julia Grant Kitters. When he searched her, Hines discovered she was the sister of William Grant. Grant was a senior partner of FMG -

Foster, McWillis and Grant Advertising. Hines knew FMG was a well-known Portland ad agency and that they had represented Graham Developments prior to Synergy.

"Bingo," Hines said to the computer monitor. He immediately headed for Powell's office.

After Powell received the briefing from Hines, he went directly to the ready room where he found Mac Kierney.

"Let's mount up in fifteen minutes. We need to make a call."

Mac shrugged and gave Hank the thumbs-up. Nothing pleased him more than traveling with Powell to weed-out some trouble. They both armed themselves, selecting from the weapons each possessed in their tactical gear lockers, though they were just as deadly unarmed. Kierney also loaded up four surveillance bugs Hines had brought into the room.

As Powell drove the black Ford Raptor, he briefed Kierney on Kitters. Hines had pinpointed the location of Kitters' car with some earlier fieldwork by the Kirkpatrick brothers. Powell further explained Kitters worked as a longshoreman and would be off at five, which is when they would follow him and seize the opportunity to confront and question him, preferably at his home, without witnesses.

They didn't have long to wait after arriving at the Portland shipyards in the northeastern corner of the city. As Hines foretold, at 5:10 p.m. they watched Kitters walk quickly across the parking lot towards his Chevy pickup, Oregon plate BAM599. His red plaid shirt was tucked into his tan work pants and he wore black suspenders and heavy boots. He was as his driver's license described: six-foot-tall and 190 pounds, forty-eight years old, dark-haired with a swarthy complexion. He carried his hardhat and a black metal lunch pail.

They followed Kitters truck from the shipyards across the St. Johns Bridge and through the twists and turns of Germantown Road as it wound its way across the West Hills to Beaverton. They stayed well back and it wasn't difficult. Traffic was heavy.

"He's heading for home as expected," Powell said to Kierney.

He was right. Kitters had driven straight home only to meet his wife and two kids coming out of the house. From across and down the street, they watched Kitters park next to the Subaru, get out of his Chevy and talk with the three. It didn't take long. Kitters watched his family load up in the SUV, back down the drive, and depart. He waved to them as they drove off.

"Let's go," Powell said to Kierney as they watched Kitters enter his home. The Raptor tilted left and right under their weight when they stepped out of the black truck.

Powell and Kierney strode to Kitters door. Powell knocked and when the man opened it, he said, "Mr. Kitters, I'm a private investigator and I want to ask you a few questions about a situation we're looking into. Is there anyone else at home?"

Kitters appeared confused and said, "No, I'm alone. What did you say you wanted again?"

After the man's question, Powell flat-handed Kitters hard in the abdomen, sending him backwards into the living room onto to his ass, gasping for breath. Kierney pushed passed Powell and grabbed the helpless man by his arms, jerking him to his feet.

Powell quietly closed the door as Kierney dragged Kitters to the kitchen. They didn't need civilians watching from the street through the living room windows. Kierney sat the pale and panting Kitters roughly down on the wooden chair and then headed for the back rooms of the house to verify they were alone and to install the surveillance gear Hines had given him.

Powell came up to the seated man and said sternly, "Mr. Kitters. It's nice to meet you and as you may have already suspected we are not men to be trifled with. My associate and I are very concerned about some of your recent escapades. Specifically, a small matter involving some MacBooks and hard drives taken from Synergy Advertising."

He paused, making sure he had the undivided attention of Kitters. "Please take a moment to gather your thoughts, Mr. Kitters," Powell said patiently.

Kitters glanced up at Powell, who stood menacingly before him. "I don't understand. What do you want?" the man asked worriedly.

"Thank you for not beginning with a lie, or an I don't know. I respond poorly to those types of answers. But, to answer your question, I want to know the details of your adventure at Synergy and the woman you assaulted there. Mr. Kitters, I advise you to be very clear and forthright in your responses. It would be a poor decision on your part to do otherwise. I will video your answers for the record."

Powell pulled his iPhone from his jacket, selected the video record option of the camera and aimed it at Kitters.

Kitters licked his lips, blinked nervously and began. "I'm not a criminal. I've never been in trouble. I got messed up in some bad deals and I was behind the eight ball on the house. My old lady was bitching and moaning all of the time to ask her brother for help. He's this bigwig at an advertising agency. He's a real turd. Said he wouldn't help me unless I did him a big favor. He told me he'd give me ten thousand dollars to grab the hard drives and computers from this business in the southeast. He said I could sell the stuff once they had what they wanted. He even had a key to the front door. He bragged about only spending a hundred bucks to score it from one of the cleaning crew that did the office."

Kitters coughed and asked, "Can I have a glass of water, please?"

Powell was amazed at the twerps' request, but he complied, signaling Kierney, who had just come into the kitchen, with a nod.

"Here ya go, bud," Kierney growled at Kitters when he passed him the glass.

"Thanks," Kitters said gratefully. He drank deeply and then continued. "I went to the office and had already gotten the Macs and the drives from the first three rooms, only there wasn't a computer in the third. I went to the last office, the big one on the end. I was being real quiet the whole time and I didn't even hear her come in. I was on my knees, bending over to unclip the drive when I get hit by this giant fucking purse. This crazy lady is screaming at me and I slug her. Hard as I could. It fuckin' hurt.

The bitch's teeth cut into my knuckles. I think I knocked out her front teeth, but she wouldn't stop. Oh, no. She gets up and swings the fuckin' purse at me again. I left-hooked her and she went down. I said, 'enough of this shit' and kicked her in the ribs. I didn't mean too but she wouldn't back-off," Kitters whined to Powell. "I didn't know what I was thinking. I knew she wouldn't be able to recognize me with the mask on, but I panicked. I didn't want to hurt anyone. It just happened. Anyway, I left her unconscious on the floor. I then went back to the other offices and ransacked the desks. It was supposed to look like a random burglary, not only a heist of computers and drives," Kitters explained as he squirmed on his chair, inspecting his hands.

"So, let's be clear. Your brother-in-law, William Grant, offered and paid you ten thousand dollars to steal the hard drives and MacBooks from Synergy Advertising?"

"Yes," Kitters answered. "They wanted the business they'd lost to them. Bill told me it was personal. He said they were determined that no small-time, all-woman agency would beat them at their own game."

Powell believed everything Kitters told him, except the panic part. "Why did you leave your name at the electronics store?"

Kitters looked up at the ceiling and then back at Powell. "It didn't even dawn on me. I was in a hurry and I didn't think the guy wouldn't give a shit because the price was so cheap. He didn't ask for ID and I didn't think he'd remember what I said."

Powell nodded his head. "Mr. Kitters, have the statements you've made been under the threat of death or violence to you?"

"No, it's the truth. I needed the money to help my family. I'm sorry I ever did it."

Powell turned off the video recording on his phone.

"Mr. Kitters, thank you for your cooperation. If you say one word to anyone about what we've discussed, you'll suffer the consequences. The police will be sent your video, you'll be arrested, and you'll end up in prison. But here's the upside: You can keep the money, because we want nobody the wiser, especially your wife, Julia, or her brother. Oh, and if you think we won't know if you tell someone of our little encounter, think again. We'll be monitoring everything about you: your phones, your email accounts, your friends and relatives, your bank, everything. Am I clear?"

Kitters nodded without answering.

"Good. This is for what you did to the woman," Powell said as he stepped towards Kitters and seized his left arm by the elbow and wrist. He then cracked the man's arm over his raised knee. Kitters' head flopped back, his screams muffled by Kierney's hand covering his mouth.

Powell bent down and peered intently into the man's eyes. "Better get that fixed. You've obviously had a bad fall. And remember, not one word. Oh, and by the way, that's a simple fracture you have there, bud. If I was trying, I could have broken your fucking arm off. Get the message now? Is it loud and clear?"

Kitters nodded - his anguish and pain evident.

They left Kitters whining on the floor clutching his arm.

Chapter 20 • Confrontation

Powell dropped Kierney at the Avalanche office before he headed to Graham Developments. When he arrived, Gretchen buzzed him in. She was on her headset, talking, but pointed and gestured for him to proceed to Marcus' office.

Graham was at his desk when he saw Powell enter the room.

Powell didn't hesitate to begin. "I have the info on the caper at Synergy. I believe you're going to be surprised to learn the mastermind behind the break-in was Bill Grant of your old ad agency, FMG. He conspired to steal you back as a client. He needed the info contained on the Macs and hard drives to analyze how Synergy acquired your media business and how to counter existing creative efforts by the agency. I'm guessing they also wanted to see what new clients Synergy was working with so they could make moves on those as well."

Powell sat down and watched Marcus mulling over what he had told him. He then pulled his phone from his pocket and passed it to Graham. "Watch the video. It's the perp who did the theft and beating."

Graham watched silently until it concluded. "You know, Grant and McWillis are predators. Ever since Foster died last year they've been very aggressive in the market, Grant particularly. He's known to be ruthless and there have been rumors he isn't afraid to take extreme measures to get what he wants. Well, this time he's crossed a line that will have a profound negative effect on their future. I think we need to have a conversation with our friends at FMG. What do you think?" Graham asked, smiling.

"LT, I couldn't agree more."

Graham dialed the number from the phone on his desk. On speakerphone, he asked for Bill Grant. It took only moments for the man to answer. "Marcus, it's good to hear from you. What can I do for you?"

"Thanks for taking my call. It's been a while. I was hoping we could meet tomorrow. I've been considering some issues about our media and I want to talk to you and Fred about it. Do you have time?"

"It would be our pleasure, Marcus. We've been reviewing some of our media planning and I think it would be good for us to sit down. How about ten, tomorrow morning?"

"Sounds good. I'll bring Hank Powell with me. He's considering some new challenges, too."

"Very good. See you both at ten."

He hung up the phone and leaned back in his chair. Graham smiled at Powell. The ambush was set.

The next morning Powell and Graham drove to the offices of Foster, McWillis and Grant. They were quickly shown to the conference room where Grant and McWillis were waiting. Both men were in their sixties, dressed in dark suits, jackets removed, white shirts and power ties in place. Grant was six foot tall and slender. Clean-shaven, he had dark gray hair, brown eyes, a thin nose and a sharp jawline. His ears were long, close to his head and almost pointed. Graham always thought he looked like an old wolf. McWillis was the opposite of Grant. He was short, balding and overweight. He had a round, jowly face that was offset by a pencil-thin mustache. Brown, horn-rimmed glasses framed his blue eyes.

Both men smiled at Graham and Powell.

"Welcome, Marcus. And it's good to see you again, Mr. Powell," Grant said as he approached them, extending his hand. McWillis was close behind. The four exchanged handshakes and returned to sit at the conference table.

Graham sat next to Powell across the table from the two. He removed his cell phone from his jacket pocket and tapped in a selection.

"Before we begin, I want to play you a video we've recently obtained. You may find it interesting."

He slid the phone across the table to them.

Grant picked up the cell and held it in front of McWillis. For the next few minutes they watched and listened to the interview of Carl Kitters, their expressions quickly changing from curiosity to concern. When the video ended Grant passed the phone back to Graham.

"That's rather awkward to say the least. I'm not sure how I should respond," Grant said quietly.

McWillis sat there, the color draining from his face, seeming to hold his breath.

Graham frowned and then lowered the boom on them. "Thanks for not denying the obvious. Now, we have some interesting choices for you to make. I would advise you both to consider very carefully what I am about to say. In the next week you're going to make a major announcement about downsizing the agency due to health concerns. You'll shift fifty percent of your client business to Synergy Advertising, and you'll do it with glowing praise for Synergy. The remaining fifty percent you can keep for one year, but then you'll close your doors forever, passing them along to Synergy, too."

Graham paused, letting them absorb his demands. They both looked stunned.

"If you believe that to be too harsh or unrealistic, consider the alternative: we send this recording to the police, you'll be arrested and you'll both end up in prison. Oh, and your families will be ruined financially by the lawsuits that would be filed against your firm."

The silence from Grant and McWillis was short-lived. McWillis was quickest to respond. "I speak for the both of us when I say your offer is very fair. We will comply with your terms."

"Excellent," Graham replied. "I'll look forward to seeing you do that. One other condition: do not imply to anyone that we had any involvement in your selection of Synergy. You develop a story on why you chose Synergy and make it a good one. Ditto for the press. Don't involve us in any manner."

The two men nodded.

Graham and Powell strode from the conference room. When they reached the hallway, Graham stopped and faced Powell. "Foster, McWillis and Grant have been in business since 1972 and have seen it all come and go in the Portland and Northwest markets. Now it's their turn to go. I believe you may agree with me when I say our solution isn't exactly legal, but it's justified. I also believe Susan Arcadia will appreciate having the new business, now, rather than having to wait years for the criminal trial and appeals to conclude before she could bring them to civil court and collect for damages."

Powell nodded in agreement. "No doubt about that, LT. Hitting their wallets and egos is true justice for those bastards. We don't need lawyers and courts to drag this out and decide what's right. In this particular case, it's our call."

Chapter 21 • First Steps

McGee and Hines finally had the time to review the entire bundle of e-mails containing the investigative reports on the murder of Jason Fischer. It was very thorough. McGee didn't know how she had obtained copies of the murder book from the police in Hawaii, but he was beginning to appreciate the reach and commitment of Judith Fischer.

Hines was of a like mind. "The investigation was very complete, although it revealed little about the killer. The autopsy concluded Fischer's blood alcohol level was 1.6 - he was really drunk. He also had ecstasy, seconal, and marijuana in his system. There is no doubt he was having a party, but I'm not sure he was conscious towards the end. The specific method of his murder I also find most interesting and disturbing."

McGee nodded his head in agreement. "I do as well. But it wasn't just a castration, it was a complete emasculation. All of his genitalia had been removed. It isn't exactly the most common way to kill someone. It indicates a high degree of purposeful anger and specific intent. It was a message to Fischer and I believe it was from a woman."

Hines rushed to comment. "I concur, John. First, I think we should revisit the two friends he traveled with to Hawaii. Maybe they can provide us some new insight. I found the police interviews with them to be somewhat vague and I think there's more there. They may also give us a clearer picture of Jason Fischer."

McGee nodded. "Okay. You make the list of people Powell should interview along with their relevant contact info. I'll also need summaries of the investigation files. Once you're finished, I'll do an overview and then we can brief Powell."

Without responding Hines turned back to his keyboard and monitors.

It took a little more than two hours before they were standing in front of Powell and passing him their four-page report.

McGee began, "As you'll read, we're suggesting three courses of action to begin the investigation. The first involves the re-interview of the men who accompanied Fischer to Hawaii. Their names and current contact info are included in our summary. The second is a detailed look at who Fischer actually was - the interviews will help with this, but Andy will also conduct a deep background search on the man. The third step will be our search for similar crimes. The method of his murder was unusual to say the least, so we'll look for others like it. Our explanations for each recommended course of action are also listed."

Powell sat quietly and read the report. After a few minutes he returned his attention to them. "Solid work on this. I'll see if I can arrange the interviews immediately. Luckily, they're both still in the Sea-Tac area, so they're close. John, I want you to accompany me when I've set them. Andy, go ahead and get the work-up done on Fischer and the search you described."

Hines and McGee nodded and left the office.

Powell began dialing and was quickly rewarded. Howard Jamieson and Mark Rafferty were both still friends and cooperative. They agreed to meet him the next day in Seattle at Rafferty's office, 11:00 a.m.

•

Rafferty's Architecture was located in a modern office complex in south Seattle. When Powell and McGee entered their office, they were immediately greeted by two men standing in front of an empty receptionist's desk. Both were dressed casually in slacks and sport shirts.

"I'm guessing you're Hank Powell," said the taller of the two men. "I'm Mark Rafferty and this is Howard Jamieson." Both men shook Powell's hand. Rafferty was six-foot-tall, athletic, with dark blonde hair and a ruddy complexion. He was polished and gregarious, and Powell was reminded of the term "city slicker." Jamieson was shorter and squarely built with thinning brown hair. His beard was closely cropped and his eyes squinted when he smiled. He appeared fit and tough. He was slim-hipped and his thick neck, arms and chest belied his athleticism.

Powell gestured to his right. "This is John McGee, my associate."

Handshakes were exchanged between McGee and the two.

"Come on, guys. Let's go sit in my office where we can talk," Rafferty said cordially, gesturing to the glass door behind the reception area.

Powell and McGee followed the two men into Rafferty's office, which was more of a lounge - display room, containing numerous miniature replica models of modern multi-story buildings, lavish homes and shopping complexes. There was no desk. In the middle of the room sat plush, black leather couch and two green overstuffed leather chairs. An elegant, slender chrome floor lamp illuminated the area and shed light on an ebony black table that resided between the couch and chairs. Several copies of Architectural Digest were fanned on the table.

Powell and McGee sat on the couch, while Rafferty and Jamieson settled into the overstuffed chairs.

Powell didn't hesitate to begin. "Thank you both for taking the time to meet with us today. As I've explained, we've been asked to look into the circumstances surrounding the murder of your friend, Jason Fischer. I'm interested in hearing what you may remember about Jason and your time together in Maui."

Jamieson and Rafferty looked at each other like they were sharing a private joke before Jamieson answered. "Eight years ago we were pretty wild. We'd gone through four years at UW and we did everything together. And Jason was the wildest of us all. To put it bluntly, Jase was a big-time pussy hound and he loved to party. Money was never an object for him. He always picked up the bill. We lived in a big house his parents had rented for him near campus. It was awesome. There was something going on every night and as you may suspect, we always had a boatload of women hanging out. By the time we were seniors, we felt like we owned UW and its finest ladies. We threw the best parties and Jase always led the charge. He was a legend on campus."

Rafferty added, "Howard's right. Everyone liked Jase, but hell, who wouldn't back then? Yeah, he had a rep all right. And truthfully, some of it wasn't good, but as his best buds we didn't care. He was handsome, loaded and given how we lived, he had his choice of girls, but he never had a relationship that lasted more than a few weeks. In fact, he preferred one-night stands. He was one of those guys who thought of women as sex objects and he was owed the perks. It was something he took for granted. He told us both, I don't know how many times, that he'd never get married. He didn't see the point of it. He always laughed. 'I have so many choices, why bother? I'm not in a hurry and she'd have to be very beautiful and have the approval of my mother."

"Tell us about Hawaii, specifically the night Jason was killed," Powell asked.

Rafferty responded. "The first few days in Hawaii were a blast. We surfed all day on the North Shore and partied every night in Lahaina. Our condo was in Kihei, right on the beach. Jase's parents owned the place. It was deluxe. We'd been there four days and it was Friday. Jase was really jazzed and told me he was ready to cut loose. I knew what that meant: booze, pot, ecstasy, and pussy. I was wasted from surfing and being out the three previous nights."

Jamieson interrupted. "We both were. But not Jason. Shit, you would've thought he'd slept all day he was so wound up to go out and party. I'm pretty sure he was already high and with Jase, it could have been from anything. He always had a stash. He called them his "party supplies" and he always had plenty. He left about six or six-thirty that evening heading for Lahaina. It was the last time we saw him alive."

McGee didn't hesitate. "Let me back you up a bit. What about the first three days and nights? Did Jason have an altercation with someone or an incident that he was involved in? Any locals give him trouble?"

"No, I don't think so. Jase always got along well with dudes and he'd practically grown up on Maui. He spent every summer there since he was five or something. He always sort of bragged about it and his local 'brahs'. He was a man's man. I'd never seen him even have cross words with another guy. He was just that way. He was pretty cool."

Rafferty quickly interjected. "That's true. But, thinking about it, I do remember one odd thing he said to me before he left that night. I didn't think of it until now. He said he'd met a real dog and was looking forward to seeing her again. He said she was gorgeous."

Powell leaned forward and asked, "Dog? He said he was going after a dog? I don't get it."

"You're misinterpreting me. He meant D-A-W-G. He was referring to a girl from U-Dub: the University of Washington. The Huskies. Our alma mater. We're called the dawgs. Do you get it?"

Powell and McGee both nodded.

"So, you think he was going to meet a girl from your school in Lahaina that night?" Powell asked.

Rafferty looked at the ceiling before he responded. "I do. I didn't mention before. I don't know why."

"That testimony was not in your police interview and I find it hard to believe that you just now remembered that information," McGee said skeptically.

Rafferty at first hesitated and then admitted to them, "I was pretty scared about what had happened. When they first questioned me they just said Jase was in trouble, not that he was dead. The last thing I wanted to do was implicate him in something I knew nothing about. I guess you could say I was protecting him, but I was used to doing it. Jase wasn't always careful with his money or drugs. We had pot in the condo, plus, god knows what he had in his stash. I thought for sure I was being arrested for possession and that Jason already had been. So, I didn't say shit to them. I was freaked out."

"I was too," Jamieson quickly added. "I was afraid they'd charge me for something I had nothing to do with other than being there and getting a little high. Those Hawaiian cops are no bullshit with male Haoles - white guys, especially white guys with money. They held us for eighteen hours and I felt lucky to get the hell off that island. I did tell them that Jason told me he was going to see if he could find a local girl he'd talked to before. But I didn't tell them he meant 'local,' as in a girl from Seattle. It was just a guess on my part anyway, so I didn't mention it. I felt bad for Jase, but I didn't know anything about how it happened."

Powell frowned before he said, "So you both protected Jason, and yourselves. Did it ever cross your minds that maybe you should have helped with the police investigation? Maybe call them when you were home and safe? Didn't you owe that to him?"

Neither Rafferty nor Jamieson responded. Both men were looking at the floor.

Powell simply nodded with a frown at the two men. "Do you remember anything else he may have said or implied about the girl to either of you? Hair color, build, eyes, height, weight? If he'd met her before? Anything?"

The two men glanced at each other, shook their heads, and said nothing.

The interview ended.

Three hours and a car ride later, McGee, Hines and Powell sat together in the operations center at Avalanche to discuss the Fischer case. Powell was intrigued by the information they'd obtained in their conversations with Rafferty and Jamieson. McGee briefed Hines in detail when they'd first returned and the two had spent the last hour compiling a new report.

Hines began. "As you know, John and I have reviewed all of the police files in depth. Hawaii is a dead end. They have no forensic evidence and too much time has passed to believe that we could garner any information by going there. In fact, based upon your interviews today, we believe our next course of action should be to look elsewhere. Specifically, we should search for any unsolved murders reported in Seattle during the years 2005-2008, the years Fischer attended college at the UW. We'll pay particular attention to anyone who was a student or worked there."

McGee added, "We'll be focusing on the mutilation angle. It's the only unusual marking on this case and about all we have to go on. We'll also do a deeper background probe on Fischer and hopefully discover other people he knew at college who may know something about the girl. It's a long shot on that. There's just not a lot to go on."

Powell hesitated for a moment before responding to the two. "I think you're right. We don't have much, but we do have what the police never did: we know he met a girl from his school that night and she, more than likely, knows about his murder." Powell paused and then said, "Get back to me when you have more details."

Chapter 22 • Portlandia

Franklin was amazed by how much Portland had changed in twenty years. The only features he still recognized were the bridges over the Willamette River and some of the older buildings that sat along its waterfront, but the businesses they housed were now gentrified and trendy. Stores were now called boutiques, and restaurants were eateries or carried a foreign name he didn't recognize.

The people had changed even more than the city - it was now a fucking zoo. There were an unbelievable number of vagrants, crazies and drug addicts of every kind. The TV news called them "campers" because of their tents and makeshift lean-to's. But they were just squatting in places where they wouldn't be hassled. As soon as one tent was erected, the next day there'd be fifty. Then the crime, the panhandling, drugs, and public pissing and shitting would begin. They disgusted him. In his opinion they weren't even worthy of living - they were just oxygen thieves.

The young millennials of Portland were also strange to him. Piercings, blue hair, clothes that were more like costumes, and cell phones stuck to everyone's hand were the norm. To these people, he was invisible; some had even bumped into him, oblivious of where they were going, intent only on their text messaging.

The straights, the coat-and tie-crowd, were different, but only in appearance. He couldn't blend in with them, even if he wanted. It was as if he had the word EX-CON tattooed on his forehead and they all saw it. He felt he was nothing more than an interloper in their perfect, ordered world. That was his imagination and he knew it was something he needed to get over, but he did see the need to change his appearance.

The clothes Franklin purchased were not like what he wore back in the day and he initially was confused about what to buy. He shopped at Nordstrom and Macy's, but in the end, he decided on the affordable, middle-of-the-road styles JC Penney offered. It was also kinder on his budget and he enjoyed the freedom of picking what he wanted and having people wait on him.

The old man who rented him the furnished apartment on the northwest side of town was a pain in the ass. The fucker was suspicious and had questioned him why he had come by taxi. He had to lie and say his car was being repaired and he had moved here for work at a local box plant. He was fearful that if the man suspected he was an ex-con he'd never get it. But he did. He paid the motherfucker first, last, and a security deposit to seal the deal with no credit checks. He really had no choice.

He spent almost two thousand dollars for a bedroom, a small kitchen and a bathroom. It pissed him off, because the apartment was nothing more than a converted basement with a side entrance door. The furnishings consisted of a wooden kitchen table with two chairs, a twin bed, nightstand, and a small desk with a lamp and a small chair. He still couldn't believe how much it had cost him. Twenty years ago, he could have rented the entire house for what he had paid for the room. The kitchen, which he wouldn't use except for making coffee, was an extra he didn't give a shit about. There were too many local pubs, eateries and small markets where he could catch a meal. The last thing he wanted to do was sit in his room. He'd done enough sitting in small places to last him a lifetime.

After renting the apartment, his next purchase was a car. Craigslist made it easy. The guy even delivered the '99 Honda to him. It was a beater, but it ran good. It was also invisible, being one of those models you couldn't tell from others. It cost him nine hundred dollars, but it worked for him.

He was nervous about driving, so decided to check out downtown Portland and get a feel for the metro before heading to see his brother in Vancouver. He knew he'd made a mistake shortly after he started. It seemed to take forever to go anywhere and parking was virtually impossible. The streets were all the same, but they had reached a saturation point with the heavy traffic. He hated it and quickly abandoned his exploration.

On the drive to Vancouver, Franklin again realized how crowded Portland had become. When he had lived in Vancouver in '96, a trip to Portland was nothing more than a ten-minute drive down I-5. Not anymore.

The freeway was now clogged with traffic and it took him over an hour to reach and cross over the Interstate Bridge on the Columbia River.

After the bridge, he took the fifth exit off I-5 and ten minutes later he was on the street he knew like the back of his hand. He slowed as he approached the familiar mailbox and address. The house was smaller than he remembered and it was also better taken care of than when he had lived there. It was obviously a family home; there was a trampoline in the front yard and two bicycles were leaned up against the front porch. His brother had moved in shortly after he had been sent to prison and he and Doris had raised their two boys there. Randy obviously took pride in the home because it was neat as a pin, as were the grass and flowers surrounding the yellow two-story house with white shutters.

Franklin opened the car door and stood next to it, looking over the property. He knew from his earlier call to Randy the kids were at school and Doris was shopping for the day in Portland.

The front screen door of the home opened and his brother, clad in a black t-shirt and jeans, stepped onto the porch with a smile. "How's it look after twenty years, Ray?"

"Man, you've got yourself a real nice home here. It looks better than it did when I lived here, that's for damn sure. But I was never much of fixer-upper kind of guy, and you always were, Ran. You've done real good for yourself."

"I appreciate that, Ray. Let me get your stuff. I'll be right back."

Franklin went to the porch and sat down on the front steps. The smell of the freshly mowed grass and the chirping of the birds in the nearby willows reminded him again of how much he had missed while being in prison.

His brother's returning steps caused him to turn in time to see him push through the screen door carrying the black Wilson sport bag.

"I gathered all the stuff you gave me, Ray, including your stash," he said, handing the bag to his brother.

Franklin unzipped the bag and removed the paper sack that contained his future: $2,000 in hundreds, his Washington State driver's license, and a VHS videotape.

"Thanks, Randy. It's all here, just like I left it."

"It's the least I could do, man. So, what's your plan? I'm hoping you've reconsidered trying to go after that girl. I could use your help at the shop, you know? It's not like you need to look for a job. You've got one with me, man."

Franklin stuffed the paper sack back into bag, zippered it and said, "I know and I appreciate it. I'm not going to be crazy and fuck up my life again, trust me. I'm just trying to get used to being out and I'm in no hurry to do something that'll land me back in the shithouse. Thanks for the job offer though, but I've got plans of my own."

"Ok, ok. I'm just concerned, that's all. Say, why don't you come in? We can hang out for a while and have a few beers."

"I'd like to, Ran, but I'm trying to wrap up a few things today and get settled. How about a rain check?"

"No worries. I understand. We'll do it some other time."

His brother sounded disappointed, but he had somewhere to be this afternoon. He stood and pulled the sport bag from the steps. "Ok, man. I'm outta here. Say hello to Doris for me. I'll be in touch."

"I will. Take it easy, Ray. Be safe."

He had every intention of taking the advice to heart. "No worries, brother," he shouted, waving out of the window as he drove away.

The Lakemount Golf and Country Club was his next place of business.

It took him an additional fifty-five minutes to complete the side trip to the golf course, but it was worth it. After carefully checking that there were no video cams in the parking lot or pro shop to betray him, he'd made his personal appearance. It felt good to him to do something positive, and it was interesting to see the man Evan had become. The boy had turned out just fine. Evan also didn't recognize him, which didn't surprise Franklin. Twenty years changes people.

Thanks to his brother's care he was now richer by $2,000 and more importantly the videotape was once again in his possession. He had everything except the final details of his plan, but they were developing. His visit today with Evan would certainly have an additional effect upon her. It would rattle her cage and that's what he wanted. He needed her jumpy and willing to do anything to get rid of him.

Chapter 23 • Lost and Found

Saturday did not begin for Stephanie as any other. She'd stayed over at Marcus' and she'd been snoozing on and off, as she loved to do. Marcus had already left for his morning coffee and she knew he'd be in the front room listening to the television and reading the newspaper in front of the fireplace. It was her third sleepover and she was starting to get a feel for his routine - he called it the "daily prep."

She lazily rolled over onto her back when her phone began to chime and vibrate. She clutched the iPhone from the nightstand and saw that it was only 7:00 a.m. and that it was Diana. She answered sleepily, "Di, it's early. What's up?"

"I'm sorry Steph, but I can't find Evan. Not anywhere."

She yawned, still trying to wake-up. "Really? Okay, but it's early. He's probably working at the club."

"Are you serious, Steph? Wake up. I haven't been able to find him for the last two days. Today is number three. He's not answering his cell. It goes straight to voicemail. I'm worried. He never does this. He always checks in with me every few days. You know that."

She did. Diana was very protective of Evan and watched out for him constantly.

"Well, I think he'll be fine. He's twenty-nine years old for Christ's sake. He has his own life to live. He's probably run off to play golf somewhere or something."

"Really? Without calling me? I don't think so. He would never do that, especially with the holidays coming up."

"Okay, relax. God knows he wouldn't do that, right?" she jibed at Diana.

"I get it now, Steph. No big deal, right? Is that what you're thinking? Still unable to feel anything, Sis? It doesn't seem that way to me with you living it up with Marcus. I have a life, too. I'm cruising right now, but it doesn't make me distant or vacant. And in case you've forgotten, Ray is still out there."

"Okay, I understand you're upset," she said calmly, trying to soothe her sister, but at the same time she was suddenly again worried about Ray. "I really don't appreciate the Ray reference, Di. I don't think he'd go after Evan, do you?"

"No, I just said that. I'm sorry. I'm worried to death. The little bastard didn't tell me he was going anywhere. Oh, shit. Wouldn't you know it? He's calling me on the other line. I'll call you back after I skin him alive."

The phone call ended. Stephanie stood up and slid into her 49'ers jersey knowing it would only make the conversation easier with Marcus.

He was right where she expected him to be. She joined him on the circular couch and set her phone and coffee down. She then bent over and kissed him on the cheek. "Morning, LT."

"Oh-oh," he replied. He'd seen that look from her before.

"What? What do you mean 'oh-oh'?" she said with mock concern. She tried her best to frown and not smile. She did squirm a bit though, just to make sure he was listening.

"Okay, what's up? It must have been the phone call. Is there some new disaster or plot underfoot?" he joked.

"The call was from Diana. She hadn't heard from Evan for almost three days and she was worried sick. Evan always checks in and would have told her if he was going somewhere. I was going to tell her that you could find him when her phone rang and he was on the other line. She's going to call me back."

She could see him thinking. The LT wheels were spinning, she guessed.

"Really? And what info would you have supplied me on Evan so I could find him?"

"His phone, address, where he works, places he frequents, and people he knows. Di would've helped me."

"Look at you," he said, a small laugh beginning. "Apparently, you know exactly what to do."

It surprised her, too. It really wasn't like her at all. She immediately suspected *Beth* had joined the conversation. Before she could think further about the why, her phone buzzed. She reached for it and saw it was Diana.

Clutching the phone, she bent down, kissed him on the cheek and sprinted for the bedroom. She could hardly wait to hear what Evan had been up to. She answered on the fourth ring. "What? What have you heard? Is he dead? Was it a car crash?"

Di laughed openly at her mock questions before saying, "No, he's alive. And even better than that, he has a suntan and a girlfriend."

"Are you kidding me? He has a girlfriend?"

"That's the report. They went to Maui to golf and play. It was their second time this year. Isn't it wonderful? He may have finally found someone who can handle the golf thing and you know, the other stuff he worries about."

"Wow, I'm in shock. What did he tell you about her?"

"Not much. He just said we'd have to wait to meet her in person. I'm going to strangle him when I see him."

"Oh my god, that is so rich. But just think of it this way: it could be worse. He could be a golf bachelor, or whatever they call those guys. Seriously, thank you so much for the info on Ev. Love you."

"Wait. I have other news and it's a little strange."

"What now? Another surprise?"

She heard a pause from Di and then a slight sigh. "Before he left for Hawaii, some man was in his pro shop shopping for clubs. Well, Evan helped him and just before the guy left he told him there was a man in the parking lot who'd given him twenty dollars to give Evan a message."

"What? That's weird," she replied as she felt the hairs on the back of her neck begin to tingle.

"Steph, the message was, 'Tell Stephanie, Ray said to say hello and that he looks forward to seeing her real soon.' Evan said the man who gave him the message was older, about six-foot tall, had short dark hair and was built like a weightlifter. Evan didn't think he was a golfer, but he was real nice."

She knew the moment Di described the man that it was Ray. Her hand trembled on the phone and she felt bile rising in her throat. Her head spun with the thought of Evan being in the presence of Ray.

"Settle down. He didn't hurt Ev. It's an opening gambit by him," Beth said confidently to her, ever so silently.

Tiffany wasn't amused. "Pump it up, Steph. I can smell his tricks. Di can't, but we can."

She complied. "Why? Why didn't Evan call me and tell me, or you? This isn't some joke."

"He didn't think much of the message, other than it was weird and then his girlfriend arrived and they were off to the airport and Hawaii. It didn't really dawn on him that it was our Ray. You know Evan: if he isn't on the golf course, he doesn't have much of an attention span. I told him it could have been Ray standing in front of him, but he has no memory of what Ray looked like. He didn't know. He said he was sorry he didn't call about it sooner, but he didn't want to stress us out about nothing."

"Nothing? It scares the hell out of me, Di. You know that. You better start being careful. If he knows where Evan works, he could know about you, too."

"I will Steph, but I'm more worried about you. Ray never hurt Evan or me like he did you. I'm so sorry. I love you."

"Di, I love you too. I'm going now. I need to think."

"Not me!" Tiffany said gleefully, internally to her.

"K. Love you. Bye."

She thumbed her phone to end the call and when she glanced up she saw Marcus standing there. "How long were you listening?"

"Just at the end, when you were saying goodbye. Why don't you give me the details I don't know?"

"It's Ray. He went to Evan's job at the golf course and left a message for me with him. He said he'd see me soon. It didn't even dawn on Evan that it was a serious threat to me. He kept it to himself, while he was in Hawaii for three days with his new girlfriend. Three days, and he didn't say a word."

Marcus walked to the bed and sat down. He placed his arm around her. "Steph, I've got this. I'll get Hank and the crew working to get this situation stabilized. I promised you that Ray wouldn't hurt you again and I meant it."

She rested her head on his shoulder. "Okay. Go ahead and call Hank. I'll be okay. I just need to rest and think for a while."

Marcus kissed her cheek and rose from the bed. "I'll be back in a bit." He then walked purposefully from the bedroom dialing Powell as he did.

Powell picked up on the first ring. "What's up, Marcus?"

"Apparently three days ago Franklin visited Stephanie's brother at his job site. Left a message for Stephanie. Said he'd be seeing her soon. I want us to get on top of this bastard. No waiting."

"Roger that. I thought he was still in Walla Walla at the halfway house, but I'll find out where the scumbag is located. I'll call you back when I have more. In the meantime, why don't we put the badger boys on a rotation and have them keep watch over Miss Courtland coming and going to work?"

"Good, Hank. Let's do it. But I don't want her to be escorted. Keep the men back. She doesn't need to feel their shadow, and Franklin doesn't need to suspect it."

"Roger, LT. I'll get on it and get back to you about Franklin."

"Okay. Later."

Powell clicked off and dialed the halfway house.

"Jim Lowell," the man answered.

"Jim, Hank Powell."

"Hank, I'm glad you called. I tried to reach you, but I had no luck. I didn't want to leave a voicemail."

"Really? I didn't see your call. So, what's up with Franklin? I've heard he's been in Portland."

"I'm not surprised. The Parole Commission took my six-month report and they terminated his parolee supervision early. We're too damn crowded to hold someone longer than the minimum anymore, especially if the guy has been solid. Franklin wasn't trouble and he went out of his way to follow every rule. We cut him loose last Tuesday," Lowell said flatly.

"You have a forwarding address?" Powell asked, trying not to sound pissed.

"Nope. He said he didn't know where he was going and didn't give a damn about any mail. Said he didn't know anyone anymore."

"All right. Thanks for the info, Jim. I appreciate it."

"No worries, Hank. Good luck with this guy. He's got a chip on his shoulder for sure. He doesn't show it much, but it's there."

Powell hung up. He needed to consult with Marcus and develop a contingency plan for what was sure to come, but first he needed time to think. There was no doubt in his mind Franklin was going to be trouble.

Fifteen minutes later, Powell called Graham. "We definitely have some issues, LT."

"Ok. Let's hear them. What do you have?"

Graham sounded irritated. He could hardly blame him.

"We have zip. He's off the reservation, full release. I suspect he's in Portland, though we have no address. We'll keep looking, but unless he makes a mistake or does something we can trace, I don't expect much. I'll send Kierney over to the golf course to check if they have any video, but I'm not holding my breath. Of course, he could try to make a move on Miss Courtland, but I doubt he'll be dumb enough. If he does, we'll have him. Given his threat, I think we'll soon know what he wants."

"Yeah, you're probably right. Just make sure Stephanie is covered from Monday to Friday, from the moment she leaves here until she's back. I'll take care of the weekends. I don't want any loose ends or surprises, Hank. Get back to me when you have something."

The call ended and Powell tossed the cell phone down on his desk. Graham had sounded all business, and he couldn't blame him. Powell was also concerned and decided the assignment to oversee Miss Courtland would begin that afternoon. He also knew it was time to press and press hard to find Franklin.

Chapter 24 • Wake-Up Call

Powell liked his plan, and taking the *honey badgers* to do the work fit it perfectly. The Kirkpatrick brothers were always his first choice when it came to potentially mobile, hostile engagements. Their experiences in MOUT (Military Operation in Urban Terrain) and capture intelligence tactics were the best he had.

The three left Avalanche headquarters, when Hines confirmed that he finally had Franklin's location; it had shown up on an application for a Wi-Fi connection through Verizon. It had taken almost two weeks for it to post. Hines learned that Franklin was renting a basement apartment in a home owned by a man named Gary Simpson. Further searches detailed that Simpson was a Vietnam veteran and had retired after thirty years with Portland General Electric. He was a widower and lived alone, renting out a downstairs apartment for supplemental income to his retirement. When Powell received the information about Simpson, he believed they had an angle they could possibly use to their advantage.

It took them less than fifteen minutes to arrive at the address. Powell left the Raptor and walked up to the front door and rang the bell. He noticed next to the ringer was a circular decal that read "Vietnam Veterans of America." In the center of the sticker was a green, yellow, and red ribbon Powell recognized: the Vietnam Service Medal.

An older man with graying hair and a mustache answered the door. The man had a large scar running from the corner of his mouth to his chin. He was wearing a red and black plaid shirt and blue jeans.

Powell flipped open his identification wallet and introduced himself. "Mr. Simpson, I'm ex-Master Sergeant Powell. I served with Special Forces during my four tours in the Middle East. I'm now a full-time private investigator with Avalanche Investigations. I was wondering if I could have your help on a case I've been assigned."

Simpson carefully scrutinized Powell's ID and then noticed the small, pale blue ribbon with the five stars on Powell's safari jacket. "Jesus

H. Christ, are you a Medal of Honor recipient? That's what the ribbon is, isn't it?"

Powell nodded. "It is. I earned it in Afghanistan."

"Alright, Master Sergeant. Come on in and tell me what you're up to. I could hardly deny a man with your credentials." Simpson opened the door wider and gestured for Powell to enter.

As soon as Powell came into the living room, he saw a giant black and rust colored Rottweiler coming around the corner from down the hallway. The massive hound was at least 200 pounds and had a head the same size as that of a brown bear.

Simpson called to the big dog, "Rajah! Come meet our new friend. You can relax, Powell. He's going to check you out."

Powell laughed and put his hands down, palms open. "I have no problem with big Rotts, Mr. Simpson."

Powell was then under the control of the giant dog as he was sniffed, drooled upon, and generally molested, as giant dogs love to do.

"This is quite a beast, Mr. Simpson," Powell said, rubbing behind the huge, floppy, black ears of the dog.

"Yes, he's a German Rottweiler. Comes from an exceptional breed, near Stuttgart. He's 210 pounds and a formidable animal. So, what's up, Master Sergeant?"

"I wanted to thank you for your infantry service in Vietnam. We both wear a Combat Infantry Badge for our troubles," Powell said, extending his hand to Simpson. The dog returned to Simpson's side and heeled, looking at Powell.

Simpson shook Powell's hand vigorously and smiled. "Thanks, Powell. It's always good to meet a fellow brother from the dark side. How did you know I was an infantryman?"

Powell smiled at the question and replied, "Yes, it is good to be us. As far as knowing your infantry background, I can usually tell when I see a *Vietnam Veterans of America* sticker on the front door and the CIB on a truck bumper in the driveway."

Simpson laughed. "So, what can I do for you? I'm guessing it could have something to do with my tenant?"

"That's a big 10-4. The man you know as Franklin is an ex-con who was recently released from the pen at Walla Walla. He killed the mother of our client and now he's a little too close to her for our comfort."

"Goddammit, I'm not surprised. The guy was very flakey when he applied for the place. There was something wrong about him I couldn't put my finger on. So, what can I do to help you?"

"This is off the record. I don't want any blowback for you. I need access to Franklin's apartment for about five minutes. If you have a key, place it on the table over there, and leave the room for a minute. I'll borrow the key and have my two associates do a quick look-see, while we visit about our tours."

"I have no problem with that, Powell. We'll keep it between ourselves," Simpson replied. He then took his keychain from his pocket, removed a key, and set it on the coffee table next to the couch. He then left the room.

Powell retrieved the key, went to the front door, opened it, and signaled to the waiting Kirkpatrick's.

The brothers quickly marched from the Raptor to where Powell waited on the front porch. Powell then flipped the key to Liam, went back into the house, and closed the door. The brothers proceeded to the entrance of Franklin's apartment, opened the door and entered, closing the door behind them.

Aiden then pressed his earpiece. "We're inside. Keep an eye out for us, Mac."

"Roger that," he heard Kierney reply. Kierney was their watchdog ensuring they wouldn't be surprised with a sudden arrival by Franklin.

They then conducted their search of the small apartment. There weren't many places to hide things. A Mac laptop, a few clothes hanging on hangers, a suitcase and a laundry bag were the only personal effects they could identify. On Liam's search of the bed, however, he found Franklin's hidey-hole where he discovered an envelope with $1800, which he left in-place.

Aiden spat out. "Let's roll. We're done here. I'll call Mac and tell him we're out."

He then heard Kierney in his ear bud. "We have a problem. Our boy is coming down the block. Exit the location. You have thirty seconds."

With the warning, the brothers checked the room and straightened anything out of place. Liam smoothed the bed and then stopped. He looked over at his brother and said, "Fuck it. Let's brace this bitch and see what he's made of. Powell said we had options."

Aiden nodded to his brother and asked, "Rock, paper, scissors?"

Liam grinned and they played, Aiden winning in the third round.

They then heard Franklin's car in the driveway.

Aiden stood shoulder-to-shoulder next to Liam as they listened to Franklin's steps approach the door. They heard the sound of a key being inserted into the lock. The handle turned and Franklin came through the door and then suddenly stopped when he saw the two black-hatted brothers. "What the fuck..."

"Welcome home, buddy. We've been waiting for you," Aiden quipped at the man, smiling broadly.

Franklin momentarily stood there, shocked. He then rushed towards Aiden and took a wild punch at his face. Aiden ducked under the punch and savagely elbowed the man in the jaw. Franklin rocked back from the blow. Aiden then stepped forward and, in a blur, side-kicked Franklin, crumpling him to the floor.

Liam walked over to Franklin and said, "You were warned about fucking around with our clients, specifically Miss Courtland. And you being in Portland visiting her brother is not to our liking. Well, we're here to give you a wake-up call."

Franklin shook his head, pushed himself up and stood. He looked at the older Kirkpatrick. "Go fuck yourself, you want some of me, come get it."

Liam smiled. "Sounds good to me, man. Let's see what you have."

Franklin shrugged his arms and sneered as he stepped forward in a boxer's stance, his fists clenched in front of him.

Liam just waited, bouncing up and down slightly on his toes. Franklin rushed him and threw a flurry of punches at his chest and stomach. Liam absorbed the blows and then slapped Franklin brutally across the face, breaking his nose. He then front-kicked Franklin in the chest knocking him flat on his ass.

"My, my, did you have a bad fall?" Aiden said as he reached down and grabbed Franklin's chin. Clenching it, he raised Franklin to a kneeling position. Franklin was pained, his eyes filling with tears, his breath coming in wheezes and bubbles through his broken and bleeding nose.

"I could break your neck right now, old man, and I will if you move. Just listen to what my brother has to say to you."

Liam leaned down, scowled, and said in a threatening tone, "This is your last warning, Franklin. We don't like you in Portland. Not at all. If we hear one report of you engaging or threatening Miss Courtland, her sister or brother in any way you'll find out how long you can hold your breath underwater. We like that stuff, so be wary. You don't want to see us again, do you, boy?"

Without waiting for a reply, Aiden shoved the man's head back, knocking him backwards onto his back.

The brothers exited the apartment leaving Franklin on the floor. They hurried up the steps to the main door of the house and knocked.

Powell opened the door and came out with Simpson. Aiden handed the apartment key to Powell, who in turn passed it to Simpson saying, "Mr. Simpson, thank you for your time today. We think all veterans are important and thank you for your service. Welcome back, brother."

Powell then shook the man's hand, and as he did Simpson said, "Master Sergeant, it was a real pleasure meeting you. I'm very honored. Thanks so much for your heroic service."

Powell nodded, turned, and walked down the stairs with the two Kirkpatrick's close behind, heading to the parked Raptor.

When they crawled into the big Ford, Aiden called Kierney, "We're clearing this twenty. Meeting you back at base."

"Roger, I'm out," Kierney radioed back.

Aiden turned to Powell. "We're good to go, Top."

Liam joined in, "We didn't find anything of value in the place. He had some cash and a computer and that was about it. But we bounced him around for good measure to make sure he was reading us clearly not to hassle Miss Courtland. What a pussy."

Powell just laughed.

As Liam wheeled the black Raptor away from the curb, Simpson waved at them from the front porch. Powell waved back over the top of the truck.

Powell also saw Franklin peek out from the door of his apartment. He was holding a towel over his nose, staring at them.

Powell turned away, leaned back and smiled. He wished he could have seen the man's face when the badgers had confronted him. "Good stuff," he thought.

Franklin closed the door to his apartment and limped to the small fridge. He opened the freezer door and removed four small ice cubes from the plastic bucket he kept there. He took the towel from his nose and wrapped the cubes in it as he walked into the small bedroom and sat slowly down on the bed. His grunted as he sat. His chest and hip ached from where the two assholes had kicked him. He then laid back and placed the towel and ice onto his throbbing nose. He winced at the rough, square edges of the ice as he positioned them on either side of the break. He felt out of it, dazed.

He knew he could blame Simpson for probably helping those two assholes get into his place, but he couldn't prove it. Worse, the old bastard had a hard on for him already and the man's dog wouldn't tolerate him confronting Simpson.

He could blame Graham, his bitch, and those fuckers from that investigation firm. She hated him and he would bet she put Graham up to it. Probably gave him the big old sob story about what a mean, bad man he was. He thought again of the two hard-asses who smacked him around and the way they grinned at him before leaving. They were smirking as if they were sharing a private joke. And they were. He was the fucking, dumbass joke.

No, the blame was on him for thinking he could act indiscriminately. He pounded the bed with his fists. Everyone was against him. There were no good choices left, but he'd be damned if he would sit and let everything he'd planned slip through his fingers. Not again.

He was lucky in one regard - the videotape was stashed in the car, hidden behind the spare tire. He'd at least been smart enough to do that right.

He closed his eyes and imagined how it would be with real money in his pocket. Then and only then would he be able to leave this shit hole and everyone else behind. He'd start a new life and find a woman or women. It was always a problem for him in the past to decide if he wanted one or many. Even with Alice it had been hard for him not to fuck around. Alice, sweet Alice. His thoughts drifted to sex and then gradually faded as he fell into a deep sleep.

Hours later he woke slowly and stretched. The towel on his nose was wet but no longer cold. He lifted the towel gently from his face and grimaced from the pain. The apartment was dark, as night had already come. He lay there until he thought of his stash.

Franklin sat up slowly and then reached over and turned on the light that sat on the desk beside his Mac. He then dropped to his knees next the bed and slid his hand between the mattress and box spring until he found the cut he had made. He slipped his hand inside and found the envelope. He pulled back his hand and quickly counted his cash. It was all there.

He rose from his knees, sat on the bed and fumed. He held his head in his hands and rocked back and forth, attempting to quiet the demons in his head. Right then and there he decided he wouldn't wait any longer; she had to pay now, not later. He began packing.

Chapter 25 • Options

Grant flipped on the light as he went into his garage. It was one of the places where he did his best thinking. It relaxed him to putter with the boat and his fishing gear. He enjoyed fishing, but he loved money. He'd never had time for marriage. He'd tried it early and hated the expense and responsibility of a full-time woman. When he needed to get laid, the friendly ladies at his favorite escort services were always willing and able. No, a wife wasn't what he'd ever needed or wanted.

After mulling over Graham's demands for days along with how he could make things right again, he finally came to a solution and it had been right before him the whole time. It would be a gamble, but he knew this was no time for him to sit on the sidelines and let the dice fall where they may. Taking risks hadn't stopped him in the past. He'd never hesitated to use dirty tactics to gain and keep new business for the company, and without his creative intervention FMG would never have grown to be as large as they were. It usually didn't take more than a simple blackmail here and there: a photo of a perspective competitor caught in an awkward, but telling situation usually did the trick. Foster was all for it when he was alive, but McWillis feared one day they would step over the line and be exposed. Now that it had happened, McWillis told him he was done with any further foul play.

Grant considered his options. For one thing, regardless of McWillis, he wasn't going to lie back and let their forty-year history end abruptly for health reasons, while passing the last of their hard-earned dollars and client base to those bitches at Synergy. "Not while there are still alternatives," he said sternly to himself.

Graham and Powell had been very clever. There was no evidence of their involvement in coercing Kitters or blackmailing FMG. They'd scrubbed the interview so it appeared Kitters was giving a spontaneous confession and accusation of Grant. There was also no record of Graham's demands made to McWillis and him.

The video was the real problem, but only as long as Kitters admitted it was true. Susan Arcadia couldn't identify Kitters and didn't know that he was behind the caper. Only Graham and Powell knew, but they could never admit it for fear of being charged for withholding evidence, let alone conspiracy and blackmail. The ten grand he'd paid Kitters could never be traced back to him. In the end, any court would be challenged to decide if Kitters' confession was nothing more than an elaborate hoax Kitters concocted to extort money from him and FMG. All Kitters needed to admit was that he read about the break-in and decided to take advantage of the situation, but didn't. Without Kitters' confession as fact, the video would have no value and Graham would have no future leverage without exposing his own misdeeds. The advertising clients passed to Synergy would be the last. Synergy could keep them, and that might satisfy Graham, pondered Grant.

He'd make his next move after waiting a few months, long enough to let the dust settle. He'd then announce that due to the miracles of modern medicine their health problems were cured and they would remain in business for the good of their clients and employees. His plan was not without risks. Kitters would have to be convinced if push came to shove and the video surfaced, he would have to admit to at least making the tape, but nothing more. He and McWillis would back him by saying they'd never seen the video and had never been blackmailed by Kitters. Graham and Powell would be helpless to object. They couldn't even use the connection between the stolen MacBook's and Kitters because it encumbered them with knowledge that could be considered withholding evidence.

He took a deep breath. The last thing he needed was another careless mistake. His strategy depended on Kitters buying into the plan and standing firm on the story. He would have to offer Kitters a big bonus, but it would be worth it. He already knew where he'd have the conversation with him.

Carl loved fishing and the Columbia River was their favorite place for salmon. They'd started fishing together soon after Kitters married his sister. It was the only thing they had in common, but it worked for them.

Over the years they'd fished many different locations on the river in Grant's Alumaweld Stryker. He'd learned to respect Kitters' fishing skills and grew to trust him handling the boat unless he'd been drinking too much. Kitters was more than happy to drink on the boat when he fished, and it wasn't unusual for him to be drunk by the end of the day. Grant had driven him home enough times to know.

Grant pulled his phone from his pocket and called his sister on her landline.

"Good morning, Julia."

"Hi, Bill. How are you?" his sister answered cordially.

"I'm good. How are those little monkeys of yours, sis?"

"They're good. What's going on? It's not like you to be calling to catch up."

That comment was more the sister he knew. "Well, thanks. I'll cut to the chase, girl. Is Carl at home?"

"Yeah, he's home nursing his broken arm since his flight down the steps. He's not working. He's been watching TV and complaining. Thank God we have insurance and that bonus from work. Not that you would understand how people on a paycheck make ends meet."

"Thanks, I appreciate that. Anyway, I can help. I was thinking Carl might enjoy getting out of the house and doing some fishing. He can still fish, can't he?"

"It would probably do him some good. Here he is. You can ask him yourself."

There was a long pause before Kitters said, "Good to hear from you. The motherfuckers broke my arm after they forced me to tell them about your scheme. Why didn't you tell me those kind of people were involved?"

Kitters was whining and he hated it. He'd spent ten thousand dollars to have a royal fuck-up, and now he had to sound patient and understanding. "How in the hell did I know? They came to my office after they saw you and played your video confession. It cost me more than you can imagine, so we both fucked up. At least we're not in jail, thanks to me. I got us both off the hook and you have ten grand to show for your troubles.

That's not why I'm calling. Can you fish? I need to get on the river and clear my head. Salmon are running and Bonneville Dam has big Chinook counts. You want to go?"

"Fuck, you think I wouldn't? If it weren't for my insurance coverage and the dough you paid me, I'd be fucked. But thank God, your sister is at least happy. She was killing me."

"Okay, good to know. We both suffered. So, what do think of this Saturday? The weather looks perfect. We can launch at Caterpillar Island and troll down river from there and then back up to Frenchmen's Bar."

"That's a good strip of water. Fishing the edge of those pilings where they jut out along the shore has always been good. I can do that. I need to get out of the house and we can talk."

"Yes, we can. Be over here by 5:00 a.m. and help me hook up the boat. I'll see you then."

He'd made his cast and thrown his lure. His fish was rising.

Chapter 26 • Windfalls

Stephanie watched Susan slowly recover from her injuries, although she seemed to heal more quickly physically than mentally. She'd visited her every day in the hospital and later at her home. Susan's stitches were now out, leaving two small, pink scars above her left eye. Her ribs were better, and her new dental prosthesis now filled the gap where her two front teeth had been. Susan said she hated it because it made her lisp, but it was all she could do until her gums healed completely and she was able to get implants. Regardless of the lisp, Susan was very upbeat and excited when she returned to work.

During Susan's absence Stephanie had been more than busy managing the agency, in addition to overseeing the new media business from Foster, McWillis and Grant. It'd shocked and surprised her when Fred McWillis called their office to ask if he could come by for a meeting with her. His announcement of FMGs forthcoming retirement and selection of Synergy to represent some of their largest clients was still astonishing to her. When Susan heard, she couldn't believe it. It meant an increase of almost two million dollars to the agency's revenue. The new business leapfrogged Synergy into the headlines when FMG's announcement appeared on their agency website and in both the Willamette Week and the Oregonian newspaper the next week.

When she told Marcus of the surprise windfall, he insisted on tightening security for them at the office. Avalanche installed cameras, alarms, and new locks. It was the first time she met Hank Powell. He was accompanied by Liam and Aiden Kirkpatrick, who after being introduced by him, began measuring the office and discussing "fields of vision." She was quickly impressed by the giant man and how kind he was to her. He also went out of his way to make Susan and the media girls feel comfortable with what they were doing. Powell stayed for the entire six-hour installation process, and when it was completed he patiently explained and demonstrated how it all worked.

Avalanche. She recalled how Marcus explained to her his involvement with the company. It was right after she heard the detective mention it the night of the break-in. It scared her at first, sounding so militaristic and ominous. She'd never considered there were people and companies who did the things Avalanche did. Now, she was comforted by the knowledge of Hank Powell and his team being part of Marcus' life and indirectly, hers.

It was almost September and the pace had seemed non-stop since Susan's return. The former clients of FMG were extremely pleased with their new campaigns, along with the smarter and more cost-efficient use of their media dollars. But that wasn't all. They'd taken on three additional clients since FMG's retirement announcement. Synergy was definitely on a roll and it wasn't going unnoticed in the press. Willamette Week had just featured them as "Portland's Hottest New Ad Agency."

The staff had grown to accommodate the new business and now occupied another large office upstairs. That's where the media girls - all four of them now - cranked out the budgets, trends, algorithms, and things she really wasn't interested in knowing. Susan loved them and called the girls her "ATM Department - All the Money."

She was busy with the Harborside restaurant chain and the Cascade Wine Growers Association, both new clients, in addition to the Mt. Hood Villa campaign and the elaborate themes and renderings required for the Gorge Project. To assist her with the increased workload, Susan had hired her an assistant: Jill Barton was a USC grad and came with a stunning portfolio from two years at McGowan and Associates of San Francisco. She was grateful for Jill; otherwise she'd only see Marcus when they were working. She smiled at her white lie. She saw him every night.

"My goodness, Steph, you look positively blissful," Susan said, walking into her office as she sat dreamily staring at her monitor.

She smiled at her boss and said, "I'm creating your next big success, and at times I have to take a deep breath and let myself drift."

"I think the only thing you're drifting on is that Graham boy, and I couldn't be happier for us."

"Us? So, this is part of your grand plan?"

"My sweet girl, everything is part of my plan. Well, almost everything." Susan laughed at her own remark and continued, "What I meant is that you're so much happier and it shows in everything you do. You've never been better."

"Thanks, Boss. Good to know." She too, could play that game.

"Thought you'd appreciate it, Steph. Why don't you get out of here? It's 4:30 and it has been a long week. Go see your man."

She grinned, unable to help herself. "You could be right. I'm ready. I'll see you Monday. Any plans for the weekend?" she asked.

"Not really. Roger and I will probably go to the coast. We're considering getting a place at Rockaway beach. It will give the kids a reason to visit us. I hope, anyway."

"Me too, Susan," she said quietly as Susan turned and left her office.

She didn't wait. She shut down her MacBook and zipped it up in her computer case. She shrugged into her new black leather coat, its suppleness and silk lining caressing her. She reached into the pockets and pulled out her black calfskin gloves. Both the coat and gloves were gifts from Marcus. She picked up her purse and computer bag and strolled out of the building.

It would be good to be home early, she mused, thinking of Marcus and his newest houseguest, Skinnykitty. It made her smile; he'd been so understanding and gracious and at the same time worried about the clawing and most of all, the cat box. In the end, he didn't have much of a choice. All she had to do was patiently explain to him Skinnykitty was part of her and her family.

She breezed through traffic heading for the Tower, though she was careful not to speed. She didn't want to lose her guardians. She then stole a look at the woman in the rearview mirror. Part of her still doubted her life could be this good, this easy and complete. That's why she'd kept her apartment, although she was now living with Marcus.

She felt safer because of him, but there was much more to it than that. Their lovemaking was over the top. She shivered and smiled at the same time thinking of him and how he made her feel lately; her life was a fairy tale with all of the charity events and dinners Marcus and she had attended. They'd even been in the Oregonian, photographed at the Mayor's Ball. Diana thought it was wonderful, but she didn't yet feel comfortable being in the public eye. She still hated publicity remembering the ordeal with Ray. "Stop it," she said to herself. "You're safe and at home. Marcus is here."

She wheeled into the underground parking and found the spot with her name on it; right next to Marcus' parked Mercedes.

She rode the elevator up to 22 and stepped across to the door. She inserted her key card and entered to see Gretchen talking into her headset. Gretchen nodded and waved. She hurried down the green-carpeted hallway, glancing at the working shapes of Cothren and Turner behind their glass walls.

Stephanie reached the doors of her new home, placed the keycard in the entry portal and opened the door to find Skinnykitty waiting for her.

She bent down, stroked the cat and said, "Missed me, boy? I know it's new, but it's nice, isn't it? Look at all of the room you have to roam. And I know Valeria has been giving you treats. Look at your fat tummy."

She heard footsteps and glanced up. She couldn't help but smile at the approaching figure.

"Hi, gorgeous. You're home early. What a nice surprise," he said with a warm smile. He approached her and kissed her on the lips before she could think again.

She kissed him back and said, "It's good to be home. What's that delicious aroma? Is it Valeria in the kitchen or you?" She batted her eyelashes at him because he loved dramatic expressions from her.

"You're so perfect. See what you've become? You're now the ruler of your domain. How easily you ask is it Valeria or me?" he said, a slight laugh escaping.

He helped her off with her coat and hung it on the hooks near the doors. "How about a cocktail and we can see what's cooking?" he asked.

She knew his routine and it didn't vary much, unless he'd decided to surprise her, which he enjoyed doing.

"I'd love one. It's been a long, busy week. I'm glad it's Friday. How was your day?"

"It was great. We closed on some new property that I've had my eye on. The one I told you about in Vancouver. Come on, we can talk after I pour us a drink."

He held her hand and guided her towards the kitchen where she saw Valeria busy washing spinach. The woman glanced up from the greens she was cutting and smiled at them, her cheeks rosy, her dark eyes squinting in joy. She was heavyset, in her late fifties, and was dressed in a black skirt with a white apron and a starched white blouse.

In a clipped, eastern European accent she said, "Marcus, Miss Stephanie. Very nice to see you. I have something special for you both. It's a favorite of Marcus': smoked trout pasta with truffles, served with a salad of delicate, baby spinach. So beautiful. I would recommend the Chardonnay. It will be perfect. So good. Please enjoy while I finish."

"Valeria, that sounds ideal. How are you today?" she asked.

The woman smiled at her and said, "Da, Miss Stephanie, I'm so good. It's Friday for me as well and I have grandchildren this weekend. I will have everything warming for you. You may serve when you wish to eat. So easy. Da?"

"Yes, it will be easy Valeria. Thank you so much."

She peeked over at Marcus who had been watching the exchange between them. He was always observing her and in a strange way it pleased her.

"Valeria, please go and enjoy your grandchildren. Stephanie and I have this handled."

"Da, Marcus. Bless you both." Valeria then removed her apron, put it over her arm and quietly left the kitchen.

Marcus smiled at her and said, "Finally. Just us two."

The cat suddenly skittered into the room, meowed and rubbed against Marcus' legs.

She laughed and said, "No, it's just the three of us."

He glanced down at the cat and said soberly, "Of all things, I never imagined I would ever have a cat here. But to be honest, I don't think we ever have to worry about mice."

She laughed at his remark and then kissed him on the cheek. For the first time in her life she had a connection with a man she didn't want to run away from or keep at arm's length. He made her vulnerable in a way she'd never experienced, but at the same time she felt stronger about herself.

The dinner didn't delay him long from asking, "Come with me?" His eyes locked into hers. She knew it really wasn't a question. She followed him. She wanted to. She held her hand out to him. He entwined his fingers in hers and led her towards the bedroom.

When they reached the closet, he playfully pulled her towards him, pressing himself into her. He kissed her ear and nuzzled into her neck, the smell of her was primal. All he could think of was getting her naked, vulnerable to him. "You look like you may need some help. Turn around."

She did as she was told; this was no time to argue. She wanted his hands and mouth to touch her, taste her, and tantalize her.

He unzipped her dress, slipping it off of her shoulders. She shrugged out of the garment wordlessly, luxuriating in his touch and attention. His fingers glided feather-soft over her bare breasts and then to her waist. He slipped his hands deftly into the sides of her lavender thong panties and slid them down to her ankles. She shivered as she stepped away from the lace and dress surrounding her feet. He heart was beating out of her chest. His touch was hot on her skin; she wanted to give him everything.

Marcus stood and leaned into her, inhaling her essence. "Steph, you're like Christmas. You're a graceful red gift sitting underneath my tree. Your ribbons are black satin. Every time I unwrap you, layer-by-layer, I'm excited and in awe of what I find. I'm humbled by your beauty. I'm so lucky. You're a very sexy woman."

She turned and snuggled into his chest, her breasts naked against him. She yearned for him, her hips moving involuntarily: rhythmic and seductive. "You're very nice to say that, Marcus, but it's the way you make me feel. I'm starving for you." Stephanie reached up and entwined her arms around his neck, pulling him towards her. She closed her eyes and kissed him deeply, tempting him with her tongue. She wanted to taste him, to devour him, but most of all she wanted to surrender to him.

As their kiss ended, Marcus delayed her with a whisper. "Let me catch up." He quickly undressed as Stephanie waited impatiently for him on the edge of the bed. Her legs were slightly parted and she was flushed with anticipation.

Sitting next to her, his hands gently caressed her breasts and as he bent to kiss them, she moaned and pulled his lips harder against her nipples. She was ravenous. Her desire swept and engulfed them. It was like no other night in her life and it was the love she had waited for and wanted her whole life. Acceptance was her response to his every touch and want. She surrendered, hesitation lost to her.

Later, they were clinging to each other and breathing in that way lovers do when they have emotionally and physically spent themselves.

"Whatever the hell that was, it was damn amazing."

She rolled over, sniggered at him and said, "You got that right, LT."

"I know, right?" He laughed at his own remark and gazed at her beautiful, long-legged nakedness. "What a piece of ass."

"There you go again, but I believe your enthusiasm is justified in this particular circumstance," she replied smartly.

"I'm absolutely right. You're a very naughty girl," he said wickedly as he pulled her into him.

"I am. But only with you." It was true. Stephanie moaned, drew closer to him and kissed his neck knowing her need for him was as strong as his want for her. She trembled as his hand slid down her waist and caressed her. She arched her back and waited for something she had always wanted; a man she could trust and give herself to completely.

Beth silently questioned the decision. Tiffany was excited and wet for his touch.

Chapter 27 • The River

Hines smiled. "Nothing escapes me," he said to himself. Mac Kierney had done a very good job in the Kitters' home. He'd heard everything. The conversation between Grant and Kitters lit him up.

He didn't hesitate to tell Powell what he'd learned. "We have a situation, Top. Kitters and Grant are going fishing, and Grant has implied they're going to talk. I assume it's about their next move on Synergy. It's something that probably deserves our attention," he said, although as soon as he did, he wanted to pull it back.

Powell raised his left eyebrow, frowned and said, "Well, I appreciate your opinion, Mr. Hines. Your research is excellent, but your reccos aren't really necessary. Thanks though. When are they meeting?"

"Sorry, Top. It's Saturday. Kitters will meet Grant at his house to grab the boat. They're going out near Frenchmen's Bar. They're launching at Caterpillar Island. They talked about where they're going to fish. The recording is sitting in your email."

"Good deal. I'll put the badgers on this. I'll send them over to you for some gear after I brief them." Powell knew they grew up fishing in Oregon, had their own boat, and fished whenever they could.

He texted them to his office. He guessed they were probably in the gym, doing god-knows-what to each other.

Not forty-five seconds later, dressed in gym shorts and sweaty t-shirts, the two brothers pushed into his office. Both tried to fit in through the doorframe first. It didn't work. Aiden pushed against his brother and said, "What the fuck, Liam?"

"Relax, little brother. Give me space," he said, jostling his way into the room first.

Powell didn't wait for them to settle down and got right to the point. "It's good to see you, gentlemen. I've something you may enjoy."

The two smiled. Liam spoke first. "It's good to be up again, Top. What do you have? New security detail?"

"Not this time guys. How about fishing?"

The Kirkpatrick's looked at him quizzically.

Powell explained the backstory of Grant and Kitters, and about the details gleaned from the recording Hines had taken. After playing the tape, Powell outlined their mission. "As you've just heard, they're going fishing together tomorrow, leaving from Grant's. I don't want you to follow. I want you to take your boat to the same launch, tag their boat there and then fish and observe them. I want everything recorded. Cut them loose when they've left the water. Hines will give you the gear."

Liam replied quickly, "That sounds fun to me, Boss. We've fished that stretch of the Columbia many times. We even launch there at Caterpillar Island. I bet we've seen this guy's boat, especially if he fishes as much as he says in the recording."

"Yeah, it's our kind of job, Top. We know this place," Aiden said with a grin.

"Okay. I want that info back here ASAP, especially if you hear they're planning some shenanigans. Here's the info on Grant's boat and truck."

Liam nodded, taking the sheet. He said, "We've got this. Anything else?"

"Nope, that's it. Enjoy your fishing," Powell said, dismissing them.

The two turned and left Powell's office heading for Hines in the operations room.

It was still dark at 5:30 a.m. when the Kirkpatrick brothers arrived at the Caterpillar Island boat launch. Liam wheeled the Ford Excursion that towed their 22' Duckworth Pacific Navigator into the empty lot and parked. They took their time as they put on their coveralls, custom Swimsafe jackets, and prepared the boat for launch.

Liam nodded to Aiden when they saw the brown Chevy Tahoe driving into the lot. It towed a red-sided Alumaweld Stryker and the rig parked right next to them. Kitters was easy to ID. When he opened the Chevy's door and jumped out on their side, they could see the cast on his left arm. Powell's work.

Kitters nodded at them and said, "Nice boat. I think I've seen you guys out here before."

Liam answered, "Yeah. We like this spot and with the fish counts being good we might have some luck today. We're hoping anyway."

Grant came around to their side and said to the three, "It's going to be a great day for fishing. Not much company either, which is good."

Aiden piped in, "Yeah, we're ready to kill some big ones."

Aiden then pointed at the Stryker and went over by its stern. "Is this one of the jet boat models?" he asked.

Grant ambled over to him and said, "Yeah, it has a 175 Mercury SportJet. We can run in water as shallow as twelve inches. We side-drift the Lewis and Cowlitz with it and some spots on those rivers aren't very deep."

As Grant talked, Liam came up to the side of the Stryker and rested his elbows on the black-topped, rubberized gunnel between the two rod holders. He leaned in and pretended to listen.

Kitters was still admiring the Duckworth, looking into its plush interior as Liam placed the transceiver he had palmed in his hand underneath the gunnel's lip of the Stryker. Its adhesive bottom instantly attached itself to the aluminum hull.

Aiden watched Liam plant the device and then looked back at Grant, encouraging an end to the conversation with the man. "You've got a real nice set-up to be sure. I always wondered how shallow these boats could go. We're not that lucky, but we do enjoy our Duck. Thanks for the info. Let's go fishing! Sunrise is coming."

"I agree. See you out there. Good luck," Grant responded.

Kitters muttered, "Good luck," as he walked back to where Grant was standing.

Fifteen minutes later both boats had launched and slowly made their way down the narrow, shallow, kelp-infested channel that led to the main river.

While Liam drove, Aiden listened on his ear bud to Grant and Kitters, recording every word.

Both boats soon settled into fishing mode, back trolling one direction and trolling the next. There were only two other boats on the river, and there were another half-dozen, heavily clothed and booted fisherman casting and fishing from shore. Here, the Columbia River was about a half-mile wide and the current varied on the tides. On an outgoing tide as it was today, the current was pushing three knots, and there were plenty of rips and bubbling eddies where the lighter, green slack shore waters met the darker, gray-green black current of the main river. It was in this line of turbulence they trolled their boats. It was fifty-four degrees at 6:30 a.m. and the water temperature according to their boats' Lowrance system displayed a cool sixty-two. The wind was a steady six to eight knots and there were small rollers and whitecaps.

Conversation between Grant and Kitters was minimal. Both were concentrating on their rods and occasionally speculating on which lures would be best. The Kirkpatrick's were doing the same, while keeping a watchful eye on their targets.

"Fish on," Aiden announced calmly as he reached for his rod, the line screaming from the reel, the rod tip bent and jerking downwards at the dark green of the river. Liam took the trolling motor out of gear and watched his brother stand and begin to fight the fish.

"It's a good one!" Aiden exclaimed, the rod tip dancing from the powerful tugs of the fish.

"I think you're right. It figures you'd hook in on a work assignment," Liam replied.

After fifteen minutes and three major runs by the fish, Liam reached the net down into the river and scooped up the gleaming salmon. It flopped on the deck entangled in the knotted squares of the net, its gills blood red and gasping. Its bright silver color and clipped adipose fin marked it was a keeper.

Liam high-fived his brother. "Right on, Aiden! It's a good twenty-five pounder."

"Good fish. Nice color," they heard yelled at them from off the bow. They both turned and saw it was Grant and Kitters. Grant was sitting on the motor box of the Stryker and steering the small trolling motor with his left hand. Kitters sat on the opposite side facing the back of the boat. They were coming up right next to them continuing to troll.

Kitters turned towards them and held up a beer, toasting them. "What were you using?"

"Super Bait with some tuna on the inside. He hit it hard," Aiden shouted back to the two.

Kitters nodded and gave him another toast. As Grant's boat continued downriver past them, Aiden heard Kitters say in his ear bud, "Lucky fuckin' bastard. He's using the same set-up we are."

"Relax, Carl. It's still early. We're not done yet," Grant said reassuringly.

Kitters spat at him, "You've said that before, Bill. Your plans and confidence got my arm broke. I don't need cheerleading; I need to hook into a fish like that prick did."

By 2:00 p.m. no additional fish had been caught and Aiden was listening to Grant explain to a somewhat drunken Kitters about their lack of luck. "The best laid plans sometimes rely upon luck for their success, Carl. Your little foray at Synergy was not supposed to involve beating the crap out of the owner, and the downside of that was pissing off some very heavy people who, as you know, didn't respond well. That was poor luck, largely because of your fuckup. We both paid a price. Me more than you," Grant lectured.

"Fuck you, Bill. You and your fucking agency and money can go straight to hell." Kitters sneered.

Hearing the change of tone in the conversation, Aiden pulled out his binoculars to see Kitters stand, stumble, and then regain his balance.

"Relax, Carl. Sit down before you fall down," Grant ordered. "I have a plan."

"I've had enough of your plans. Here's my plan," Kitters shouted as he punched Grant squarely in the face.

Grant reeled from the blow, his legs banging the side of the boat and flipping him backwards. As he fell, Grant's left knee hooked under the trolling motors' steering handle and it slowed him long enough to be able to reach out and grab the front of Kitters' jacket before the momentum pulled them both overboard. As they splashed into the water, their boat immediately turned to starboard, away from their fall.

"Liam! Kitters and Grant just went overboard. I'm cutting the lines. We gotta go!" Aiden yelled, reaching for the knife strapped to his side.

Liam raised the trolling motor, locked it and ran forward. He sat and fired up the Duckworth's motor. Aiden came up next to him, sat and said, "The lines are cut. Let's roll."

They raced to where the Stryker was circling and scanned the water for the two men. It had taken them almost forty-five seconds to arrive on scene.

"You see anything on that side?" Aiden asked.

"No. Let's track down river; they'll be moving in the outgoing rip. Did either of them have life jackets on?"

"Grant had a survival vest on. Kitters had nothing, the dumbass. Wait, wait - what's that? Off the bow."

They both saw an arm with a cast reach out of the water, fingers grasping at the surface before disappearing into the darkness.

Liam sped the Duckworth to the spot of Kitters' struggle. There was nothing but the rip and swirl of bubbles along the gray-black and green path of the eddy line.

Aiden spotted Grant first. "There! Over there next to the pilings - it's Grant!"

Grant was hugging onto one of the twenty broken-topped, moss-covered pilings extending from shore. He was visible from the waist up, the lower portion of his body hidden in the river.

Liam slapped the boat into gear and raced for the man.

As they approached the pilings Liam shouted at Aiden, "Throw him a line! We'll get pinned against the pilings by the current if I get any closer!"

Aiden went to the stern, pulled out the spare docking line, and threw the coiled rope towards Grant. "Hey, swim for the rope! We can't get any closer!" he shouted.

Grant nodded and pushed out from the piling, reaching for the orange-and-white-striped line floating in front of him. Just as he clutched it, the line went taut and he momentarily submerged. He quickly resurfaced coughing, but still holding the rope in both hands.

Aiden slowly reeled him in to the Duckworth. Grant was pale and panicky, his eyes wide with fear as Aiden pulled him to the side of the boat. He then reached down and grabbed Grant by his vest and in one fluid jerk brought him on board, landing him flat on his ass.

Grant was shaking and breathless. Snot and blood ran from his nose and there was a small piece of green moss hanging on his ear. He sat there shivering with his legs splayed before him, pale as a dead man, his lips purple with cold.

"Dude, you're lucky you had your vest on. Your buddy didn't make it though," Liam said flatly.

Grant replied weakly, managing to say through chattering teeth, "Tha - tha- thanks. Did you see what happened? The SOB swung on me and knocked me overboard."

"Yeah, I saw it. I first thought you had a fish on. What was the beef about? You guys have an argument or what?" Aiden asked, already knowing the answer and expecting a lie.

"He was drunk and got pissed at me when he thought I hooked into a fish. The dumbass. I told him to sit down, but he was out of control and punched me in the face. I tried to stop from falling overboard by grabbing his jacket, but we both went in."

"Well, he was the dumbass for not wearing a PFD," Liam responded harshly. "You don't last long in that water, not out here. The shock makes you immobile in a heartbeat. Add stress and the lack of proper training and you've got a drowning. Simple math. He didn't have chance, especially with that cast on."

Grant said nothing as he continued to shiver and shake, his eyes now closed.

"It's time to call the sheriff. Aiden, make the call and I'll go corral the Stryker. You can drive it back for our friend," Liam told his brother.

"Roger that, I'm on it."

After notifying the sheriff of the situation and their location, Aiden piloted Grant's boat to shore and retrieved their transceiver before docking. Two hours later, they had concluded their interview by the sheriff. Grant had been taken into custody, but they both knew no charges would be forthcoming. When they drove out, two boats from River Rescue were still out searching for Kitters' body.

When Powell heard the news from the younger Kirkpatrick, he was surprised but not relieved. He knew the LT would also be concerned. The drama of Foster, McWillis and Grant was not over, and if anything, it was now more complicated.

Chapter 28 • Unexpected

Stephanie strolled along Broadway; the dazzling window displays of Nordstrom tantalizing her every step. She loved the store and all it contained. She could browse the clothing, shoe and make-up departments for hours and never tire of it. It was one of her favorite things to do. It was also a beautiful fall Saturday morning and she was thinking that she had two or three hours before Marcus would be done for the day. She smiled to herself thinking of how she'd convinced him that she didn't need him to escort her to go shopping downtown at Nordstrom.

She was finally alone and free to do what she wanted without someone watching her every move. She felt somewhat apprehensive though, and she didn't know why.

She stopped and gazed at the beautiful winter coats and imagined which one would look best on her. She was so absorbed in her own thoughts that she didn't notice a man come up from behind her.

"It's been a long time, Stephanie," she heard in a voice she instantly recognized.

She turned and stepped into the past, her breath taken from her in a gasp.

Franklin was dressed in blue jeans and a black hoodie. He wore a baseball cap and his face was wrinkled with age, but she still recognized the devil who had haunted her childhood and created her nightmares. She couldn't speak as she stared at him, trying to breathe.

Franklin lowered his voice, the last thing he needed was her screaming and attracting a crowd. "I'm happy to see you recognize me. That's good. You were easy to find and even easier to follow. You should remember that. Now listen. I've waited twenty fucking years to tell you that you were wrong," he said quietly.

Stephanie couldn't talk. She couldn't even move. She was frozen, listening to him. At that exact moment, *Beth and Tiffany came forward and began their internal conversations.*

"I've got this, Tiffany."

"No, you don't Beth. This is my guy."

"Okay, okay. Let's see what he has to say to our Stephy."

"You think your mother was so sweet and so great, such a good mommy? I owned Alice. She was mine. Why would I want to kill her? It was an accident. She worked for me and made me a lot of money. And you know what? She loved it. Why do you think she ended up with me? And you, little missy, I saved you and your brother and sister. You had nothing when I let you all move in. But that's not why I'm here."

Franklin paused, letting what he said sink in.

Beth waited patiently, plotting.

Tiffany was inside out anxious and pushing. "I want to do very bad things to him, Beth. Don't make me wait too long; you know I won't like it."

"I'm sure you've enjoyed the pictures of your mother that I had sent to you. They're pretty sweet. And your brother is all grown up working at that golf course. Good for him."

Franklin then pulled a DVD from his jacket and passed it to her.

Tiffany giggled to Beth. "Here it comes. His big moment. I'm so excited. Just watch."

"I've brought a little present for you and I think you'll enjoy it," Franklin sneered malevolently. "Your mother loved posing and being the star. You'll see. I brought you the movie we'd been working on together. It was originally a VHS tape, but I thought you'd find it easier to watch as a DVD. I think your boyfriend and all his big job connections will love it, too. Oh, and one more thing. You look so much like your mother most people will have a hard time believing it's not you."

Tiffany, now fully forward, held the DVD. It was cool in her hand. She raised her eyebrows as she read the plain cardboard cover. "XXX - Filthy Housewives" was scribbled across it, smudged and sloppy in handwritten black magic marker.

Tiffany lifted her attention from the box and smiled at him. "What do you really want, Ray? Me or money?" she asked in her most seductive Stephanie voice as she melodramatically batted her eyes and squirmed.

Franklin stared at her, stupefied by her question and mannerisms.

"What's wrong, Ray? Cat got your tongue?" she asked, rocking back and forth, smirking at him as she twirled her hair with her right hand.

Franklin gawked at her not believing what he'd heard or seen. It took him a moment to compose himself enough to reply gruffly, "I want money and I'm sure that's not a problem for you. I'm also going to be reasonable. Give me twenty grand and I'm out of your life forever. It's not a lot for you, but it can restart my life, which is the least you owe me. I also think the last thing your boyfriend needs is a scandal to ruin his big plans for the Gorge. I read all about it."

Beth returned in a heartbeat and silently planned it out for Tiffany, "Tell him, we've got to go to the bank and you'll meet him at Lloyd Center, in the underground parking garage for Macy's."

Tiffany sneaked a peek at her watch and then turned to Franklin. "Okay, Ray. I get it, but it will take me time to get the cash. I have to go to the bank. It's 10:30 now. How about I meet you at noon at the underground parking garage for Macy's at Lloyd Center?"

Franklin frowned at her. "That sounds real good if you think I'm an idiot. I'm sure that if I showed up there, I'd be greeted by the police. Restraining order violation and all that. I've got a better idea. Give me your cell number. I'll call you at twelve and meet you at the parking garage you described. From there, I'm going to give you directions as you drive along. Sort of a point-to-point thing. Oh, and I'll be watching you the whole way, so if you have those bad asses from Avalanche or the police tagging along, you'll never hear from me again, but your boyfriend and all of your clients will get copies of the video and I'll post it on the Internet."

Tiffany coolly replied, no longer needing, or waiting for Beth. "Ok, Ray. I'll be at the parking garage at noon. Just make sure you bring the original tape. I'm not paying for a copy. My phone number is 503-255-5120."

Franklin tapped the number into his cell phone and warned her.

"Don't forget what I said about bringing anybody with you. And if you think my phone can be traced back to me, think again. It's a burner from Walmart."

He turned and walked away.

Tiffany took another look at the DVD's title before slipping it into her purse.

"Get moving, Tiffany. We need to get prepared," Beth ordered.

"Roger, that," said Tiffany with a snigger.

"Very funny. I see that you've been listening to Marcus."

"I love what that man does to us. He makes me feel dreamy."

"Everything makes you feel dreamy, Tiff. Now, let's get moving," Beth implored.

"Ok. Ok. I know just what I need. Three stops should do it."

One hour and twenty-five minutes later, Tiffany sat and fidgeted in the underground parking at Lloyd Center. Waiting. A stop at Sportsman's Warehouse took her almost an hour to find everything she needed. She wasn't in a hurry; the store was huge and it had a broad selection of supplies and equipment. After careful consideration, she purchased a small backpack, a 5-inch wood handled knife and a 9.8 million-volt stun gun. The clerk who helped her with the stun gun had shown her various models and their effectiveness at incapacitating a human being. She thought it was most helpful and revealing. The stun gun she selected was no larger than a pack of cigarettes but it could effectively put someone on the ground in less than a half second. If it was applied for one to two seconds it resulted in a dazed mental condition for the person, and if used for three seconds it caused loss of muscle control, balance and extreme disorientation. Longer than five seconds and it could induce heart failure. It would be perfect for their intentions. Beth was enthusiastic about her selections.

Her phone rang at 12:05. It was him. "I'm here, Ray," Tiffany said calmly.

"Good. I see you," said Franklin.

She looked around when he said that, but she didn't see him and she didn't know what kind of car he was in.

"Do you have the money?" he asked gruffly.

"Yes, I have the money, Ray," she sing-songed to him, lying.

"Good. Now listen carefully. You're first going to drive to 31st and East Burnside. There's a music store there. Park in front of the store and wait for my call. I'll be right behind you the whole way and if I see you pick up your phone or begin talking through your Bluetooth connection, our trip will end. If I see anyone suspicious behind you, or trailing us, I'll disappear. Got it?"

"Yes, Ray. I do. I'm leaving now, I look forward to getting this done" Tiffany said sweetly. She had no intention of calling anyone for help. And she did want him done.

It took her almost twenty minutes to get to Music Millennium on Burnside. She parked as instructed and waited for his call.

It didn't take long. "I see you've made it. Good. Now you're going to 26th and East Belmont. Park near Hannigan's. It's a restaurant. You've got five minutes to get there, so you better hurry."

She did as instructed and again waited, rocking in her seat, anxious and hungry.

"Laurelhurst Park is where you're going next. It's ten minutes away from you. Park on Southeast 37th near the corner of Oak Street."

It didn't take her long to find the street location and park where he described. She checked the backpack to ensure everything was where it should be. She then rolled her hair into a tight ponytail and tucked it under the black baseball cap. It went nicely with the black sweatpants, red sweatshirt and black Nike's Beth had instructed Stephy, ever so subtly, to wear that morning.

"Always be prepared." Tiffany giggled.

"I can see that you're excited, but remember, we have to be careful. No mistakes and no getting carried away," Beth reminded her, ever so patiently, knowing that Tiffany could suddenly get very out of control. She'd seen it.

"I promise. I understand." Tiffany cooed, drooling at the prospect

of what was to come.

Her phone rang. It was him.

"I see that you're alone and have been. Good. Now, get out of the car with the money and walk straight ahead down Oak about 100 feet. Take the first trail to your right. After about 50 feet you'll see a small path off to the right that leads to clearing that has a bench at the water's edge. Wait for me there."

She grabbed the backpack and left the car. She advanced purposefully down the dirt trail through the trees. She felt lucky. She saw no one on her walk to the place he described: it was off the main trail, down a small, twisty path about twenty-five feet long. It was wooded and brush covered along the path until it reached a small open area that looked out upon the lake; it wasn't much larger than the wood bench that sat there.

Tiffany set the backpack on the bench and sat next to it. She quietly rocked back and forth and began reciting her favorite old nursery rhyme written in 1828 by Mary Howitt. "Will you walk into my parlor? Said the Spider to the Fly. 'Tis the prettiest little parlor that ever you did spy. The way into my parlor is up a winding stair, and I've a many curious things to show when you are there."

Her rhyming was interrupted when she heard his steps on the path coming towards her. She stood up to face him. She took a quick glance over her shoulder at the lake. There was no one within eyesight.

Franklin stepped into the clearing and stopped. His dark eyes squinted at her, appraising her, leering. "I thought about you on our little journey today. You look fabulous. Maybe I should've changed my demands to include fucking you first. You remember our times together, don't you girl?"

"Oh, Ray, don't be so silly. You're much too old for me, I'd kill you. I'd fuck you so hard you'd die," she said, smirking, conceit in her voice.

He glared at her. *But she could see the confusion in his eyes.*

"You said you had the money - show it to me!" he demanded, the worry evident.

Tiffany lifted the backpack by its plastic wrapped handle and stepped around the bench to face him. She placed the bag at her feet and crossed her arms. "First, I want to see the original video tape, Ray. Prove to me you have it." It was Beth, helping make the demand.

"I've got it, hold on," he said as he turned his head slightly to the back, reaching to his rear pocket to extract the video cassette.

She didn't wait. She pulled the cigarette-pack sized stun gun from her waistband and slammed it against his chest, just below his neck as she depressed the ON switch.

9.8 million volts coursed into Franklin. He collapsed to the ground making an "arghh" sound. He was shaking and shuddering uncontrollably.

She knew it wouldn't last, and she couldn't wait to hurt him so she leaned down and slammed the gun into his neck and held it for a count of four.

The effect was devastating and cruel. He was completely incapacitated, twitching, and foaming from the mouth. He had also wet himself.

"Poor baby," Tiffany chortled as she slid the stun gun into the backpack and withdrew the knife from her sock. She flipped the five-inch blade open. It gleamed wickedly in her hand. She knelt next to him and grabbed his chin roughly. She held the blade in front of his face so he could have a good look. She could tell he saw it; his eyes went as round as saucers with fear.

She bent down, kissed his cheek, and whispered in her most breathless, sexy, fuck-me-now voice, "Ray, this is for all of the terrible things you did to Alice, Stephy, Di, and Evan."

She grabbed his neck and pinned his head firmly against the dirt. With her other hand she carefully inserted the tip of the knife into the corner of his eye. She drooled just before burying the blade into his eye socket with all of Beth's strength.

It went all the way into the handle.

His whole body went rigid and twitched. His one eye was locked open, wildly staring at her. With a shudder, he gasped, gurgled, and died. His body collapsed like a leaky balloon, wheezing as it did.

Tiffany chortled and pulled the bloody blade of the wood handled knife from his eye. It made a sucking sound when it came out, dripping bloody, gelatinous eye and brain matter.

"Don't even think about it. We don't have time." Beth ordered.

"I know this is different. I won't do what I really, really want to do, but he deserves another good mark," Tiffany cruelly said as she inserted the knifepoint into the corner of his ruined eye and ripped it viciously down and across his face. His flesh opened like a ripe peach, garishly exposing his cheekbone, teeth and jawbone.

"Good girl. That's enough. Now get this cleaned up and let's go," Beth worried to her impatiently.

Tiffany wiped the ruin and gore from the knife on Franklin's chest, folded it, and slipped it back into her sock. She then carefully padded him down and removed his cell phone, wallet, and the videotape. She added them to the backpack. She hurriedly stepped to the water and rinsed her hands of him. She checked the lake again. Still no one.

Returning to the lifeless body of Franklin, she grabbed his wrists and drug him over and into the bushes at the edge of the clearing. She backed into the shrubbery and pulled him in behind her. After several steps she stopped and dropped his arms. She stepped around, over and past his body, pushing her way back out through the foliage into the clearing. When she turned and checked her work, Franklin's booted left foot was partially exposed.

"I'm going to leave the foot, Beth. I like the shot for the news. It's a nice touch."

"Ok, Tiff. You've got everything. Let's roll."

She picked up the backpack and left the clearing. Tiffany checked her watch. Start to finish it had only taken one minute and fifteen seconds. She hurried to her car.

On her way back to the Tower she stopped at a 7-11, parking in front of the dumpster on the side of the store. She went inside and bought a Big Gulp, plastic kitchen gloves, and two bags of chips. When she returned to the Lexus, she slipped on the plastic gloves and meticulously wiped down Franklin's cell phone and wallet, the videotape, and the plastic covered handle of the backpack. She knew Beth was a stickler for details so she worked carefully. She opened the bags of chips and dumped half of their contents in the empty backpack. She broke Franklin's flip phone in half and put it into one of the chip bags. Franklin's wallet went into the other. She closed and tightly rolled up both. "A thing for every place, a place for every thing," she mused. Tiffany checked right and left. No one. She slightly opened the door to the Lexus and stuck the videotape in the corner of the door jam and crushed it. She placed the broken videotape cassette box into the backpack after removing the two small white plastic rolls that the film was wound upon. She dropped the rolls of film into the large Big Gulp and closed its lid. She reached over and snatched the backpack and chip bags from the seat and took them to the dumpster, depositing them all under the black lid. The dumpster was almost full, so she spread the items out along the edges, disconnected from one another. She pulled the DVD from her pocket, broke it in half and added it and the Big Gulp to the dumpster. The plastic gloves were the last things she discarded.

As she drove away from the 7-11, she hid the stun gun deep under the front seat next to the metal rail where it wouldn't slide around. The knife was already tucked safely away in her purse. She'd hide it later at home.

"Great job, Tiff. Strong work, girlfriend. That devil bastard is finally where he belongs. No more bad dreams for our Stephy," Beth said happily.

Tiffany smiled, batted her eyes one last time and withdrew.
Then Beth, with a sigh, did as well.

Stephanie arrived at the Tower and parked her car next to Marcus' wondering how her shopping could have passed so quickly. She looked into the back seat and didn't see any of things she imagined purchasing. "Oh, well," she said to herself. "Anyway, it's more about the shopping than it is about the buying."

She walked away from the Lexus feeling strangely pleased about her day. She inadvertently twirled her hair and giggled.

Chapter 29 • Complications

Graham quietly slid out of bed. He didn't want to wake Stephanie. She loved her sleep and Sunday was her day to make the most of it. He studied her as he stood beside the bed. Her red hair was sprawled on the pillow and she had one foot sneaking out of the covers. Her arms wrapped the pillow, her shoulders relaxed. He smiled at her sleeping form; she was so slender, freckled, pale, and perfect. He'd never seen anything so beautiful, naked, and in his bed.

He pulled on his robe and silently stole from the bedroom heading down the hallway past the kitchen and the aroma of brewing coffee. The living room was quiet and still dark. He opened the front door and retrieved the newspaper before returning to the kitchen. He enjoyed the weekends when it was quiet and just the two of them at home.

When he reached the kitchen he poured himself a large cup of coffee and returned to the living room. He picked up the remote from the table and opened the blinds covering the windows. The morning light of Portland streamed into the room, flat and white.

He sat on the couch and unfolded the newspaper. It was one of the small pleasures he'd learned from his father. He enjoyed the texture of newsprint in his hands and he preferred the detailed news reporting the paper provided. The Sunday morning edition of the Oregonian in the Metro/Northwest section led with the headline: "Ad Exec Rescued in Boating Mishap."

Graham read the article with interest. When Powell called him the previous afternoon and told him how the Kirkpatrick brothers saved Bill Grant from drowning, he said it would probably make the papers. And it had.

His cell phone buzzed. It was Powell, ever diligent and up early.

"Marcus, did you see it? I told you it would make the news."

"I just read it. The boys looked good."

"Yes, they handled themselves well. No connections to us. But I'm sure you've been thinking about our new loose end. Grant could become a difficulty again. With Kitters dead, the videotape of his confession is all but worthless. Grant could say Kitters made the whole thing up to extort money from him."

"I know, I've been thinking about that, too. But I don't want to overreact or overcorrect the situation. I think we need to take a wait-and-see-approach."

"Yeah, we'll see how big his balls are now. There's a good chance the other guy, McWillis, could chill him out. Maybe the whole drowning thing will spook Grant back to his senses. It's also a family crisis for Grant. His sister probably will have a lot of questions about how her husband died."

"There's no doubt about that, but Kitters got what he deserved. His first big mistake was taking the job. His second was beating Susan."

"Roger that, LT. I've got something else. Hines picked up some info on Franklin early this morning from our contacts at Portland Police."

"What's he done now?" Graham asked.

"Nothing. He's dead. His body was discovered in Laurelhurst Park late yesterday afternoon. Foul play apparently. Stun gunned and stabbed. The Blues think it was probably gang work given the injuries and robbery, as there was no wallet or cell phone on him. It didn't take them long to identify Franklin. His car was parked a short distance away from where his body was found and his prints were in their database."

Graham paused and said, "Well, I'm sure Stephanie will be relieved. I know I am." And he was. It was somehow ironic that he felt the way he did: his biological father was dead and he didn't care. Not even a little bit.

"I think we all are. It's funny how things work out. You never know what he was up to. Probably a drug deal gone bad or similar. In any event, it's done. You okay?"

"Yeah, I am. I appreciate the update, Hank."

"No worries, LT. I'll be in touch."

He heard her bare feet walking towards him as he ended the call. He turned and smiled at her approaching form. Her hair was wild and red. She had on the beautiful, green silk robe he'd bought for her and it shimmered as she moved. She was carrying a steaming cup of coffee in one hand and her glasses in the other.

"Good morning, gorgeous. What are you doing up so early?" he asked.

"I don't know, I woke up and wondered where you were," she said, sitting next to him, setting the coffee cup on the oval table. She turned and kissed him on the cheek and whispered, "Morning, handsome."

"Thanks. It's good to be me," he beamed back at her.

"Listen to you. Are we feeling god-like today?"

"Always with you, little miss. And I've got some big news."

"Ok. Don't make me wait. What's happened?"

"Franklin's dead. His body was found last night. Robbed is what the police reported."

Stephanie was shocked by the revelation. "What? Ray's dead? I can't believe that. Are you sure?"

"Yes, I am. Hank just told me."

"Easy there, girlfriend. Let's keep this celebration under control. Happy is okay, delirious is not. He got what he deserved." Beth setting the tone.

"Oh, Marcus," she said as she leaned over and hugged him. A small tear trickled down her cheek. "I'm so happy. I hate to say that, but I am. I'm happy that he's dead. He deserved it after all of the things he did to my family."

He held her, knowing exactly how she felt. "I've got something else."

She pulled back from his embrace.

He then passed the newspaper to her and pointed to the article about Grant. "Check this out; it features a former competitor of yours."

When she saw the headline she quickly put on her glasses. For the next few minutes she read silently. He watched her re-read some parts and stop to study the picture taken at the boat launch at Caterpillar Island. The photo was of Grant's boat being pulled out of the water by a big Ford Excursion. A uniformed sheriff was standing next to the boat. A sheriff's patrol boat was visible in the small channel at the end of the boat ramp.

When Stephanie finished reading the story, she folded the newspaper on her lap and said to him, "Bill Grant has certainly had a rough go of it lately, hasn't he? First, they have the health issue and now this; his brother-in-law drowns after assaulting him. How weird and tragic."

Her take on the story was as he expected until he heard her say, "But isn't it interesting who saved Bill Grant? Why, it was those two handsome brothers who work at Avalanche. What a coincidence they would be there. And I find it particularly interesting Grant's misfortunes began after the break-in at our office. Oh, and let's not forget FMG rewards our agency with a small fortune in new business. And now Ray is dead, too."

She looked at him skeptically.

He shrugged his shoulders and said, "Why are you looking at me that way? You don't honestly think I had anything to do with Franklin's death, do you?"

"No, of course not. But the whole Grant thing seems awfully suspicious to me, mister. Have you been up to controlling things again? Are you, Hank, and those brutes at Avalanche involved in this?"

He smiled at her and touched her cheek gently. "I think you're a funny, sexy woman who enjoys making grand assumptions. That's what I think."

"Good answer, LT. That's what they all call you, isn't it? LT?" She asked, mimicking Gretchen and Hank.

He smirked and said, "You're very funny."

"That's me," she laughed before throwing her arms around his neck and kissing him. "I'm just so happy having Ray out of my life, Marcus. I'm sorry if I sounded suspicious."

"It's okay, darling. No big deal. Now let's get some breakfast going. Would you like me to make my favorite, Eggs Benedict?"

"Yes, I would, LT, but finish your paper first. I'll get things started."

Walking to the kitchen, she was almost afraid to believe what she now suspected to be true: Marcus was manipulating everything around her and in her life. She believed he wasn't involved in Franklin's death, but the so-called retirement of FMG he'd so casually brushed aside were definitely his doing. He'd somehow discovered Bill Grant was involved with the break-in and had made him pay for it. She was equally certain Hank Powell and his men were also involved, probably following the LT's orders.

"LT," she said to herself. It was now clear to her he was the ultimate controller. He'd used charm, money, and his powerful friends to ensure his goals. Even with her. She wondered what else she didn't know about the depth and resources of Marcus Graham. All the hmmm's.

She paused her thoughts as she poured herself a cup of coffee. As she inhaled the rich, warm aroma she heard *Tiffany* silently tell her that Marcus had never done anything to harm or diminish her in any way. Quite the opposite.

"You're right," she said to herself.

Stephanie then took another sip of coffee and suddenly laughed, choking and dribbling several drops from her lips. She couldn't help but be joyous. Ray was dead! She shivered at how wonderful it felt to have the nightmare of him gone from her life forever. It seemed too good to be true.

Chapter 30 • A Crime of Passion

Hines and McGee had been buried with cases and it had taken them several weeks to find something significant on the Fischer investigation and report to Powell. Powell had his own ideas, and had brought in his buddy, Dr. J, in for a listen. Dr. Jim Galloway was a clinical psychologist who had a successful private practice in Lakewood, Washington. He worked there every other week - he called them his "money" weeks. The "off" weeks he worked for the Veterans Administration at their numerous outreach clinics and hospitals in Washington State. He'd spent the past 15 years traveling from one VA location to another helping veterans. He had a full plate. America's involvement in Vietnam, Iraq, and Afghanistan provided him with more than enough patients that needed his counseling. He was dedicated to the work.

Galloway was forty-five, six-foot-tall, and a slender 165 pounds. He had a swarthy complexion, dark curly hair, and he was bearded. He had striking blue eyes and he squinted when he talked or laughed. He was as handsome as an actor and he used it to disarm both men and women. He considered it an edge - his advantage. Funny and engaging, Galloway had a natural, easy-going manner that suited his looks. People liked him.

Powell first met Galloway at the Seattle VA when Powell was being evaluated for PTSD. Over the course of their consults the two became friends. Powell liked Galloway's off beat sense of humor and his lack of psychological flim-flam. It went both ways. Galloway enjoyed Powell's no-nonsense manner and greatly admired his military accomplishments. He was also interested in what Powell did for a living and frequently queried Powell about his work.

Galloway was smart and experienced - he'd seen it all during his years of practice. At least he thought he had until Powell invited him to consult with Avalanche on "The Invisible Man" murders, when they were hunting for Frank Morton. Galloway provided key insight into Morton's motives and methods, which allowed them to unearth a new, previously undiscovered lead that eventually led to Morton's capture.

McGee began the briefing. "We searched through a number of unsolved murders in Washington, but only one fit the same profile as Jason Fischer. In September 2005, a man by the name of Ken Staubb was killed at Lakeland Marina on Lake Washington. His body was discovered on his parents' 54-foot motor yacht that was moored there. The police found no witnesses who could verify seeing him at the marina the previous two nights, but Staubb was well known to have a steady stream of women visitors, so I doubt it would have caught anyone's attention to begin with. When the police interviewed other boat owners at the marina, they provided descriptions of at least six different women who were seen there in the last few weeks before his death. The forensic team was buried in evidence. They collected hair samples, fibers and prints from over thirty different people on the boat, but all the prints proved negative. DNA testing back then was slow but even if it weren't, given the traffic, it would have been a crap shoot for them to pinpoint anyone from the hair samples. There was also no DNA evidence on the body, so that was a dead end. There wasn't much of an investigation from there. Staubb was no angel. He'd been accused of rape in 2003, but nothing came from it. In 2004, he was arrested for cocaine possession, but the charges were dropped due to a technicality. I suspect some very talented and expensive lawyers represented him because his family is wealthy. I assume that's probably what got him out of the rape charge as well."

Hines was up next. "Even though the autopsy by the medical examiner reported the cause of death as knife wounds, there were anomalies. We had to dig to get this, luckily, we have a great contact at the ME's office. The autopsy revealed that the body had been partially mutilated, specifically his genitals, and he'd suffered a blow to the head significant enough to incapacitate him. He bled to death from the emasculation. This was not given to the press, apparently the influence of his parents extended all the way to the Seattle PD."

McGee interjected. "It was your buddy, Givens, who passed these pics to us." McGee spread out three photos in front of Powell. "Note that in the shot of the galley there are no dirty glasses, even though there are two bottles of champagne, one empty, one half-full. Ditto for the shot in the bedroom. No glasses. Another interesting thing was that there were no prints taken from the nightstands in the master bedroom or from the dining table in the galley. They were wiped clean."

Both men looked at Powell and Galloway waiting for their input.

Powell and Dr. Galloway examined the photos. The two from the bedroom were gruesome. Staubb lay naked on his back in a giant stain of blood that had seeped into the bed covers under his buttocks and thighs. His legs were spread, as were his arms, crucifixion style. There was bloody gaping wound where his genitals had been removed. His head had a large gash above his right eye and it looked to Powell that there was no doubt the man had been rendered unconscious from the blow.

After a few moments Dr. Galloway responded. "She was very careful. Quite fastidious. Meticulous. She's got style, and I admire that. I say she, because given the mutilation, I believe this was more than likely a crime of passion. She's an angry little thing. Again, I say the obvious. She needs to incapacitate them first, so it leads me to believe she's smaller or believes she lacks the strength to overpower them. She exhibits extremely impulsive behavior when she's stressed, probably physically. The genital mutilation indicates a desire and a need for like-revenge. She wants to return the favor: fuck me? - I'll fuck you up. We have a woman who reacts violently to men who, more than likely, treat her with great disregard. I say that because she's killed two men who have a track record of treating women badly, maybe even criminally. I think we also have a preliminary profile: she's white, thirty to thirty-five-years old, attractive, and she's mobile. You're possibly looking at a serial killer."

Dr. Galloway ended his overview. The three then looked at Powell waiting for his input.

"I agree with your assessment, Jim. Thank you." Powell set his hands on his knees, hesitated for a moment and then eyed McGee and Hines. "I think we need to expand our search. Let's look from '08 until present and see if we can find similar homicides. Concentrate on Oregon and California."

McGee and Hines nodded in compliance and left the office. When the door closed, Galloway said matter-of-factly to Powell, "I suspect she won't be easy to find. She's been very careful thus far, but there's one thing that's on your side - she's impulsive. It will be that spontaneity that will lead to her downfall."

Chapter 31 • Islands in the Stream

She was ecstatic. "Islands in the Stream" had just received a full approval by the Gorge Commission! Her concept would be coming to life in the summer of 2020. The call from Marcus lifted the entire agency into a euphoric state. Susan was literally dancing for joy. The project would propel Synergy to the next level along with all of their paychecks.

It was 4:00 p.m. when she put on her coat, picked up her purse and headed for the door. She quickly said goodnight to Jill, who was bent over her keyboard, typing furiously. Jill only waved and that was fine for her. She wanted nothing more than to see Marcus and hear all about the meeting he'd attended. When he'd called, he was in Troutdale, and that was forty-five minutes ago.

She peeked into Susan's office and said, "I'm on my way out boss lady. Congratulations on 'Islands.' Have a great weekend."

Susan smiled at her broadly and replied, "Stephanie, you have a wonderful one as well. Tell Marcus we're so proud of his vision and for including us."

"I will, Susan. See you Monday."

She breezed through the reception area after saying goodnight to Melody. Walking to her car she considered how her relationship with Susan had changed. She was now a partner in the agency and it had given her new confidence and made her less afraid of what was next for the agency and her role there.

It took her a scant twenty minutes to reach her parking space. Marcus had already arrived. She slid out of the Lexus, closed the door, and leaned over and touched the hood of the Mercedes. It was still warm, almost hot. It was a trick she'd learned from him and it told her he hadn't been home long.

When she slipped her card into the entry slot at GD, she opened the door to a celebration. Gretchen was pouring Paul Roget' champagne into glasses held by Marcus, Hank, Robert Cothren and Clay Turner.

"Stephanie, you're right on time." It was Hank Powell.

Powell walked over to her, bent down and gently kissed her cheek. She felt like a small girl when he did. "Marcus just scored the Gorge project, and I've heard you had everything to do with it. I'm so happy for you both!" Powell was exuberant. She'd never seen him smile so broadly.

"Thank you, Hank. I'm happy, too."

Marcus winked at her as he came towards her and then said to Powell, smiling at the big man, "Excuse me, Hank. I'm going to steal Stephanie away from your large presence."

Hank smiled back. "No problem, LT. It's my pleasure."

She waited for him. He came up to her and hugged her, his hands around her waist. He then kissed her full on the lips. She swooned at his public embrace.

She smiled at him, pulling slightly back. "Look at you, mister," she said, breathlessly.

"I am so happy for us, Stephanie. And it's your inspiration that has led the way. I am so proud and pleased with you." He was smiling - no, he was beaming at her.

Gretchen interrupted them when she handed her a glass of champagne and said in her most snarky, receptionist, guard-dog voice, "Look at you two in the office. If I didn't know better, I would say, 'Whoa, slow down kids, we're still in the room.' I mean, really!"

Both Graham and Stephanie laughed at the remark.

Powell had heard Gretchen. He strode over to her and said, "You're not trying to harsh the LT's mellow, are you, beautiful?"

Gretchen grinned at Powell and batted her eyelashes at him. "Why, what do you mean, big man?"

Powell bent down and whispered to her, "I mean, finish your champagne and let's blow this popsicle stand before you get into trouble."

The blush that grew on Gretchen's face was priceless to Powell. "I see I still have what it takes," he said with a broad smile.

Marcus then clapped his hands a few times and said, "I have an announcement."

He waited for a moment until he had their attention. "I want to thank everyone for contributing to our great victory today. I'm also happy to announce the staff of Graham Developments just received a healthy bonus for their work."

Graham studied each of the puzzled faces in the room before reaching into his breast pocket and extracting four white envelopes.

He passed one to Gretchen, Robert, Clay, and lastly, to Powell.

"It's a small token of my gratitude for each of you. Thanks so much."

Stephanie could tell by Gretchen's gasp it must have been something special in the envelope, because she immediately came over and kissed Marcus on the cheek. "Marcus, this is a beautiful gesture. I'm overwhelmed. Thank you so much." She kissed him again and returned to where Powell was standing and smiling.

Powell winked at Marcus and gave him a thumbs-up.

Clay and Robert both came up to Marcus and shook his hand vigorously. Each warmly thanked him.

A glass of champagne later, Marcus leaned in towards Stephanie and whispered in her ear, "You don't think I've forgotten you, do you?" Before she could answer he reached into his jacket and pulled out a circular black velvet box. "This is how I feel about you, Stephanie," he said softly as he passed it to her.

She hesitated before opening it and then gasped when she did; a diamond tennis bracelet lay coiled and twinkling against the black velvet of the box. Each diamond was huge and was set in white gold to further enhance its glittering presence. The total carat weight on the box read 8.4CTW. It was breathtaking.

"Oh, my god, Marcus. What have you done?"

She lifted the bracelet from its box and laid it across her left wrist.

"Let me help you with the clasp - it's tricky," he said. He held her wrist, turned it over and snapped the small clasp and its safety chain. "There you go. It's beautiful on you."

She extended her arm and squinted at the diamond's sparkling back to her. It was the most beautiful, most outrageous gift she'd ever received or hoped to. She turned and hugged Marcus. She then kissed him on the lips and said, "It's the most wonderful bracelet, Marcus. I'm speechless." She kissed him again.

Gretchen came over and softly touched her on the arm. "Show me your sparkles. I could see them shining from where I was standing."

Stephanie held out her arm and turned her wrist. "It's pretty spectacular, isn't it?"

"Stephanie, are you kidding? It's the most stunning tennis bracelet I've ever seen in person. It's gorgeous." Gretchen then looked over at Marcus and said, "You're the best guy, Marcus. We all love you."

Marcus thanked her and then proclaimed, "I think everyone is happy. I know I am."

The party continued for the next hour in the office and when Robert and Clay's wives arrived Marcus invited everyone back to their home at the end of the hallway. The evening turned into one of the most delightful nights of Stephanie's life, especially when they were finally alone.

After seeing the last of their guests out and locking up, he accompanied her to the bedroom. He had one more surprise for her. "I wanted to show you something, Steph."

Marcus stepped next to the bed, reached up and pushed against one of the painted stones that decorated the walls. The stone opened and behind it was a metal door with a combination dial on its front. He spun the dial several times and pulled the door open. "This is where I want you to keep your bracelet and jewelry when you're not wearing them. There's also some emergency cash I keep in here. It's my mad money."

She peered into the safe and saw ten or twelve bundles of $100 bills. Each bundle's wrap was labeled $10,000. "You want me to keep my bracelet in there?"

"Yes, love. The combo will be easy for you to remember. It's 8-22-8-22-0."

She said the numbers over again to herself. "I think I've got it, but I have to ask you, what's all the money for? What's mad money?"

He was quick to respond, "It's for whatever the need: last-minute vacation, investment opportunities, new car, whatever. It's not a big deal." It was to her. She'd never seen so much cash, or heard such an outrageous explanation for having it. It's so different with him, but she already knew that.

He then helped her remove the bracelet from her wrist. He placed it in the black box and carefully set in the safe. He closed the metal door and the hidden piece of the wall. He then smiled at her and said, "Let's get you out of those clothes. You know how I feel about you. Don't you, darling?"

She did, and it wasn't long before the night wrapped them both in its embrace.

Chapter 32 • Ramming Speed

Grant pushed into McWillis' office and passed the press release and letter to him. "Fred, I'd appreciate it if you'd read these and tell me what you think."

McWillis scanned the papers and then began reading them. When he finished, he took off his glasses and said, "So, this is your next big move? You want to declare our health issues are over and we have a renewed commitment to keep moving ahead for our clients? Oh, and we offer a flat fifteen-percent guarantee that our media department can beat anyone?"

"That's it in a nutshell."

McWillis put his glasses back on and shook his head softly. "You don't honestly expect me to believe that our *friends*, specifically Graham and Powell, are going to idly stand by and allow us to do this?"

"That's exactly what I expect they'll do. The Kitters confession is a dead issue. They got what they wanted from us and now they're fucking stuck. Conspiracy, withholding evidence, blackmail and God knows what else would be the charges against them. So, what good is their video? The answer is nothing. It's good for nothing, Fred. All we have to do is stand tall and look them in the eye. What's to lose?"

McWillis appeared exasperated and said, "Stand tall and look them in the eye? Are you out of your goddamn mind, Bill? This isn't the movies. Did you suddenly forget who these guys are and what they do for a living? Graham is a powerful man and with Powell and his Avalanche crew they become the type of people you don't want to screw with. They are obviously not afraid to act as vigilantes if the cause suits them."

"Fred, don't be such a pussy. Are you really ready to retire and walk away from what we built?"

"I think that's exactly what I'm going to do. You can buy me out for fifty cents on the dollar. I'll be tendering my resignation officially in the morning. I'm done. You can now stand tall and look them in the eye, Bill.

It'll just be without me."

McWillis stood and walked to where his jacket was hanging on the coat tree. He pulled his jacket on and left the room.

Grant was relieved by McWillis' decision. The idea of being exclusively in charge appealed to him. There would be no more whining to slow him down. He'd have to change the press release citing the new development, but that wasn't a problem. Taking risks hadn't stopped him in the past.

Grant considered his options. For one thing, he wasn't going to lie back and let their forty-year history end abruptly for health reasons, while passing the last of their hard-earned dollars and client base to those bitches at Synergy. "Not while there still alternatives," he said sternly to himself.

He went back to his office and settled behind his desk. He hadn't told McWillis about his entire plan and its two distinct stages. The press release was only an opening volley. The only way to eliminate Graham and Powell from the picture was with his intellect. He was done with using heavy-handed methods and it wouldn't work with those two anyway. He was lucky Kitters hadn't landed them both in prison or worse. No, it was time for him to be smarter than he'd been in the past.

He picked up his desk phone and called Susan Arcadia. He tapped his foot as he waited for the receptionist to connect him.

"Mr. Grant, it's nice to hear from you. How may I help you?"

"Susan thanks for taking my call. Please call me Bill. I've heard grand things about what you've been doing for our former clients. I'm very pleased we made the right choice with your agency."

"Thank you, Bill. That's very kind of you to say."

"Not a problem. The reason for my call is business. I know this is a little late in the day, but could you meet me for lunch? I have something you may be interested in."

"That's a little unexpected, but how can I refuse our biggest benefactor? I'm curious about what you have in mind."

"Great. Shall we say Jake's Restaurant in an hour?"

"Yes, that's fine. I'll leave in a few minutes and meet you there."

"Alright. See you there, Susan."

Grant drove to Jake's and dumped his car at valet parking. It was crowded as usual, but he slipped the hostess a twenty and was rewarded with a booth. He waited. He was chilled; the October east winds had started and it reminded him of how late in the year it was.

He was already on his second gin and tonic when Arcadia arrived. He rose from the table and shook her hand saying, "I appreciate you coming on such short notice, Susan."

"Well, I'm intrigued, Bill. I'm curious what you have in mind," Susan said as she sat down and waited for him to join her.

The waitress approached their table and asked if she could bring her a cocktail. Susan declined but asked for the menu.

After the waitress departed, Grant got right to the point. "I want to make you an offer, Susan. I want you and your staff to join FMG. You would have a full partnership with Portland's most prestigious and enduring agency. Your salary and partnership would be equal with your value and those of your clients. We're prepared to offer a twenty percent partnership, a $100,000 signing bonus and a salary of $175,000 annually to begin. All of your employees would be brought on with their same salaries, but with a ten percent bonus."

Susan sat back. She was startled and totally unprepared for what he'd told her. "Wow, that's quite an offer, Bill. I'm flattered. I thought you guys were retiring due to health problems and all that?"

"Fred McWillis is retiring. It was his health in question, not mine. At first, I didn't know if I wanted to continue without him, but since the boating accident, I feel renewed. Now I want to take the agency to the next level. I believe you and I would be better as a team, instead of being competitors. Why split our efforts over the same turf when we could have it all?"

Arcadia looked at him and smiled. "That's a very interesting idea, Bill, but I need to think about it. Can you send me a draft this afternoon outlining the specifics?"

"Absolutely, Susan. I appreciate your thoughtful consideration." He was pleased. A soft maybe was always better than a hard no.

The remainder of lunch passed with small talk between them about commercials they had seen and the new clients that were constantly popping up from the tech industry.

Now, Grant would have to wait.

Chapter 33 • Reflections

The first mirror Stephanie ever remembered looking into was the one at Ray's house. When she saw the girl looking back, she almost jumped. She approached the mirror again, and was surprised the girl in the mirror seemed so dissimilar. She didn't smile, or frown, or anything. She just stared back, expressionless.

"That was then," she thought. The mirror was huge now and the woman in it was stronger, less afraid and more importantly, open to the future. She left the executive washroom and click-clacked her way back to her office. Just as she sat down, Susan peeked her head in the door and then approached the front of her desk. "What's up, Susan? You have something you want to tell me?" she asked, knowing that she did.

Susan smiled and said, "Yes, I do. Guess who I met for lunch?"

"I'm guessing your husband? Come on, don't make me wait."

"It was Bill Grant, our former benefactor. He wants to put us out of business by offering me a partnership, big signing bonus and a huge salary. Everyone would come with me with a ten percent bonus and all is good, right? Oh, I forgot to mention, all of our clients would come with us in his 'offer.' We'd be one big, happy mega-agency."

"I'm not sure what you mean. He wants to put us out of business?"

"Steph, it's a scheme. I'd be gone within a year and you and everyone else would be as well. Our clients would remain, of course. Now, what do you think?"

"I think it's wrong. I've been suspicious of FMG ever since they passed all of their media business to us, but I didn't say anything. You've told me before not to look a gift horse in the mouth. So, I didn't."

"Well, we're looking this one right in the mouth, girl. Fuck Bill Grant and his offer."

She'd never heard Susan swear before other than to say hell or damn, which weren't really swear words. She couldn't help but laugh. "Gosh, Susan, don't hold back."

Susan frowned slightly and said, "Get back to work, partner. I have a call to make." With those words, Susan turned from Stephanie's desk and briskly walked out.

She considered what Susan told her about Grant and his offer. It was upsetting. For some reason the man seemed obsessed with hurting Susan and indirectly, everyone in the office.

"Don't you worry your pretty head about Bill Grant, Stephy. I have a feeling his days are numbered," Tiffany assured her.

Stephanie smiled to herself. *They* were always there when she needed *them* most.

She quickly decided she couldn't work or wait any longer. She needed to find out what Marcus would think of Grant's latest move.

After a quick goodbye to Susan, she drove to the Tower.

When she arrived home, Marcus was on the phone with Powell and Valeria was cooking in the kitchen. She chose to be with Valeria and the two talked for twenty minutes before Marcus joined them.

"Sorry, baby. I was on the phone with the man. Catching up."

"Uh-huh. I bet you were. Are you hungry? Valeria is preparing that pasta dish we both love. She went to the Vietnamese fish market and retrieved some smoked salmon. It's not trout, but it'll be wonderful just the same."

"Sounds delicious," he said. "I'll pour us some wine."

"You do that, I'm thirsty. So, what's Hank Powell up to? A new mystery to be solved?"

Graham went to the fridge and removed a chilled bottle of chardonnay. He opened it and poured two glasses. He saluted her with his and they both took a deep drink.

"That's tasty. This Stoller is so good. I love it," Stephanie said smiling.

Graham smiled back. "It is refreshing. Not quite Russian Standard vodka, but I like it."

She laughed at him. "You and your Russian Standard. Now tell me about the new case."

"It's an interesting one. Come on and I'll tell you all about it.'"

The fire was dancing in the fireplace and the early evening of Portland was beginning to sparkle and shine through the windows.

"Okay, what's up?" she asked as they settled into the couch.

"Hank's working on another mystery no one else has been able to solve. That's why this woman came to him, because of his reputation for solving those "Invisible Man" murders I told you about. This woman's brother was murdered in Maui, Hawaii in 2008. He'd just graduated from the University of Washington and was over there celebrating with some buddies and ended up dead one night. Murdered. Powell found a comparable murder that took place in 2005, in Seattle. Both had similar, though not exact, causes of death."

Stephanie involuntarily shivered, and goose bumps rose on her arms.

Marcus noticed immediately. "What the heck are you so excited about?"

She didn't know why she was reacting the way she was. She then heard *Beth silently say, "Settle down, Stephy. We're here. You're fine."*

She shook her head. "I'm okay. I just find talking about murders to be unsettling. But I'm interested in hearing more. Does he have any leads?" she asked.

"I think they're in the process of expanding their search for any other similar killings. They're sure about one thing: it's a woman they're after."

Stephanie heard *Tiffany suggest a change of subject to her. "I'm hungry. Let's go eat."*

She agreed. "Marcus, I hope Hank is successful, but I'm starving."

"Me too. Let's go see if dinner is done," Marcus replied, right on cue.

She relaxed. Her composure returned and she laughed at herself for being so giddy and introspective. "You're right, LT. Let's go."

Valeria's dinner was sumptuous and the wine brightened her spirits. Their conversations about work evolved into their shared visions for the

Gorge project. Marcus' enthusiasm was contagious and they both ended up making notes on their phones.

The remainder of the evening passed quickly for her and when Marcus suggested they retire, she didn't have to be asked twice. She wasn't tired, she was *hungree* for him. "Where the heck did that come from?" she wondered, but she knew it was *Tiffany*.

The next morning Marcus was standing beside her in the bathroom. They were each at their own sink in front of the giant bathroom mirror. He was shaving. She loved watching the faces he made in the mirror as he worked carefully with the razor. When he noticed her watching him, he paused, his face half-covered in shaving cream, the multi-bladed razor poised in his hand. His foam-covered reflection beamed at her in the mirror. "You are a beautiful, sexy woman. Last night was a downright mind-bender. Stephanie, you're so amazing. I think you may have exactly what I've been looking for in a sex slave. I mean, you've got the job, baby, if you want it!"

"Sex slave? I don't think so, LT. I see it the other way around. You can be my pool boy." She grinned at him with her hands on her hips, naked and pink as the day she was born. She then slowly wiggled her ass back and forth, her breasts shimmering with the movement. It was wrong of her, but she loved what it did to him.

"Stop that or we'll be going back to the bedroom. I'm warning you."

"I see who wins this contest. Sex slave, huh? Gotcha again, LT."

She was giggling and teasing at him as she twirled, spanked her bare bottom with a slap, and marched from the bathroom heading for her closet. She missed a step when she heard *Tiffany say lustily, "I love that man. He's so naughty. He makes me all gooey and creamy inside."*

Stephanie nodded her head without thinking. "Me, too," she said silently.

She loved talking with Marcus when she was naked. He was so happy and reasonable when she did. She smiled at her secret thought; she loved that about him. Skinnykitty then strolled into the closet and rubbed up against her leg, wrapping his tail around her ankle in the closet. She bent down, stroked the big cat and said, "That's how I managed to get you in the door, fluffy guy. I just asked him when I was naked. That poor man never had a chance."

She laughed again, more at her confidence than anything.

She then heard *Beth* and it startled her. *"Good girl, but let's still be careful. Tiffany is a little too excited for my way of thinking. We don't need any more outbursts from her."*

Stephanie shivered. "No, we don't," she said to herself.

Chapter 34 • San Francisco

Powell closed the door to his office, travel bag in hand. He looked to his right and saw McGee, dressed in a brown suit, white shirt and brown tie exiting the operations room. McGee carried an oversized valise, which Powell surmised contained his notes and laptop.

"Minimizing again, John?" Powell asked.

"Not at all, Hank. I've already placed my overnight bag in the truck," McGee said seriously. "I was just making sure that I had everything from Andy."

Powell nodded and headed across the gym to the Avalanche lobby door.

Kierney was sitting at the reception desk. Mac took his meet-and-greet duty seriously, and no one would ever dishonor him by calling him a "receptionist."

"Off to SF, Top? You're right on time. I see that it's on your schedule today," Kierney said, pointing to the printout on his desk.

"Roger that, Mac. Hold down the fort with Andy while I'm gone. I'll have the coat-and-tie with me," Powell said with a smile as McGee came through the lobby door from the gym.

Kierney smirked at the two men who were now standing side by side. "I'll be sure to keep on top of things, Top. John, have a pleasant trip. Good hunting."

Powell and McGee's flight from Portland to San Francisco took less than two hours. During the flight they reviewed the report Hines had assembled.

Powell found it interesting that mutilation killings were almost exclusively limited to female victims and were referred to as "honor" killings. Hines' notes came straight off the Internet. "Hidden among thousands of nondescript murders and cases labeled as domestic violence in the United States are a mounting number of killings motivated by a radical and dark interpretation of Islam. Honor killings and violence, which typically see men victimize wives and daughters because of behavior that has somehow insulted their faith, are among the most secretive crimes in society. These cases in the U.S. are often unreported because of the shame it can cause to the victim and the victim's family."

Hines' last note in the report was compelling. "The last reported mutilation killing of a man in Washington, Oregon, and California was in 2012. Marvin B. McMasters."

Powell and McGee arrived at 1:33 p.m. to meet Detective Jim Miller of SF Homicide. Miller had agreed to privately meet with them after Powell explained to Judith Fischer why they were going to San Francisco and the help they could use. Apparently, her contacts were as good as her money because three days later Powell received a call from Miller agreeing to meet with him and McGee.

They met Miller in the lobby of the Mosser Hotel in downtown San Francisco. Hines booked rooms at the Mosser because it was near the crime scene and Powell wanted to take a good look at the area. Hines suspected there was another reason, but he kept it to himself.

Miller was short, balding and wore a tired gray suit. Bushy, dark eyebrows framed his dark eyes. His droopy mustache was streaked with gray. Powell was reminded of Danny DeVito with an attitude. He carried a dark green folder.

Powell was surprised by Miller's voice when he'd heard the man call out to them, "Powell? McGee? Avalanche Investigations from Portland?" He was barrel-voiced. His greeting sounded like it came from a man twice as large.

"That's us," McGee replied as the man approached them.

They exchanged handshakes and Powell said, "I appreciate you agreeing to meet with us."

Miller shook his head. "This is not a social call, Powell. Everything we have I've hard-copied for you per my Captain and Mayor's instructions. There's also a couple of DVD's in here that contain our database searches of people who attended the conference. It wasn't my call on providing this info. I'm just the delivery boy. The two detectives who worked the case back in 2012 retired a few years ago, but their notes are all in here."

Miller passed the folder to Powell and left abruptly.

McGee and Powell exchanged glances with each other.

Powell then said, "That was nice and friendly."

"It's not hard to understand. They're protective about their work and think our inquiry is a bunch of bullshit. We're outsiders from Oregon."

"You're right, John. Not a big deal. Let's get to the room and see what he gave us. I'll take the hard copies first and you check their database reviews."

The files were very complete. It took them over two hours to finish their review.

Marvin B. McMasters was thirty-two, single, and was an advertising executive from Seattle. He died from bleeding to death after being emasculated. The autopsy also reported he had a near-lethal dose of oxycodone in him, enough to make him seriously intoxicated. The crime scene photos were gruesome. A large pool of blood was in the middle of the bed and from there it smeared and slid its way down the sheets to the floor and slowly spread across the room to the door where it stopped and pooled under the waist of the man. It was the man's face that disturbed Powell. He'd seen pain and anguish before, but this seemed far different: McMaster's eyes and mouth were wide open in a silent scream. He was frozen in agony from his torment, his arms extended towards the door, his hands reaching out in vain.

McGee broke Powell's focus on the grisly images. "There were over 2,500 people who attended the conference and there were also almost three hundred vendors. The police ran all the vendors and show officials through NCIC and got what you may expect from their search - nothing of value. There was no real search of the attendees, the information was just too limited and they were way too spread out geographically."

It was Powell's turn. "I didn't find much of interest here, either. There was no surveillance in the hotel. There were plenty from outside, but there so many people it was useless. The police CSI report stated the only physical evidence discovered at the scene were hairs: blonde and red - from two different people. The hair samples indicated he was either with two people different people in the room, or he'd picked them up randomly earlier that day. Can't tell. No prints either. Whoever killed McMasters was very careful. The only person who reported seeing him with a woman was a bartender at the hotel where he was staying and he couldn't remember if she was a blonde, a brunette or whatever. He only remembered her as being beautiful."

Powell was disappointed and McGee noticed. "Do you still want to walk over to the hotel where it happened?"

"I will, but I'll do it later. You take the files. I'll meet you downstairs for dinner at 1900 hours."

"Okay. I'll see you in the lobby at 7:00 p.m. sharp."

Powell didn't walk to the hotel. He went to an afternoon Giants baseball game at AT&T Park. He'd always wanted to see a big-league game and he wasn't disappointed. The park was beautiful and green sitting on the edge of the Bay. The Giants beat the Phillies 5-4, but Powell didn't really care; the hot dogs and beer were the best he ever had.

When Powell joined McGee for dinner he'd barely sat down when McGee said, "I did find something that could be helpful. When I reviewed the police database of conference vendors, I found a man listed as the official photographer for the trade show. I looked him up, but he's not in business anymore. I'm betting Hines can find him and when he does maybe we'll get lucky and snag a photo of McMaster's with someone. It's a long shot and not much of a lead, but you never know. That's all I found of any interest. How was your walk?"

"I didn't. I went to a Giants baseball game instead. They were playing the Dodgers. I always wanted to see a pro game and today I marked it off my bucket list. Best hot dogs I've ever had." Powell smirked at the memory before returning to business. "I don't think we learned much here, John. I'm not sure what I expected to find, but I'm batting a big zero right now. I do think there is a high probability that the murder of McMasters is connected to the Hawaii and Seattle killings. The similarities are there. I didn't see much of a work-up on McMasters though. We really don't know who he was. I think we should head back to Seattle and check out the people who worked with him. Maybe we'll get some insight."

"I don't think we have anything else," McGee replied, but he was thinking something else - luck has a way of turning things around.

Chapter 35 • Challenges

It took Grant more than a week to think of his next move after receiving the call from Susan Arcadia. She'd been polite but firm when she declined his offer. He was slightly surprised, but if he'd been in her position, he probably would have nixed the deal as well. If she'd accepted the offer, it would have been easy for him to phase her and her people out within a year.

"And I would have," he said to himself. "No doubt about it."

What he really wanted to do was finish what Kitters had inadvertently begun and kill Susan Arcadia. With Synergy Advertising leaderless, FMG would be the natural choice for their clients, including their new ones. He'd drag the staff from Synergy along to ensure there were no defections from their client base. Having the return of companies like Graham Developments would also ensure FMG's and his continued success. The only obstacles to the plan were Marcus Graham and Hank Powell. They wouldn't hesitate to come after him for harming Arcadia or any member of her staff. No, they were definitely not to be provoked in that manner.

He then heard his receptionist over the intercom. "Mr. Grant, you have Marcus Graham on line one. Shall I put him through?"

"I've got it. Thanks, Stella."

Grant sat there thinking about what he was going to say. It wouldn't be smart to antagonize Graham, but on the other hand he had to be firm in his resolve to move ahead.

He pushed the blinking button on his desk phone and answered, "Marcus, good afternoon. How can I help you?"

"Thanks for asking, Bill. I'm calling about your generous offer to Susan Arcadia at Synergy Advertising."

He's getting right to the point. "Yes, I thought it was a generous offer I made. I'm disappointed she didn't find it to be appealing enough."

"You're kidding me, aren't you, Bill? She would have lasted a year and then she'd be history. So would her staff. So, for a small upfront investment, you capitalize on retaining her new clients and regaining the ones you lost. I'm guessing you'd reap twenty million dollars a year, at the minimum."

Grant said nothing in response.

Graham continued. "We both know how this all started. You hired your brother-in-law, Kitters, to steal the computers and hard drives at Synergy and then he beat the crap out of Susan Arcadia. You were after their business records so you'd have the information you needed to steal their clients."

Grant interrupted. "That's not true, Marcus. I have no idea what you're talking about. Fred McWillis has health problems, and at first we were going to call it quits - that's why we passed so many of our clients to Synergy. But in the end, I received too many requests wanting FMG to continue. So, I am. I also want to make you an offer in good faith. I want to extend to you a fifteen percent incentive to give FMG another try at your media. I know you're happy with Synergy's creative approach, so keep it. I only want a shot at your media budget."

"That's interesting, Bill. But I'm sure you know I have a contract with Synergy and I'm quite satisfied."

"Contracts are made to be broken, Marcus. You know that."

Graham exploded at him. "You think it's that easy? Who the hell do you think you're talking to? Do you honestly think I'm going to do business with you after everything you've done, Grant?"

"Marcus, I don't understand why you're so angry. I'm a businessman. Susan Arcadia's misfortune had nothing to do with me. I'm sorry you think I was involved."

"Involved? It was your idea!"

"You think so? Was there anything else, Marcus? I hope you'll consider my offer."

The line went dead. Graham had hung up.

Grant sat back and relaxed. He believed it went fairly well with Graham. He smiled when he thought of how Graham was ready to explode when he played it dumb about Kitters. Graham and Powell may have the tape, but it was worthless and he just proved it to them.

When he ended the call, Graham looked over at Andy Hines and asked, "You get all that?"

Hines nodded and passed the small digital recorder to Graham. "Just push the play button. I've already sent a copy to McGee."

"Thanks, Andy. I appreciate your help."

Powell, always the gracious one, added, "Show yourself out, Mr. Hines. Thank you."

Graham then asked Powell, "What do you think? Do we have anything?"

Powell shook his head and said, "Not that I can tell. He's a ballsy motherfucker. I'll give him that. Smart, too. He didn't admit to anything, even when you asked him who the hell he was talking to? Good stuff."

Graham chuckled. "Yeah, I gave him my best tough-guy act and he didn't fold. I did have to watch my boundaries though. McGee warned me I couldn't refer to the tape. "Conspiracy" and 'withholding evidence' I believe are the terms he referenced."

"I believe they were. McGee was totally your idea, but Mr. Harvard Coat and Tie has proven to be a real asset for us, particularly on our private endeavors." Powell never minced words.

"Endeavors is it? I think of them more in terms of saving our police and government the hardships and expenses they would otherwise endure, if not for our careful and discreet interventions."

Powell smirked at Graham's remark. "Correct again, LT."

"I'm going to see what McGee makes of the conversation," Graham said as he left Powell's office and strode to the operations center that housed the tech and legal sides of Avalanche.

He peered through the wire mesh window and saw McGee and Hines at their workstations, the three monitors on sleep mode, framing them both with their random displays of colorful raindrops. Hines' work.

When he pushed through the door he heard the faint background sound of a train clickity-clacking down a track. He also heard his own voice from the recording with Grant.

McGee and Hines looked over to him.

McGee rose quickly, rounded the workstation and approached him. "Marcus, you're right on time." McGee had his suit jacket off, but his tie was firmly in place.

"John, what do you think? Is there anything there we can use?"

"Absolutely. On the surface, his offer to you sounds reasonable, but it is, in fact, a violation of contract law."

McGee waited for Graham to absorb the words.

"Okay, I like the sound of that. What are the details?" Graham asked.

"It's called Tortious interference with contract rights. It can occur where the tortfeasor - that's Grant - convinces a party - that's you - to breach the contract you have with Synergy Advertising in circumstances where Grant acts with knowledge of the existence of the contract. Then there's Tortious interference with a business relationship. This occurs when the tortfeasor acts to prevent one company from successfully establishing or maintaining a business relationship with another company."

McGee paused and then said, "That's it in a nutshell. We have two potential courses of action. Number one: Synergy files the complaint against Grant with our help and they easily win. Or, two: GD files suit and claims that Grant's offer was an attempt to prevent you from successfully continuing your relationship with Synergy for a variety of reasons we can delineate with a little help from Grant. In both cases, I believe we can put enough pressure and suspect circumstances upon him and his lawyers. They'll be hard pressed to resist us. In the end, settlement will be their only course of action."

Graham considered the detail of McGee's evaluation. "John, I believe you may be right. I'm going to cogitate on what you've told me."

"It's my pleasure. I'm glad I could be of service. I always enjoy in applying the law the way it should be practiced. I have your back, Marcus."

Graham nodded and turned, leaving the office. McGee's curious parting words pleased him. McGee's knowledge and input would discreetly help keep them within the boundaries of the law.

Chapter 36 • Justice Served

Grant heard a knock on his door. He wasn't expecting anyone so he cautiously peered out the peephole. He was surprised to see a tall, beautiful brunette and she apparently was dressed for the gym. She wore black, skintight yoga pants, and a red ribbed tank top that barely covered her exploding cleavage.

He smiled as he opened the door. "May I help you?" he asked.

She licked her lips and smiled back. "I'm Tiffany. The service said that you've been so good to us you deserve a little bonus on the house. Lucky man. I'm the bonus and you look like you need a good work-out."

"Well, Tiffany, it's nice to meet you. And yes, I do need some exercise this evening. Which agency did you say you're from? 'A Lass Insane' or 'Puss'N Boots'?"

"It's the former rather than the latter, handsome," she said in her best hooker voice, all creamy and dreamy pouts and posturing. It was well known Grant preferred his relationships with women to be of the pay-to-play kind.

"Okay, come on in. I'm alone and having a cocktail. You thirsty?" he asked as he closed the door behind her luscious backside.

"You betcha, I'm parched." She was pleased he didn't recognize her. The wig and dark make-up were obviously effective in deceiving him, but it was her nearly exposed breasts that were catching most of his attention, just as she'd planned.

"Follow me and we'll fix that thirst you have," he said, all creepy to her. She watched him walk ahead. He was dressed casually in khaki pants, a green sweater and brown moccasin-style slippers.

He led her through the entryway into the living room, which was furnished in dark leathers and woods. The floor was a paneled in strips of honey-colored oak. A small semi-circular metal-framed wooden bar sat opposite the furniture, against the wall. A large crystal ashtray with a smoldering cigar sat on top of bar's shiny black glass surface and three blue leather stools were positioned in front of it. She chose the middle one and sat.

Grant went around the bar and asked, "What can I get for you?"

"How about vodka, Bill? On the rocks."

"No problema. Grey Goose okay?"

"Sounds good," she relied, buttery smooth.

"I'll have one, too. It's my drink of choice," he said as he stared at her breasts lasciviously.

She felt repulsed, but she had plans - plans that wouldn't wait. She inadvertently drooled at the prospect.

"Slow down, girlfriend," Beth silently scolded her.

She brushed Beth's comment aside and patted the seat next to her. "When you have that poured, Bill, come over and sit your ass down next to me and we can talk about how I can make this the night of your life." She wasn't kidding.

"I'll be right there, uh, what's your name again?"

"Tiffany. It's Tiffany, Bill." She hated him even more for forgetting her name.

"Sorry, baby. I've been drinking a bit, as I said." Grant then passed her drink across the bar and joined her at the seat she'd indicated.

She kissed him on the cheek, leaving a big red set of her lips on him as she'd planned. She picked up her glass and took a big swallow, grimacing at the taste. She coughed and caught her breath. "I'm not quite used to that. It's pretty strong."

Grant guzzled his vodka before responding in a slur. "It's an acquired taste, like many of the finer things in life."

She gave him a loopy smile. "I'm sure you know all about those things, Bill. It reminds me, the service asked me to bring you a small token of their appreciation for all of your business over the years."

"Really? What do you have for me?'

Tiffany reached into the back of her yoga pants and extracted the black stun gun from her waistband. It was small and rectangular like a cell phone. She held it in the palm of her hand and said, "This is for you."

"What is it? A new type of vibrator?" he asked wickedly.

"Why yes, yes it is, Bill," she said calmly, as she slid the ON button forward, igniting a vicious blue-white electric spark that snapped and crackled between the two metal heads of the gun.

Grant seemed hypnotized by the dancing voltage right until the moment she jammed it against his chest. He fell immediately to the floor, shaking and thrumming from the gun's discharge.

Tiffany bent down and zapped him again for a count of four. "No fooling around this time," she said aloud.

The effect of the second dose of the gun was what she expected. He was nothing more than a quivering mass at her feet. She looked down on him and shoved the gun back into her waistband. She then withdrew the wood handled knife from her sock and opened its five-inch blade. It gleamed sharply at her.

"You said you'd be careful. They'll catch us if you aren't." It was Beth again, ever the worrier.

She screamed at Beth at the top of her lungs, "I have to do what I have to do! I can't just stop. He deserves it! And now he gets it."

Grant's eyes were twitching, wide open in fear, when she glowered at him with the knife in her hand. She bent down close enough to him to feel his breath on her cheek. Tiffany smiled at him and said softly. "I know what you're thinking, Bill. Is she going to rob me? Is she going to kill me? What's next, right?"

She paused, leaned down and kissed him gently on the cheek. "Bill, this is for Susan Arcadia and all of the shit you've done to women over the years. It's going to hurt, and I don't want this to be messy, so you get another big jolt first."

She laid the knife on the ground next to her and removed the stun gun from her waistband. She slid the switch to ON and slammed it against his neck. She counted to eight and by then he was totally unconscious and still. She checked his pulse but she couldn't detect a beat.

"Just right," she said with glee.

Tiffany reached down, pushed his chin up and viciously slashed his neck back and forth. The flesh split open, carved all the way down to where she could see bloody bone and tendons. The arteries didn't spurt and spray: his heart was stopped. "Dead men don't bleed. No muss, no fuss," she said, eyeing the zipper on his pants.

"No, no, no, Tiff. Not this time," Beth ordered. "It's too close to home. You know that."

Tiffany paused, thinking of what Beth had said. Beth was right and it tormented her. She then stood and angrily stomped from the room looking for the garage and the freezer she was sure he had. "Fishermen always do," she raged, walking towards the kitchen. She found the door to the garage there.

She was right about the freezer, and it was half-full with what she could only guess were large fish wrapped in tin foil. There were also several cardboard boxes labeled chicken, hamburger and venison. She quickly removed all of the items and placed them on the floor. She returned to the kitchen and checked under the sink where she found rubber gloves, Clorox spray, paper towels and plastic trash bags.

Tiffany took a big breath and calmed herself.

She put on the gloves and sprayed and washed the knife in the sink, placing it back in her sock. She then went to the living room and with Beth's strength dragged Grant's body to the garage, pleased that there was little blood left behind. She folded him into the freezer sideways; his back bent with his head on his knees. She neatly piled the frozen fish on top of Grant's body and finished off with the boxes. He was totally hidden.

In the kitchen, Tiffany grabbed the spray and paper towels and returned to the garage where she wiped down the freezer. She then went to the living room and cleaned the blood from the floor and the drops that led to the garage. She stuffed the bloody towels into a plastic bag. She removed the two glasses from the bar and walked to the kitchen. She sprayed the glasses with Clorox and carefully wiped them down before placing both in the dishwasher. She returned the Clorox spray to the cupboard after cleaning the door. Those towels went into the bag as well.

Satisfied that everything was meticulously clean, Tiffany turned off the kitchen lights and walked to the foyer, clutching the plastic bag in her gloved hands. She flipped off the living room lights and locked the front door behind her with a satisfied smile. She checked her watch: Stephanie would be home right on time from her workout. All she had left to do was dump the bag of towels, the gloves and the wig.

Beth said one word as she walked to the car. "Perfect."

Chapter 37 • Closing In

When Powell and McGee went to Seattle looking for background information on Marvin McMasters they went to his former employer, KAMI television, where they talked with Rob Charlton, the personnel director at the station. Charlton was a small man with short dark hair and a neatly trimmed full beard. He was dressed in dark gray suit pants, a black shirt and a gray tie. Powell guessed he was in his fifties.

When Powell asked him what he knew of McMasters, Charlton was immediately forthcoming. He had a clear memory of McMasters. They were friends. "First of all, no one called him by his first name, Marvin. He hated it and he always went by his middle name, Ben. He was a popular and successful guy. He'd been here six years when he died. Probably would have ended up as our sales manager. He had everything going for himself. It was a shock to all of us, especially his fiancée, Morgan Price. She was devastated and moved back to Georgia just after the funeral. Ben was just one of those guys everybody liked. I still don't understand how that could have happened to him."

"That's what we're trying to find out, Mr. Charlton," Powell said.

"I hope somebody does. I don't think the police ever found anything. They came here just after it happened, asking if Ben had any enemies, a drinking problem, or was known to associate with prostitutes. None of that was even remotely what Ben was about. He'd just gotten engaged to Morgan two weeks before he went to that convention. And drink? Ben liked a cocktail from time to time, but I never saw him drunk or even tipsy. It wasn't his style."

"Is there anyone else he was close to at the station?" McGee asked.

"His best buddy was Dick Bell, another guy in sales. Bell doesn't work here anymore. He was at KOIN-TV in Portland last I heard."

Powell concluded the interview believing there was little more to be gained from Charlton. McGee agreed and added that he didn't see the necessity in interviewing the fiancé, but thought Bell should be next on their list.

On their drive back to Portland, McGee took a call from Hines. "I finished the sweep on McMaster's and I've got nothing: no arrests, no warrants, no trouble. I also came up with zilch on anything relating to him on social media; it's just too long ago."

McGee replied, "We don't have much either. He was popular, successful, and recently engaged when he went to SF."

Hines was skeptical. "That doesn't figure. He doesn't fit the profile of the other two vics, other than the way he was killed. Weird. I do have something else. I found the photographer who covered the convention back in 2012. It's a long shot, but he's sent me his digital files. There are over 2500 images. I'm going through them now, but it'll take a while. I'm hoping there's a shot of McMasters and maybe someone with him."

"Good luck with that. I'll help you when I get back, hang on." McGee then turned to Powell and told him what Hines had found. Powell waited a moment before responding. "Tell Andy that we're driving directly to KOIN when we get to Portland. Ask him to see if he can get us in to see Bell."

Hines called McGee back three minutes later. "You're all set. You can meet him there at 4:30."

McGee and Powell arrived at the KOIN building at 4:45. The traffic into downtown had been horrendous. When they inquired at the front desk for Bell, they were directed to the elevators and the conference room on the twenty-seventh floor.

Dick Bell was waiting for them at the door of the glass-walled room. Bell was tall and angular, in his 40's, tanned, and surprisingly dressed in tennis wear. His brown hair was casually combed. He had a big toothy smile and for Powell it was easy to see that sales were his tradecraft. The man approached them with his hand extended. "Gentlemen, pleased to meet you. I'm Dick Bell. Excuse my attire, I'm heading out to play a few sets after we're done."

McGee and Powell exchanged handshakes with the man. "Thanks for meeting with us on such short notice Mr. Bell. I appreciate it," Powell said cordially.

"Hey, if I can help you in anyway with what happened to Ben, I will. Unfortunately, I just don't know much. Please come on in, we can sit in here," Bell said, opening the door to the large room.

They sat at the closest end of the huge walnut table.

McGee began. "Can you tell us about the phone call you had with Ben the night before he was killed? The police interview indicated that he'd talked with you, but it was summarized as not containing anything of interest."

"I'm not surprised. When they came and interviewed me at KAMI, it seemed to me to be very perfunctory. I was asked if I knew anyone that wanted to hurt Ben, had a grudge with him, or was angry with him for being engaged to Morgan. I didn't. I thought the question about Morgan was strange though. They even asked me if Morgan was upset with Ben or had left town to join Ben in San Francisco. She wasn't and didn't as far as I knew. I told them my phone call with Ben had been short that night. It was just as I was leaving the office, about six o'clock. He told me that he was making some really good contacts and that the show was turning out to be better than he expected."

Bell paused a moment. "It was the last thing he said to me, but when he said it, he sounded like there was somebody in the room with him. I don't know why, but I just had that impression. I never told the police that. It would've been an assumption on my part and I wasn't about to do that. It was bad enough that he was dead. I didn't want to bring up something that would make him look like he was cheating on Morgan and got killed for it."

"Did he sound worried or afraid when he inferred that there was a person in the room with him?" Powell asked.

"No. He said it in such a way that it sounded like it was an inside joke. Like he said it for the person that was with him. And if I had to guess, it wasn't a man he said it for."

Powell asked, "Why do you say that? Maybe it was a business contact and they'd just signed a deal."

Bell nodded. "I don't think so. He would've bragged to me and dropped the guy's name and company if that was the case. No, it was a woman. Ben could be cagey when he wanted to be. He'd always been a ladies' man, but Morgan definitely turned his head and ended all of that. She kept him on a very short leash." Bell paused slightly before he added, "Let me answer the question I know you want to ask. Yes, I think Ben would have cheated on Morgan if given a good enough opportunity and the right woman."

"There it is," Powell thought to himself. McMasters was just like the others: a hunter who became the hunted when he found the wrong woman to play.

On the ride down the elevator from their meeting with Bell, Powell asked, "What do you think, John?"

"Same thing you do. McMasters was another man who angered our girl and she killed him for it."

Chapter 38 • Celebrations

It was the first week of January and the rains and wintry mixes were unrelenting in Portland. The short days and the occasional snow showers did not diminish anyone's happiness around the office of Synergy, and no one was happier than Stephanie, except maybe Susan. The agency now had as much business as they could handle and more clients were beating on their doors. It'd taken a while for the collapse of FMG to affect the market, but once it began it was a landslide. It was Marcus and Powell's discoveries that started it, but it was the death of Bill Grant that ended it.

Grant's murder shocked everyone. At first he was reported missing. Three weeks later, well after the press hype and police work had calmed, his sister discovered his body, by chance, hidden under some fish and boxes in the man's freezer. It was leaked to the press that the police missed checking the freezer on their first search of the house and found nothing of interest after a second forensic sweep. Further information revealed he'd been killed by electric shock, knifed and then stuffed into the freezer. There were no suspects, but press coverage detailed his colored past and ruthless reputation in business. It was implied that it wasn't inconceivable that Grant had accumulated a broad list of enemies in the Pacific Northwest advertising community.

Stephanie didn't care one way or the other about Grant. She believed he got what he deserved, though she expressed to anyone who asked, it was sad and unfortunate that anybody had to die. She really couldn't complain or be upset about anything or anyone in her life at the moment. A number of mid-sized agencies had grown and profited in Portland with the closing of FMG, but no agency more than Synergy. They'd grown from five to nine employees and now they were twelve. The rapid expansion forced them to move and she couldn't have been more delighted when Susan chose the Tower as their new agency home. They occupied half of the fourteenth floor, and for her it was like working from her own home with Marcus. Her commute was now a fifteen-second-elevator ride if traffic was light.

She smiled at her own joke.

Marcus and she had decided to have a small party, and for the first time in her life she was the hostess with the "mostest." At least that's what Marcus said. She loved his reference to her as "mostest." She adored the way he looked at her and commented about her charms. It was delicious for her to be embraced by his words and she reveled in them.

They'd selected a Saturday that worked for everyone. They were having a total of five guests for dinner and they were both excited about it. She'd been busy with Valeria that morning preparing the faire they'd be serving. The prime rib wouldn't be done for another hour, and Valeria had left to spend the day with her family.

She'd fussed with her appearance before returning to the kitchen. She was in charge and their guests would be arriving soon and she was ready.

Marcus had opened the doors to his home so their friends could enter directly from the office. Each guest already possessed their own entry cards for the front office. Powell was coming with Gretchen and the new guy she hadn't met, McGee, was going to be stag. Susan and Roger completed the guest list.

Not everyone was coming to their party. Marcus had invited the entire crew of Avalanche, but the Kirkpatrick brothers were busy on a protection detail, Kierney was in San Diego with his family, and Hines was at an advanced electronics and surveillance expo.

"Busy times," is what Marcus told her disappointingly.

She glanced across the butcher-block preparation bar as Marcus came into the kitchen. He was dressed in a black sport jacket, slacks, and his shirt was dark red. He smiled at her and said, "Pretty festive, aren't I? I think we're a match. You're absolutely stunning in new pants and your heels are perfect."

She twirled for him; her red leather pants and black silk blouse made her feel sensational. Her tennis bracelet sparkled on her wrist. "I'm glad you noticed, Marcus. To be honest I think it was all your idea."

"You're so funny, but yes, I have impeccable taste when it comes to you, my gorgeous Red."

"Red, huh? Listen to you. You look very good yourself, mister."

"Yes, I do, but you dressed me."

"Yes, darling, and I believe I did a fabulous job!"

Before he could respond to her obvious delight, he heard Powell's booming voice, "Anybody here at the ranch? The party has arrived!"

Gretchen and Powell were smiling as they entered the kitchen. Gretchen was stunning in a green shimmering dress that hugged her curves; her blonde hair cascaded to her shoulders. Powell towered above her in a dark blue suit jacket, gray slacks and an open collared white shirt. He carried a large magnum of champagne in each hand with labels that read 'Pol Roger Cuvee Sir Winston Churchill'.

Marcus spoke first. "Look at you two. Gretchen, you're positively beautiful. And Hank, I've never seen you look more svelte."

"Svelte is it, LT?" Powell growled at Graham, assuming his "presence with a menace" appearance, until Gretchen slugged him in the arm.

"Be nice, Hank. Or I'll take you down," she said with a growl at first and then she started laughing.

Powell was grinning as he passed the magnums to Graham. "A little joy juice for the party, Marcus."

"Good deal, Hank. Thanks. I'll get one open for us right now."

Marcus turned with the dark green bottles and carried them to the bar that separated the kitchen from the dining room. He slid one magnum into the wine fridge and proceeded to open the other with a soft pop. He poured the champagne into four, fluted Riedel glasses.

"Hello, anyone home?"

They all turned towards the voice to see Roger and Susan Arcadia enter the foyer. Susan was neatly dressed in a black cocktail dress and Roger was nicely attired in a dark tan suit, white shirt and a black sweater.

Marcus walked to where the Arcadia's were standing. Stephanie by his side.

"Welcome, Susan. Roger, it's good to see you again. I'm glad it's under better circumstances this time. Stephanie and I are very pleased to have you both join us," Marcus said as he shook Roger's hand and she gave Susan a quick hug.

Stephanie added, "Yes, we are. Susan, I love your dress. Roger, you look very handsome. Thanks so much for coming this evening."

Marcus then gestured to Hank and Gretchen. "Roger, Susan, this is my good friend and business associate, Hank Powell, and his companion Gretchen Hilde, who also happens to be my right hand here at Graham Developments."

The four greeted each other and began chatting.

Stephanie tapped Marcus on the shoulder and said, "Let's get drinks for everyone and let our guests get settled."

They quickly retrieved the champagne and returned to living room. Marcus carried a cloth-wrapped magnum, while she balanced a tray that held the Riedel glasses. They served each of their guests a glass and as they did, Marcus invited them to partake in the appetizers that sat on the coffee table. It was then he saw John McGee cautiously come through the front door. He wore a gray suit, white shirt and a gray tie. He smiled when he spotted Graham.

"John, welcome. It's good to see you."

"Thank you, Marcus. It's good to be here."

Marcus then turned to the others and said, "Excuse me, everyone. Our final guest has arrived. Roger, Susan, this is John McGee. John oversees and facilitates many of the endeavors Avalanche is involved with."

McGee raised his hand to the Arcadia's. "Good evening. Nice to meet you."

"Thanks. You too, John," Roger replied. Susan mouthed the words, "Me too" and smiled.

Gretchen stepped forward from Powell's side and shook McGee's hand. "John, it's nice to see you again. Hank let you out of the cage for a few hours I see."

McGee laughed. "It's not as bad as that, Gretchen. He's not as hard as he may lead you to believe."

Powell came up next to McGee and deadpanned him. "What's that you say, John? I'm not as hard as I should be?"

"Knock it off, Hank. Everyone knows you're hard," Gretchen said flatly with a frown, before breaking into laughter.

Marcus gestured for Stephanie to join him. They stepped over to where McGee was laughing with Powell and Gretchen.

"What's so funny, John? Hank and Gretchen ganging up on you? Marcus asked.

"No, it's nothing like that. Gretchen and I were just remarking how kind Hank had been lately. He was pleased about the comment, though he admitted he could turn at any second."

No one laughed.

McGee then added, "You had to be there."

It broke them up with Powell almost spilling his drink. Gretchen was laughing so hard she stepped away and walked to where the Arcadia's were standing, admiring the view from the floor-to-ceiling windows.

As the laughter subsided, Graham turned to McGee and said, "John, this is my dear companion, Stephanie Courtland."

McGee bowed slightly and extended his hand. "It's a pleasure, Miss Courtland."

Stephanie immediately sensed that McGee was appraising her very carefully. "Thank you, John. I've heard some very nice things about you."

"And I about you. Marcus is a very lucky man."

Stephanie smiled warmly at his remark and squeezed Marcus' arm. She then excused herself and went to where Susan was sipping from her glass, while Gretchen and Roger admired the views of downtown Portland. Out of the corner of her eye, Stephanie watched Powell go over to where Marcus was standing and say something to him and McGee. The three then headed for the kitchen.

"Not so fast," she thought as she looked at Susan and said, "Can you help me with the champagne?"

"Sure, what's up Steph?"

"Let's go see what the men are talking about. Roger and Gretchen are busy. Let's go."

When they arrived in the kitchen, she heard Marcus ask Powell, "Did you get it?"

She couldn't wait to say, "Get what? What did you get, Hank?"

Powell glanced at Marcus. "Ok, it's your call, LT. What do you want me to say?"

Susan chuckled and said, "Oh, this is going to be good. I love it when men get surprised when they're acting all secretive."

Marcus held up his hands defensively. "Easy there, ladies. You've caught us, I get it. But, do you really, really want to know what Hank has brought me?"

Stephanie knew it must be good, because Marcus was being so challenging. "I do, Marcus," she said softly as she clutched his arm and kissed his cheek.

Graham blushed ever so slightly and then said to Powell. "Okay, Hank. I guess we're busted, so go ahead and give me what I asked you to bring."

Powell knew drama when he saw it, so he played along. "Are you sure, Marcus? It's not something you can just trot out without an explanation."

"I know, Hank. But go ahead."

Powell, without expression, reached into his coat pocket and extracted a metal ring with two keys hanging from it. He flipped them to Marcus. "Here you go, Boss. As ordered."

Marcus put the ring on his index finger and twirled them, while he looked seriously at Stephanie and said, "These are the keys to our next new adventure, Steph. Are you ready?"

Susan was intrigued. "Oh, I like that. Marcus you're so clever, but tell us - what new adventure?"

"I was thinking of stealing Stephanie away for a week and taking her on a winter adventure in the Gorge. Just the two of us, roughing it in a small mountain cabin. It's warmed by a wood fired stove and the kitchen water needs to be pumped by hand. There's an outhouse though, so it has everything. And," he paused. "We can catch our own food. The fishing will be great there. It'll be a real hands-on experience. Oh, and one more thing, there's no cell service there." Marcus was smiling broadly.

Susan glanced at Stephanie and with a dour expression said, "Lucky you."

Stephanie put on her best smile. "That sounds like fun, Marcus. Just the two of us for a week isolated in a mountain cabin surrounded by god knows what kind of wild creatures, and there's even an outhouse? How can I say no?"

Graham, Powell and McGee all laughed.

Marcus bent down and whispered in her ear, "I love you for being the way you are."

Stephanie kissed him on the cheek and secretly thought she would like nothing better than to be in the wilderness all alone with her lover for a week. It was so "Jane and Tarzan."

McGee then raised his glass and said, "Happy adventures." Everyone joined in on the toast and their celebration continued late into the evening.

Chapter 39 • The Klickitat

The weather in Oregon remained cold. Marcus and Stephanie's drive to the Klickitat was accomplished under sunny, but frigid skies. When they reached the outskirts of Lyle and began the twisted climb up the Klickitat Canyon, small patches of snow along the two-lane highway gradually grew deeper on both sides of road. At the ten-mile marker, Graham knew he was close. He slowed the Lexus and searched for the driveway. As the road wound around another corner he spotted the opening. The entrance was almost hidden by the encroaching snow-covered trees and was even smaller than described to him.

Graham turned in past the "Private" sign and slowly wove his way down the snow packed drive. Fir trees drooped gloomily on both sides. After about seventy-five feet, the drive opened into a clearing that revealed a wood cabin and outhouse. Tall fir and pine trees surrounded the clearing, and their needles and broken limbs littered the snow covering the ground and the snowy cedar shingles of the cabin's roof. The outhouse stood next to the rear of the cabin and appeared to have been recently rebuilt. Marcus noticed an electrical cable running to it and pointed it out to her.

"Hallelujah!" Stephanie said exuberantly. "We have a bathroom with a light."

Graham parked the Lexus next to the front door of the cabin.

"I told you my car would be good in the snow," she said to him. "There was also plenty of room for the groceries, which we wouldn't have had in the 650."

"Correct again, my darling. It sounds like you're in full roughing-it mode. I'm sure you would have been in charge of packing the wagon had we come here with horses."

"Roger that, LT," she said with smile, getting out of the car.

Even though the walk to the front of the cabin was recently shoveled, their boots still made imprints in the snow as they trudged to the cabin door. Their breath was steamy in the cold as Marcus fumbled for the key in his pocket, found it, and inserted it into the lock. He pushed the wood door open and they stepped into the frosty interior. It was cold and the windows had a glaze of ice shining on them. He flipped on the switch next to the door and a round ceiling light flared on and brightened the room.

A wood rack with two fishing poles and a long-handled net, hanging on hooks between them, were positioned on the wall next to the door. Two old-fashioned creel boxes sat next to the poles on the wood floor. To the right of the front door was the kitchen area. A small, square, wooden table sat near the sink and four chairs were positioned around it. The metal sink had a small counter with two wood cabinets above and below it. Stephanie checked the cabinets and found dishware, pans, an aluminum percolator-style coffee pot, and several cast iron skillets. Under the sink there was dish soap, a pan and a scrub brush. There was an old-fashioned metal hand pump standing next to the sink and Marcus was warned that the water that came from it had a distinct sulfur odor of rotten eggs, but it was okay to drink.

Stephanie pumped the handle up and down. Nothing. She pumped harder; the pump gurgled and then began to spit out a slow stream of rusty water. She kept pumping until the water gradually turned clear, but it also smelled as described.

"I'm not sure we're ready for this, LT. Do you like coffee that smells like rotten eggs?" Stephanie joked to Marcus.

"That's why we brought the two cases of bottled water, love. No rotten eggs with our coffee. We got this," he said confidently.

They looked across from the kitchen to the squat wood stove sitting in the main room against the far wall. A yellow plastic box containing kindling and a few small, split logs were positioned near the side of the stove. There was also a metal trash can that contained folded newspapers, and next to it stood a brass stand with a poker and a small shovel standing in its center. Facing the stove was a brown leather couch and matching armchair, which sat upon a circular green woolen rug. A rough-hewn wood coffee table sat in front of the couch. A large glass vase with a dozen white roses sat in the center of the table. Against the far wall there were four,

Graham guessed, ten-foot long, wooden shelves mounted on the wall. Each shelf was crammed with books of all kinds: hard back reference books, soft cover novels, and entire shelf devoted to seedy, mystery-thriller, cop and blood pocketbooks from the fifties.

A small door to the right of the bookshelves led to the bedroom. They could see an old-fashioned four-poster bed in the room, but there was a new pillow-top mattress in place. Marcus' handiwork. To the right of the bedroom door was the bathroom. She stepped into the room and flipped on the light switch next to the door. A round ceiling light revealed a small metal sink, mirror, and stand-up shower. The realtor had told them the water tank supplied a limited, but hot shower experience.

Stephanie was not impressed. She turned and stood in the doorway of the bathroom with a pout. "Marcus, I hope you're not expecting miracles to come from this room. Did you see my mirror? I'll be lucky to get my lipstick on."

He laughed. "I think you'll be fine Steph. I like you anyway I can have you. Let's warm this place up. I'll get a fire going," Marcus said, rubbing his hands together.

He walked to the stove, checked the damper and opened the twin handles of the stove door. Inside the belly of the black stove he found prepared newspaper and kindling for the next fire. Marcus peered into the bucket holding the newspapers and found a box of wooden matches. He lit the newspaper under the kindling and closed the door. The fire crackled to life almost instantaneously.

Stephanie watched silently. She liked her man being a man. She shivered at the thought of having him all to herself, especially here.

She smiled and said, "Thank you for the flowers, darling. They're beautiful."

Even though it was late morning, the four small windows in the main room let in sparse light. The dense tree line surrounding the cabin shielded the windows from direct sunlight, but the snapping and crackling of the kindling from the fire warmed the setting.

They unloaded their supplies from the Lexus. It took several trips back and forth, as they'd brought sufficient food, water, toilet paper, coffee, soft drinks and booze to last a week. Two large coolers containing dry ice and some perishables completed their supplies. They had no intention of going to the IGA in Lyle unless it was absolutely necessary; they had done their shopping at Whole Foods. He also intended to remain off the grid as long as they could. It was their time and he didn't want any distractions for what he had to do.

Graham added four split logs to the stove, while Stephanie sorted and stacked their foodstuffs and supplies in the kitchen. He then moved their bags and suitcases to the small bedroom and unpacked their 2500 thread count Egyptian cotton sheets, two pillows with cases, a heavy blanket, and a black, cotton comforter. He placed them on the bed.

Graham unloaded his suitcase and strapped-on the .45 caliber M1911 semi-automatic pistol, which he wore back to the main room. He had planned to get used to carrying it while at the cabin, more for their personal protection than anything. Bears, mountain lions, and raccoons were not uncommon at the cabin, and the realtor had warned him to be particularly watchful, especially when heading for the outhouse near dusk or early morning. He had further cautioned him the same predators used the trail along the cliffs leading down to the river and that they should always be wary.

Stephanie stared at him curiously when he came back into the room. "You look like a gunfighter. What's that for?"

Graham was serious. "Well, I have no intention of letting either of us be eaten by a fucking bear or cougar while we're here."

She felt comforted by the fact that he was thinking of their safety. "Me neither," she squeaked at him.

For the first two days they spent most of their time reading, cooking, and making wild, passionate love or anticipating when they would again. Marcus was so attentive she luxuriated in how whole he made her feel. She had even stopped taking her *crazy pills* and suffered no nightmares or conversations with *them*.

She felt at long last free from her past.

They soon developed a routine with the fire and cooking on the wood stove and she hated it, but loved that he helped her. His idea of bringing six dinner meals from Blue Apron made it easier, and they both enjoyed the experience of cooking together with the instructions and ingredients supplied. It bonded them tighter than ever and she reveled in it.

On the morning of the third day, Stephanie was making their bed, her body leaning over to tuck in the sheets. Marcus came from behind her and took hold of her waist and guided her towards the cabin wall. Stephanie felt a jolt of passion, not sure what to expect until Marcus held her hands above her head pressing her wrists firmly against the wooden slats of the wall.

She turned her head sideways and looked back at him. "You please me Marcus in so many ways," she said breathlessly.

"It's mutual Steph. I'm very much in love with you."

He then turned her around and began kissing her softly. She moved against him, anticipating what he would do next. She hoped beyond hope that a diamond ring was in her future because for the first time in her life she was ready for the next step. "Nothing can hurt me now," she thought to herself as he guided her back to the bed, where they would spend the remainder of the morning.

That afternoon Marcus suggested they check out the river because he was hungry for some freshly caught trout and they needed a break from the Blue Apron regimen. It was also warmer and much of the snow in the drive had melted. It was a beautiful day.

They both dressed in parkas, hats, and boots for their trek to the river. The thermometer outside the kitchen window displayed a cool 39 degrees.

"I think we've got cabin fever, but the good kind," she said to him as she pulled on her boots.

Marcus laughed and said, "You've been very naughty and if you don't watch it, we won't make it to the river."

She glanced at him and in a voice that surprised her, said, *"Watch yourself, bub. Or we will stay here and play."* It was *Tiffany*.

"What did you say?"

Stephanie just smiled at him. "I was just joking. Let's go. I'm ready."

"Uh, no you're not. Look at your boots, Steph. They're untied."

She laughed to cover her confusion. "Silly me. I'm just excited about seeing you fish."

"Okay. Let me help you." He knelt before her and tied her laces.

She tried to make light of *Tiffany's* comment by mimicking it. "Thanks, bub."

He stood and smiled at her. "You can call me that, but only if I can call you bubbet." Marcus then turned and snatched a fishing pole from the wall, and a wicker creel off the floor. He looked back to her as he swung the creel over his shoulder. "We've a good selection of lures, swivels, weights, and hooks. You ready?"

She nodded and zipped up her parka.

The small, partially concealed path that would take them to the river was just past the Lexus, in the corner of the clearing. The narrow trail was rock and boulder strewn, slippery in spots from the snow, and it was steep and dark, shrouded from the light by the dense tree canopy. He held her hand as he led her down the trail. They had hiked a good ten minutes when the path rounded a corner and opened to what appeared to be a small grassy clearing that still held a few small patches of melting snow. The clearing flared out for about ten feet and then abruptly ended.

He stopped. "Wait here, Steph."

She watched him carefully.

He cautiously stepped forward to the edge and peered over. Loose dirt and gravel loosened under his stance and he quickly stepped back. He watched as the shift of dirt and gravel began running and slipping another fifteen feet towards a big rock jutting out from the side of the cliff. From the rock it was a sheer drop of about eighty feet to the river below. He could see the river raging and spilling over giant moss-covered boulders on the far side and flattening out into deeper water with softer, quieter riffles on the near shore.

He turned and walked to Stephanie's side. With a quick "Let's go," he led her out of the clearing to re-enter the tree-lined trail. The path switchbacked two different times before they finally reached the canyon floor and the river. He estimated the route down from the cabin was at least a half-mile.

They followed the river upstream through the rocks and boulders until they reached a small, sandy beach. As he approached the water, Marcus noticed a fish trap had been built a few feet offshore.

"Steph, look at this," he called out to her.

The fish trap was heart-shaped, about ten-by-twenty feet, with its point facing downstream. At the top, where the two halves joined together, was a narrow opening where the current passed through. The rocks forming the boundary of the heart were barely below the water. The closer to the edge of the rocks the shallower the water became. In the middle of the heart was a pool about four feet deep. It was here the fish congregated, being unable to pass back through the opening due to the rush of the current. He counted at least a half-dozen silvery shapes darting within the pool.

Stephanie was concerned. "Don't they die in there? It's so sad, Marcus."

"Baby, they don't starve in the pool. The food comes to them naturally from the opening at the top. But we do have a problem."

Stephanie made her best worried face and asked, "What? What's the problem, mighty fisherman?"

He held the fishing pole before her. "We don't need a pole, we need a net."

"Good job, LT. So, I take it that we're marching back to the cabin and getting the one that's hanging on the wall?"

He grimaced, knowing it was true. "Yes, oh powerful one. I will march back up to the cabin and retrieve the appropriate gear."

"Not without me, bub," she said, still trying to discount *Tiffany's* random remark.

He smirked at her. "Okay, woman. Let's go."

The trek up the trail was arduous and left them thirsty by the time they reached the top. Inside the cabin they shared a bottle of water before securing the net. They then trudged back down to the river, this time carefully hugging the inside of the trail when they reached the apron and exposed cliff. At the river they retraced their steps back to the fish trap.

In two scoops Marcus had three good-sized rainbow trout flopping in the net. He brought them to shore and quickly gutted and cleaned the trout while she watched. He soon dropped his catch into the creel and strapped it over his neck and shoulder.

She beamed at the man she loved as he picked up the net and they began their hike back to the cabin. The second walk up the steep path wasn't any easier than the first, but they had nothing to do for the rest of the day and evening other than to eat, enjoy each other's company and make love.

"Tomorrow will be different," was the last thought Marcus had as he drifted off to sleep that night.

It would prove to be that and more.

The next afternoon they were sitting in the living room, drinking champagne and reading when he dropped the bombshell on her. "I have something I've been meaning to share with you, Steph. Actually, there are a few things."

She instantly thought, "This is it. He's going to ask me to marry him." But when he paused, she could sense she was wrong. He was nervous and appeared worried, which was out of character for him.

Marcus then said, "First of all, when you told me about your family history, I already knew most of the details. I'm sorry I didn't tell you. When I first met you at Synergy, I was extremely attracted to you. I loved everything I saw. I then had Hank run your background for me. It was very detailed about everything - everything but one detail that I discovered last September. I couldn't tell you what I'd found because I was embarrassed, shocked, and to tell you the truth, I still have a hard time believing it."

She always suspected he knew all about her past before she had told him, and now she knew it to be true. But what was next? What could possibly have upset him so badly she wondered?

He bent over and held his head with his hands. "It's not good, Steph. Even now I'm reluctant to tell you. It fucking kills me inside. I've been afraid for months to tell you what I knew, but I couldn't bring myself to do it. Our relationship has come so far and so wonderfully - I really don't want to lose you."

Marcus paused again and gave a small sigh. "I want you to know I had no idea, until Andy Hines found something I wish he would have never dug up."

She was now seriously worried and was becoming more afraid of what he might tell her. She also had to know. "Marcus, please tell me. What is it?"

He raised his head and reached over to hold her hands. "When I first discovered your hardships with Franklin, I had Andy Hines run a deep background check on him. What he discovered were the details of my adoption records."

"I don't understand. Why would your adoption records show up?"

"Hines discovered Ray was accused of raping a girl in high school, but it wasn't rape at all. The two were boyfriend and girlfriend all the way through school. When the girl became pregnant her parents pressed charges against Franklin, but it didn't stick. She defended him. The downside was the girl was sent away by her parents to have the baby and Franklin let her go. The parents forced her to give up the baby and it was put up for adoption at birth. Six months later the girl killed herself with a drug overdose. The adoptees were Walter and Rose Graham."

It took her a few seconds to process what she'd never expected to hear, the disbelief beginning to set in. "Your real father was Ray? The same Ray?" she asked, staring at him incredulously.

"I'm truly sorry I didn't tell you when I found out, but I couldn't believe it. I also didn't want to believe it. I became more and more afraid to tell you for fear the circumstances would be too weird for you to handle.

In my defense, I may be biologically related to him, but I am not my father's son. Please believe me, Steph. I love you very much."

She sat there in shock for a moment and then she became furious. "Why didn't you tell me before? Is that why the big attraction? In some weird way are you trying to make up for what that bastard did to me and my family?"

"You know that's not true."

"I don't know what to believe right now."

She turned away from him and walked to the small bedroom, slamming the door behind her. She stood silently before their bed, her eyes fixed on the bedroom wall's horizon. She began to tremble. She'd always suspected Marcus had controlled and manipulated everything in her life for as long as she'd known him and now she knew it was true. Worst of all, he had lied, not trusting her, knowing the truth all along. She had given him everything: her body, her confessions, her soul. She wanted to run.

"I don't, Steph." It was Tiffany and she was angry, steaming.

"Me, neither," said Beth diplomatically. "But we need to be calm. There's nothing to do now and screaming will just alarm him. I need time to think. And you need to rest."

Stephanie didn't argue. She opened the bedroom door and peered out. "Marcus, I don't know what to say, but I think it best we just go to bed. I need to think," Stephanie said for the last time that she would remember.

Beth and Tiffany were already deep in conversation about the decisions to be made.

Chapter 40 • Connecting the Dots

When Powell stepped out of his office on Friday, Hines and McGee greeted him. Powell immediately sensed Hines was anxious to tell him something because the man never arrived earlier than 9:00 a.m., unless there was an active investigation that required his skills. McGee was always early.

Hines didn't wait for Powell. "It took me a bit, but I found the photographer who was hired for the convention and he was very cooperative. His photos were all digital so he was able to forward them to me online. John and I have reviewed most of them and we've found a few things that you're not going to like, Top."

"Do you want to give me a clue, Andy?" Powell asked.

"We'd rather show you," McGee said.

Powell glanced at McGee who simply nodded at him and said, "Oh, yeah."

They followed Hines back to the operations room and the bank of high-definition monitors.

"This is a whopper," Hines said over his shoulder as he sat in front of his computer.

Powell and McGee didn't sit. They came up and stood behind him.

"When I started my scan of the last of the convention photos, I didn't find anything until I came to this photo."

Hines tapped his keyboard and an image popped up on the center monitor. It was a very clear photo of a man and woman in front of a booth filled with different sizes and shapes of computer screens. It was an intimate photo that showed the woman grasping the man's arm and smiling adoringly at him. He was looking at her with the same expression. The man was Marvin McMasters. The woman was a younger Stephanie Courtland.

"Oh, shit!" Powell exclaimed.

"Hang on," Hines said. "Check this out." Another photo popped up in the right monitor. It was a screen shot from the Internet of the University of Washington graduate profiles of 2008. There were four columns of names listed alphabetically. "First read the names under C."

He did and saw Stephanie Courtland's name.

"Now go to the F's."

Jason Fischer was listed

"It doesn't prove anything. They were classmates," Powell said to Hines.

"There's more, Top," Hines said, as he punched up the scanned image in the left monitor. "When you go to each person's graduate profile you get a very clear picture of the person, although some of it is quite whimsical. Look at what it says for Miss Courtland's answer to the question of where she expects to be one day after graduation."

It read: "Celebrating my graduation with friends in Maui, Hawaii."

"I've got three more images. First, this one from the yearbook of 2005."

The photo that came up on the monitor showed Stephanie Courtland as a freshman.

"Then, there's this one."

The next photo was of the UW waterskiing club. Courtland was standing in a group photo in front of a sleek MasterCraft inboard, at a dock. A large sign was visible behind the group: Welcome to Lakeland Marina. There were two coaches shown in the picture. One was Ken Staubb.

"Jesus Christ," Powell exclaimed in disbelief.

McGee glanced at Powell and told him, "There are no coincidences."

Hines continued. "Given Miss Courtland's history with Franklin, I think it would be safe to assume that she doesn't respond well to men treating her badly. Staubb and Fischer had reputations that fit that profile to a T. In each case she had access and more than likely, opportunity."

McGee couldn't wait. "I can literally write the scenario as to what happened to McMasters. He was scoring with her at the convention, she found out he was engaged, and she killed him for being that kind of man. It isn't a big leap from there to the murders of Franklin and Grant. Motive always points the way and she had it in spades."

Hines added quickly, "Look at the method of the killings. They're all similar. First, she incapacitates them with drugs, booze, a blow to the head, or stun guns. Those are all followed by brutal knife work. Her anger is very apparent. She's also very good at this. She's never been sloppy or left any evidence behind. The police thought there was a link between Franklin and Grant because of the use of stun guns and the knife, but they never made the connection. Probably didn't know Franklin's history with Miss Courtland and they definitely didn't know about Grant's misdeeds at Synergy. Only we do. I think we all suspected it was too convenient for Franklin to be randomly killed. Grant's murder only made it obvious that someone was connected to both men. Now we know it's true."

Powell sat silently thinking of what Hines and McGee had concluded. After a moment he said dejectedly, "Goddammit. She's the last person I wanted to see involved. But I have to agree with you, there are just too many coincidences of her being with, or near, or linked to each of the murdered men. Son of a bitch." He was both pissed and concerned. "We have another problem. She's with Marcus at that cabin on the Klickitat and he told me he was going to finally clear the air with her about Franklin being his father."

"That won't be good, Hank. That's the type of scenario she responds violently to. We need to get word to the LT," McGee said adamantly to Powell.

Hines interrupted before Powell could respond. "I don't think so, Top. She's always been very careful when she's killed someone. I don't think she'll take the chance at the cabin. Everyone knows they're there. It's not in her profile to be so connected to a crime scene."

"Who's to say how rational she really is, Andy? Maybe Marcus' confession will drive her to do something erratic and off the charts," McGee argued. "I don't think we should wait to warn him."

Powell stood up and stared at the two. "There's no cell service where they're at, but I'm not going to leave things to chance. I'll drive there."

Hines asked, "Why don't we give the police a heads-up? They could have people out of The Dalles or Hood River there pretty quickly."

"Not on my watch. I don't need some bumbled-headed deputies charging the cabin and creating a situation that ends poorly. Marcus can handle himself. This is an in-house problem for now. I'll be leaving in five minutes." Powell then paused and said commandingly, "And no, I don't need any company or weapons. I can handle this. I'll be in touch."

Powell turned and left the room.

It was 0920 hours. Powell estimated it would take him almost two hours to reach the cabin on the Klickitat. As he hurried to the Ford Raptor a disturbing thought crossed his mind; he hoped Marcus wasn't so blinded by his love for Stephanie that he didn't see the knife coming.

Chapter 41 • Careening

Marcus was sleeping soundly. *She slipped out from under the covers ever so quietly and tiptoed to where his clothes were draped over the end of the bed. The gun belt and holstered gun were on the floor next to his shoes. She picked it up, surprised by its weight. She then grabbed her own clothes and crept from the room, quietly closing the door behind her. She dressed quickly, not wanting to be caught by him half-prepared. She wore jeans, a plaid shirt and her hiking boots. She strapped on the gun belt and tightened it up to its last notch.*

"So, your plan involves the gun, Tiffany?" Beth asked, worry in her voice.

"Do you really think what he's done is okay? Are you fucking serious?" Tiffany scolded her.

"No, no I don't, but," Beth started to say as Tiffany interrupted.

"Don't but me, Beth. I have to do what I have to do. I can't just stop. You know that," Tiffany hissed at her.

"Oh, yes I do. I've been there to clean up your messes, time and time again. Need I remind you? You're a fucking maniac. I'm tired of it, Tiffany."

"Oh, I do like fucking him, and the money doesn't hurt, but remember we're fucking the bastard of the man who killed Alice and molested Stephanie. Have you forgotten? Marcus didn't even tell us who he really was until now, after he's had his way with us."

"It's the first time I've felt this way," Beth said quietly.

"Felt what way, Steph? And who the heck are you talking to?" Marcus asked sleepily, peeking his head out of the bedroom door.

She turned towards his voice, stunned that he'd heard her. "Don't be silly, I'm talking to me. It's the first time I've felt like getting up early since being here," Tiffany replied.

"The gun is a nice touch. Are you going to the outhouse or just seeing how it feels?" he asked.

She laughed. "I was just curious to see what it felt like to be you. You know what I mean, LT?" she said coyly.

"I'm not sure I do, but be careful. The gun is loaded and I don't want you to shoot yourself in the foot, or me."

"Roger that, LT. I'm going to stoke up the wood stove and make some coffee. Why don't you get dressed and join me," Tiffany said commandingly, now fully forward and in charge.

"You sure you can do that? I mean the fire."

Tiffany had to think before she responded. What she really wanted to tell him was to fuck off and leave her alone but that's not what she said. "I think so. I've watched you do it and I'm sure I can."

"Okay. I'll be out in a few minutes. I'm going to shave and clean up a bit." Graham then closed the door.

Tiffany shrugged at the door. "I'll be waiting," she whispered malevolently, patting the gun. "Just me and you."

Beth was silent. Gone.

When Marcus returned from the bedroom the fire was snapping and crackling and he could smell the coffee percolating. Stephanie was standing in the kitchen, breaking eggs into a bowl. He could see a package of bacon and a cast iron skillet sitting next to the bowl. "Wow, look at you go girl. The fire, coffee, and now breakfast. How do I deserve to be treated so good?"

With a stern expression Tiffany said, "I wondered that myself after what you told me last night."

"I'm sorry. I don't know how I can say it enough times so you believe it."

"I'm not sure you can, Marcus. But let's change the subject. It's a beautiful day and I think we should go down to the river after breakfast. I can watch you fish. Maybe you can even teach me. I need to get out of the cabin."

"That sounds like a plan. I'll get the gear ready. Do you need me to help with the eggs and bacon?" He sounded eager to please her.

"No, I've got this," she said flatly, and turned back to her preparations.

Twenty minutes later they'd finished eating, passing the time with small talk, mainly his. When she rose from the table and started clearing the dishes he asked, "Are you planning on wearing the gun today? It must be getting heavy."

"No. I kind of forgot I had it on." She then unbuckled the gun belt and passed it to him. "Here, it's your deal anyway. You being the man, the LT, you should definitely have it," she said sarcastically.

"Gee, Steph. I didn't mean to make you angry. I'm sorry." Marcus paused for a moment and added. "It seems like that's all I'm saying lately: sorry. And I am,"

Tiffany studied him. She almost felt sorry for him, and he was so yummy. But it was too late for that. "I'm sorry too, Marcus. And yes, I'm grouchy. Let's just get out of here. I can do the dishes when we get back."

Marcus nodded his head. He then strapped on the gun belt. "Okay, I'll get the poles and creel."

"I'll meet you outside."

She turned to where the parkas hung on the back of the door. She selected hers and quickly put it on. She opened the door and walked to the Lexus. The stun gun was where she knew it would be; under the front seat. She clutched the black, flat, rectangular gun, stood up, and slipped it into her jacket pocket just as Marcus closed the front door of the cabin behind him.

"Forget something?" he asked walking up to her.

"I thought I left my lip balm in the car, but I didn't see it. No big deal. You have everything? I don't want to walk this trail twice like we did the first time." she said with a small smile, changing the subject by being pleasant.

"I do. Thanks for asking. Ready to catch some fish?" he asked, smiling back.

"I am. Let's go."

"Lead the way, darling," Marcus said, gesturing to the trail opening.

Chapter 42 • On the Rocks

Marcus followed Stephanie down the narrow path as it wound its way through the pine and fir trees. Their progress could only be marked by the growing sound of the unseen river below. He tried to hold her hand in the slippery portions of the trail, but *she* told him that *she* was fine and didn't need the help. *Tiffany* meant it.

As they slowly made their way down the hillside, *Tiffany began to burn inside.*

"You better settle down and be damn sure about this girlfriend." Beth cautioned.

"Hmm, I thought you died," Tiffany hissed silently back to her.

"I've been watching," Beth said, emotionless. "I'm just here to make sure you don't royally fuck this up. The whole world knows you're here with him. If you're thinking about the stun gun, don't do it. It's like your signature."

"Ta da, ta da. Really, Beth? Really? I don't fucking care. I'm just so tired of men that lie, control, shove, demand, and fuck me like a toy. I want to destroy them all. The fuckers!" Tiffany raged internally at Beth.

Marcus noticed Stephanie's grimace. Her lips were moving as if she was talking to someone. But it wasn't just talk, she was angry. He touched her elbow. "Are you okay?"

"Shut up!" she screamed at him. "I'm fine. Jesus Christ, quit trying to watch every goddamn thing I do. It makes me crazy. I trusted you."

She stopped and began to cry. Shaking.

He put his arms around her.

Tiffany pushed away from him, wiping her streaming tears. "Give me a minute, I need my space." She walked a few steps up the trail and knelt. She spied the rock she wanted, softball sized and covered in fuzzy, green moss. She turned slightly to hide her movement, placing the stone into the front pocket of her parka. In one continuous movement she stood, turned around towards him and held her face, eyes closed, shaking again.

She then heard Beth say, "You're scaring him. If this is your plan, to be the crazy fucking girl, then you're succeeding. Get it together if you're going to finish this. FYI, nice touch with the rock."

Tiffany shook her head. The tears stopped. "You're right, and now I have what I need, I can't just stop," she replied silently, patting the pocket of her parka. She then wiped her face with her hands and looked up at Marcus, her best actress flowing. "I'm okay. It's just me dealing with us. Sorry."

She didn't wait for him respond. She turned and continued down the trail.

At its narrowest point the trail reached the small grassy clearing.

Tiffany stepped into the middle of the clearing and glanced behind her. Marcus was just entering. She turned around and faced him. "Marcus, please. Let's rest for a moment. I need time to compose myself."

Tiffany cautiously stepped over to the clearing's edge and peered down. She quickly stepped back when the rim began to crumble under her feet. Shifting pebbles and dirt had begun slipping and sliding down the twenty-foot slope to a giant, cracked rock jutting out below. At the knife-edge of the rock it was a long, sheer drop to the boulders and shoreline of the river.

"Just right," she said to herself. She backed slightly away from the edge and stood there. She heard him walk up from behind her. She slipped her hand into her pocket, sliding the rock into her hand.

"Are you okay, Steph?" he asked quietly.

She turned around and faced him.

He put his arms around her shoulders and said, "You know, I love you." He looked into her eyes as he said it.

"I love you too, Marcus, but you fucking killed us with your lies," she said softly, reaching into her pocket, extracting the rock. "You should've never done that to us," she whispered as slammed the rock viciously into his temple.

The blow staggered Graham, forcing him to step back and when he did his footing gave way beneath him. He flopped hard onto his stomach, his breath escaping in a harsh gasp. *She watched in flickering freeze frames as he looked at her in disbelief and began to slowly slide down the cliff.* The loose gravel and dirt accelerated his descent until Graham stretched his legs and arms wide and dug his fingers and boot toes into the slope to slow his momentum. His slide ended after several feet.

Tiffany was transfixed on Marcus as he gradually regained his composure and refocused upon her. She then kneeled at the edge and in a voice as sad and smooth as black silk said, "We had every hope for you. We all did, especially Stephanie. We thought you weren't like the others, but you are. You lied to us right from the beginning. It was a bad, bad thing you did to us Marcus. Stephy is crushed and gone for God knows how long thanks to you."

He couldn't respond, trying to comprehend what she had said.

"But Marcus, we don't want to cut you my darling. No, I could never do that. You're so pretty to me I could never damage you like the others. You're just going to have a terrible fall, an accident. And even though I will miss your touch desperately, it has to be this way." Tiffany stopped and suddenly began to cry, tears streaming down her face. She sobbed for a short while and then rubbed her eyes. She blinked and her expression suddenly changed; she glared at him. "You ruined everything, Marcus. Now, all we want to do is just forget, forget, forget. You hurt Stephy, Beth and me that bad."

She stood and walked to where some large boulders were piled next to the trailhead. She picked one the size of a basketball and rolled it to the edge. It clunked when it rolled, half-round on two sides, Beth lifting and pushing with all of her strength and determination. Reaching the edge, she stopped and looked down at Marcus. She wiped her nose and shook her head. A small tear escaped from her eye. "And, and now, my darling, you have to pay for it."

A shudder and a deeper voice added, "Yes, you do."

She bent at the waist and cupped her hands around the boulder when she heard the man's command and question.

"Stephanie! Stop! What the hell are you doing?"

She rose up and turned towards the sound of his voice.

Dried blood was smeared across the side of Powell's forehead and cheek. The knees of his pant legs were muddy and wet. His safari jacket was blood stained in the front, the left side and arm covered in mud. He looked wild and dangerous as he stared at her. He weaved back and forth, his hands on his knees, panting and blowing like some sort of living bellows.

"Stephanie, step away from the edge. Do it now!" he ordered between breaths.

She smiled malevolently at him. "The name is Tiffany, big man," she said mocking Gretchen, Hank's love.

Powell took more several deep breaths and straightened. He waited for a moment, pausing to gather her full attention. "Tiffany is it? Where's Marcus?"

"He's paying the price for lying to us. And if you fuck with me, you'll pay it too," Tiffany snarled at him as she withdrew the stun gun from her waistband and flicked the ON button, its head instantly crackling, the spark snapping and pulsating between the chrome electrodes.

Powell stared at her and calmly said, "Stephanie, Tiffany, I don't want to hurt you, so please don't make me. This has gone far enough."

Tiffany smiled at Powell and then charged wildly towards him with the stun gun snapping in her hand. Her red hair as wild as the expression of hate on her face

Powell waited for her to be almost on top of him before he dropped to one knee, rotated his lower body, and with his right leg stiff he swept the woman's legs out from underneath her. Stephanie flew forward from the momentum before landing hard on her back with an "ummmph," the gun flopping out of her hand and landing on the ground several feet away from her.

Powell stepped quickly over to the weapon, picked it up, turned it off and shoved it in his back pocket. He looked down at Stephanie with sadness. "I'm sorry it had to end this way." He then rolled her onto her stomach, pulled the handcuffs from his belt and slapped them on her wrists.

"Stay here, and don't move," he ordered.

She said nothing.

Powell stepped over to the edge of the apron. Graham had his arms stretched wide and his fingers were dug into the gravel and dirt. His legs were also spread, the toes of his boots dug in hard to the side of the cliff. He was bleeding from the side of his head.

Powell smiled and said, "Well, you've got yourself into a fine situation, LT. Need a hand?"

Graham looked up at Powell and smiled back. "Yeah, that would be good."

Powell took off his jacket and placed it at his feet, near the edge. He dropped to the ground and extended his chest over the crumbling edge, while his left hand dug in for purchase in the grass and dirt. He grabbed one arm of the jacket and flopped it down towards Graham. The arm of the jacket landed on the top of Graham's hand.

"That's all I have, so let's make the most of it. Grab on," Powell said.

Graham lifted his hand and snatched the sleeve as his body began to slip from the movement. Powell hung on tightly and stopped the slide. He then began pulling, his huge arms bulging from the effort. Graham, now clutching the arm of the jacket with both hands, pushed with his boots and began to claw his way up the loose slope until he reached Powell. Powell leaned down and grabbed Graham's arms, pulling him to his feet and onto the safety of the grass away from the cliff.

Graham shook his head and then his arms. He bent over and took a deep breath before saying, "Thanks, Hank. I was a little worried there for a sec." Graham straightened and regarded Powell's face and stained clothing. "What happened to you?"

"When I got to the cabin and saw that you weren't there, I headed down the trail. I was running and took a fucking header over some rocks. Damn near broke my neck."

They both then looked at Stephanie who was still lying quietly, face down, her hands cuffed behind her.

Marcus' expression quickly turned to one of concern. Powell saw it and said, "She called herself Tiffany when I arrived. She tried to zap me with a stun gun. It wasn't the Stephanie that you and I know."

Marcus nodded his head, his sadness evident. "I found that out, too, but not as quickly. Once I confessed to her about Franklin and how sorry I was, she changed. I just didn't recognize it. That's how I ended up over the cliff. She totally surprised me with a rock. It knocked the shit out of me. Goddammit, it broke my heart at the same time. She told me that I was just like the others but she wasn't going to cut me. It was all so crazy, I didn't know what the hell she was saying to me."

"Well, I do. She's killed five men over the years that we know of, including both Franklin and Grant. She was highly motivated by men who treated her badly. We put it all together this morning. But there's no way we can prove any of it. It's all circumstantial. There's no forensic evidence, witnesses, or any way we can actually prove she was the one, but she was. I have no doubt."

Tiffany turned her head towards the two men and said, "Blah, blah, blah. Listen to you, Powell. So strong and sure of yourself. You couldn't find me if I was standing in front of you."

Graham and Powell were confused by what they'd heard. The woman they knew as Stephanie then said in a much deeper voice, *"Shut up, Tiffany. I warned you about doing this and now look where we're at."*

"I told you, Beth. I have to do what I have to do. I can't just stop," Tiffany shrilled, looking as if she was talking to another person.

"Well, good job. Now what?" Beth asked calmly, again in a deeper voice.

"Shut up. Just shut up and leave me alone. I'm sick and tired of being blamed for everything, when all I do is protect our Stephy from terrible men," Tiffany answered meanly. She then turned her face towards the ground and began to pound her head repeatedly.

Powell stepped forward and pulled the woman up to a kneeling position. "That's enough of that," he said brusquely. He then helped her to her feet. Stephanie's forehead was bleeding.

Marcus stepped over to Stephanie, reached up and gently placed his hand against her cheek.

She jerked away from his hand. "Don't fucking touch me," she shrieked, her eyes wild, blood dripping from her forehead and down her cheeks.

It was the last thing they would hear her say.

Chapter 43 • Decisions

When Graham and Powell left the cabin on the Klickitat, Graham sat in the back with Stephanie while Powell drove. It was eerie for Graham to sit next to the woman he loved, while at the same time realizing that she or *Tiffany* had attempted to kill him. It was difficult for him to wrap his head around the *conversations* that Stephanie had with herself in two different voices, let alone that they even took place.

Stephanie sat silently, trance-like, her handcuffed hands resting quietly in her lap.

Powell looked into the rear-view mirror at Graham and said, "Now what?"

Graham removed the small towel from the side of his head and glanced up at Powell eyes in the mirror "I really don't know. What do you think?"

"We should keep it in-house. Jim Galloway is probably the best choice. Let's see what he says."

Graham called Dr. Galloway and was told that he was with a patient. Graham left his name and requested that the doctor call as soon as he was available.

Dr. Galloway called five minutes later and after Graham explained to him the circumstances of his encounter with Stephanie. Galloway recommended they drive Stephanie directly to Providence Mental Health for evaluation and treatment. He further warned Graham that Stephanie was now possibly a danger to herself, in addition to others, and that she shouldn't be left alone. Graham assured Galloway that she wouldn't and that they would be at the hospital within two hours. Galloway said he would meet them there.

Stephanie sat silently through the phone call, oblivious, her blank stare focused on the back of Powell's head.

Graham then called John McGee and explained the bizarre end to their adventure on the Klickitat. He then asked, "What's your legal take on everything, John? Do we just sweep what we know about her under the table and say nothing?"

McGee paused for a moment. "That's a tough question, but there's no hard evidence that connects Miss Courtland to any of the crime scenes, other than a possible hair sample taken at the McMaster's killing. That would be the only link that I can think of that could possibly connect her to him. But again, it could be argued that he picked up the hairs at the convention when they were talking with one another. The photo indicates she was close enough. That's the way I'd defend her and I believe it'd stick. And of course, we're the only ones who have put this all together. And even our conclusions are based circumstantially, largely upon our belief that she had the means, motive and opportunity."

McGee paused again. "Bottom line, we've got suspicions, darn good ones, but they are suspicions none the less. There's no factual evidence. You and Powell are the only persons who have ever survived an assault by Miss Courtland and could testify accordingly. It would be within both your rights to bring charges, but given the circumstances, not likely or probable."

Marcus was silent, thinking.

McGee was sympathetic. "Marcus, I know how you feel about Miss Courtland, everyone does. Do what's best for her and take her to the hospital. That's what she really needs. I don't believe we have anything to offer the police at this time. But be mindful there is a downside to the doctor's help. If he discovers through his care of Miss Courtland that she has harmed others, he would be obliged to inform the authorities. It would still be a stretch for the police to bring charges with no evidence, but confessions are powerful."

"I'm hoping it doesn't come to that, John. Jim Galloway is going to be helping her."

"That's good. I'm relieved by that. He's smart and knows us. Let me know how it goes."

Graham thanked him and ended the call.

The next hour and twenty minutes passed without further conversations.

When Powell and Graham arrived at Providence Mental Health, they delivered Stephanie into the care of Jim Galloway. The doctor and his orderlies helped Stephanie from the car, and after Powell keyed the handcuffs and released her, she was escorted immediately inside the hospital.

Dr. Galloway remained behind long enough to tell Marcus that he would be in contact with him and that there was nothing more for him or Hank to do. He added that it would be at least several weeks before Marcus should visit.

Powell and Graham left the hospital. Neither man spoke on their way to Avalanche, both consumed by their own thoughts.

Epilogue • Lost and Gone

It took over a year for Graham's life to gradually return to normal. He'd been consumed by the Gorge project and if anything, it was good for him to stay busy; it kept his mind from focusing on his loss of Stephanie. She was gone forever and there was nothing he could do to change it.

He'd visited Dr. Galloway several times and learned the extent of Stephanie's illness. The doctor was very clear in his diagnosis. Stephanie was suffering from DID, dissociative identity disorder. Galloway explained that DID may feel like a form of possession and that Stephanie experienced memory loss that was far too extensive to be rationalized by ordinary forgetfulness. Dr. Galloway determined that the formation and emergence of her alters - *Beth* and *Tiffany,* were the direct result of her interactions with Ray Franklin when she was twelve.

"The violence conducted towards you was never really done by Stephanie, it was her alters: *Beth* and *Tiffany. Beth* on the surface displays as a pseudo-dominant and appears to be calm, reasonable, tractable and wanting to please. I'm suspicious of this behavior because of the constant internal dialogue I detect she's having with *Tiffany* - the dominant personality. *Tiffany* is the most problematic. She does not see herself as acting inappropriately or impulsively, which indicates degrees of narcissism, antisocial personality and psychopathy – she sees others as objects to be manipulated. *Tiffany* has learned, via Franklin's abuse, that they are all just bodies to be used and/or discarded. She thrives on adrenaline and aggression – they're the only things that truly engage her. My end goal will be to attempt to integrate the alters so that Stephanie is back in charge, while utilizing *their* strengths to bolster Stephanie's ego identity so it is less fractured and more cohesive. This will be a very long-term process, but I am somewhat hopeful."

Dr. Galloway's explanation didn't lessen the emotional blow to Graham and it was only made worse after his one and only visit with Stephanie. It still stuck in his mind and his heart. It had been three weeks since Stephanie entered the hospital and Dr. Galloway warned him that it was too early for him to visit, but he'd insisted so vehemently that the doctor relented, but only if he was present. He also warned Graham to keep it light and upbeat: no apologies, no questions, and no demands.

Graham thought the room where their visit was to take place was quite institutional. A utilitarian leather-like couch and matching stuffed chair were bolted to the floor and were the only furnishings. The walls were painted soft beige and the overhead lights were dimmed. Graham first believed the room was silent, but he soon detected violin music softly playing in the background. The ambience of the room was obviously intended to be as tranquil and un-distracting as possible.

Dr. Galloway and Graham were waiting for Stephanie when the door opened and an orderly ushered her into the room. She was dressed in loose fitting, blue loungewear and black slippers. He recognized them as being part of the wardrobe he'd supplied for her, all within Dr. Galloway's guidelines. Her red hair was brushed neatly and hung straight to her shoulders. She wore no make-up other than some light pink lipstick.

Marcus stood and smiled at her and she shyly smiled back.

"I'm very happy to see you, Steph," he said softly.

Stephanie ran to Graham and hugged him. "Marcus, I've missed you so much," she said to him as she pulled him closer. She nuzzled his neck and kissed his ear. "Do you remember me, baby?"

"Yes, Steph. I've missed you terribly."

Stephanie suddenly stepped back from Marcus and turned to Dr. Galloway. In a sugary-sweet voice that startled Graham, she said, *"Dr. Galloway. Honey, why don't you give me a minute with my man? I've missed him so much and he's just so yummy. We need some private time. I'm sure you understand. We just want to be alone. Tell the orderly he can go too."*

Dr. Galloway didn't hesitate to respond. "We've already talked about that, Stephanie. This is just a short visit today and it's best that we all stay together."

Stephanie's voice and demeanor changed lightning quick. *"First of all, dear Doctor, I've told you time and again not to confuse us. What do I have to do? Paint a picture? Hold up a card with my name on it? I'm Tiffany."*

Dr. Galloway replied calmly, "I'm sorry, Tiffany, but it's Stephanie's turn to visit, not yours. Don't you remember our talk?"

"Don't tell me who I have to be. I'm me. Me, me, me. And it's my turn," Tiffany raged at the doctor.

Galloway turned to Graham and said, "I think it's time for our visit to end, Marcus. Tiffany and I need to talk for a few minutes."

Graham looked at Stephanie and said sadly, "I guess I have to go now, Steph. But know that you're always in my thoughts and in my heart."

Tiffany began to cry and her pleas echoed behind him as he left the room. "Don't leave me, Marcus. Please, please. I didn't mean to be bad, I can't just stop myself. Please. I promise I'll be better."

The door closed.

Tiffany went ballistic, glaring red faced at the doctor and screeching, "You fucking bastard. All I wanted was ten minutes and you, you just can't allow me any fun, can you? Stephanie doesn't want to do anything but just stand there, can't you see that?"

Dr. Galloway was calm in his response, "Tiffany, we had an agreement. I thought you said you were fine with it. Beth was."

With a shudder Beth came forward and spoke to Tiffany, "See what you've done? If you would have been quiet and not so forceful and disrespectful to the doctor, we would have had a longer visit with Marcus. It wasn't very nice of you."

The melting to Tiffany happened very quickly. "Don't you tell me what to do. You always want to kiss the doctor's ass and be so helpful. Don't forget who runs this party, Beth. It's me, me, me!" Tiffany seethed.

Dr. Galloway intervened. "Tiffany, don't be so angry. Beth is right. She was quite willing to follow the rules and wait politely. It was you that decided to end the visit with your actions."

"You took away my man! What do you expect? Oh, I know. Both of you are always talking about me and how I should be. Well, I've got news for you, dear Doctor." Tiffany shrilled and rushed at Dr. Galloway, grabbing his hair with both hands and shaking his head. *"You bastard, I'll show you, you, you, you!"*

The orderly reacted swiftly and grabbed her arms, pulling them back and away from the doctor's head. Her hands held clumps of the doctor's curly brown hair and she had begun to laugh hysterically.

Dr. Galloway, squinting from the pain, reached into his lab coat and removed a hypodermic. While the orderly held Tiffany's arms behind her, Galloway stepped forward and quickly injected her in the shoulder.

"No, don't. Nooooooo." Tiffany moaned.

The Haldol took effect over the next minute and she slowly stopped struggling against the grip of the orderly. Stephanie soon hung her head and said, "I'm tired."

Marcus wanted to remain with Stephanie, hold her, and tell her he loved her but he knew that wasn't possible. A tear escaped from his eye as he walked down the white corridor. He still couldn't believe she wasn't in his life any longer.

Graham drove directly to Avalanche, his thoughts of Stephanie as heavy as the rain that beat against the window of the Mercedes. He wanted to update Powell and McGee about his visit with Stephanie, but even more than that he wanted to set them at ease about him.

Graham found Powell and McGee chatting with Andy Hines in the operations room. The three twisted in their chairs at the opening of the door.

"Marcus, good to see you. How did it go?" Powell inquired, hoping for the best.

"It wasn't great," Graham replied sadly. "She's not doing well. I had a few moments with her, but it changed very quickly. One of her alters took charge and I was forced to leave. It broke my heart, but it's just not my Stephanie any longer."

"I'm sorry, Marcus. We all are," Powell said solemnly. McGee and Hines both nodded with obvious concern and empathy.

Graham looked at the floor and then to them. "I wanted to thank you for your concern for Steph and me. It's most appreciated. I'm not sure if Steph and I will ever be the same, but I will remain forever hopeful." His voice cracked with sorrow and his eyes glistened.

He then turned abruptly and walked away.

•

In 2018, after nine months of intense treatment that included drug therapy, clinical re-evaluations, brain scans and psychoanalysis, Dr. Galloway determined Stephanie's DID made it impossible for her to understand the wrongfulness of her acts or even if she understood them, to distinguish them as being right or wrong. Dr. Galloway secretly confided to Marcus that Stephanie and her alters had never confessed to actually killing anyone, but he had no doubt that given *their* motive and opportunities, *they* possibly could have. Dr. Galloway offered no prognosis if and when Stephanie would ever be rational enough to be released.

The brutal murders Stephanie, *Beth* and *Tiffany* conducted over thirteen years would never be solved: Graham, Powell and the men of Avalanche vowed to remain forever silent about their discoveries and suspicions.

<END>

Acknowledgements

Terminal Impulses was inspired by some very special people I know. Don't get me wrong, this is not a true story - far from it. I do, however, suspect that the complexity of Stephanie Courtland exists within all of us to a certain degree, albeit typically absent of her impulsive and extreme reactions to stress.

I wish to thank my band of collaborators who helped bring Terminal Impulses to life:

Dr. Jeremy Senske for providing me the truth about DID and how it effects those affected by it. His keen insight into this particular mental condition was enlightening. His contributions to the dialogue and realness of *Beth, Tiffany,* Stephanie, Dr. Stoltz and Dr. Galloway were sensitive and revealing. Dr. Senske is a practicing licensed clinical psychologist in Washington State and has been for the past nine years. Dr. Senske attended graduate School at Argosy University, Seattle, and achieved a MA in Clinical Psychology and a PsyD in Clinical Psychology.

Stephanie Brovelli, my companion, inspired the vision of Stephanie. She kept me on track with woman-speak and feminine emotions. She was tireless in her editing and input.

Jayne Marchesi, Diane Kotsaris and Bonnie Schlieman - the other women in my life who were kind enough to read countless versions: right, wrong, and "what the heck are you thinking?"

Sheridan K. Low who imagined and designed the cover of Terminal Impulses in addition to providing keen marketing and promotional insight.

I cannot thank each of you enough.

Michael

About the Author

Michael McDonald-Low has an extensive writing background, having published extreme sports magazines for over twenty-five years. He has also investigated some of the United States' most important and complicated unsolved mysteries - soldiers missing in action. In September 2014, he was selected as the first-ever Southeast Asia Veteran Liaison for the Department of Defense POW/MIA Accounting Agency. Specifically, he participated in independent MIA case analysis and review of unresolved ground loss cases in Vietnam, Laos and Cambodia. His popular non-fiction book, *UNACCOUNTED,* was the end result of his five-year journey to solve a personal MIA mystery from forty-four years ago.